*"**Action-packed, sensational, and expertly told narrative**...brings top-level entertainment mixed with an important awareness for the plights of the LGBTQ community and minority groups in the US. Fans of LGBTQ action will love this large, well-woven plot that includes passionate love and sex, espionage, the FBI, terrorism, music, the media, and politics. As Steven A. Coulter's newest fan, I can't wait to see the masterpiece he creates next!"*

~ Foluso Falaye, San Francisco Book Review

COPPERHEAD

Steven A. Coulter

San Francisco

Published by Jubilation Media

979-8-9854814-1-9 paperback
979-8-9854814-0-2 e-book

Cover Design by Viktoriya Fajardo, OwlGhost Studios
Interior book design and formatting by MyBookDesigner.com
Content editing by Katherine V. Forrest

Content Warning: Please note this novel contains scenes and topics dealing with sensitive issues that may trigger some readers, including government corruption, bullying, prostitution, immigration, white supremacy, torture and casualties in a military confrontation. Despite this, Copperhead continues to make great music.

Also by Steven A. Coulter

Copperhead (Book 2) (Coming soon)
The Passageway (Coming soon)
Rising Son—Chronicles of Spartak (Book 1) (2017)
Freedom's Hope—Chronicles of Spartak (Book 2) (2018)

To Greg

1.

The foot pounding, beginning with my own, started before she finished. With her final soaring note, hundreds more feet hit the wooden floor, the room vibrating, shouts of *"Halleluiah!"* from myriad throats. She offered a demure smile, a calm acceptance of the adulation.

Her rousing version of "Take My Hand, Precious Lord" left me in goosebumps.

While she sang, my arms had pointed toward heaven. My hips swayed, my feet danced on the platform step as I sang backup with the choir. She was stunning, her skin the blackest black, "dark chocolate," she liked to purr. Tall, elegant and often wearing a pearl necklace, she had buzzed white hair. This morning she had three strands around her throat, and matching earrings. I adored the woman, a mentor. Sadie Watkins was an institution here at Emanuel AME in East Bay, across from San Francisco.

Now it was my turn. And I wanted to soar.

Pastor Smathers, another fixture at the church, a little bigger than his jacket, hair in tight cornrows, restored calm after Sadie finished. He was giving her time to applaud back to the congregation and choir. With a joyous grin he raised then lowered his palms to bring people back to their seats. It was a packed house. The lower level held at least four hundred, with a score standing in the back. Another hundred on the second level. The church had a peaked roof, dark wooden crossbeams, a giant cross on the white plaster wall behind us. The choir, fifty of us, six rows deep, stood across the back. The main pulpit was on stage right, the standby on the left. Below that was a raised platform for a glistening black grand piano and a vacant niche for the organ now undergoing repairs. Then two wide rows of pews. On either side of the nave were classrooms. All around the doors were corkboards displaying student art. It was a family focused church.

"Another special treat for you today," the pastor teased, the words slow and sonorous.

"*Tell us!*" someone shouted. It sounded like a friend in the chorus.

"Oh…I will." He grinned and waited, adding suspense one syllable at a time. He sometimes got in a playful mood. "Next… will be a performance…by a remarkable young man, one you see every Sunday in the choir. Something about him. Hmmm. What is it?"

There was laughter because my name was in the day's program.

"This will be his first starring solo before this congregation. Abel Torres, thirteen years old—that's a one followed by a three, thirteen, yeah, the precious cherub boy with the copper colored hair and cocoa skin, easy to spot, hard to take your eyes away—he will perform. Yes…he…will."

There was applause, a few "awes" and I held my face in a tight smile, not sure what else to do. I was a *precious cherub? Cocoa skin?* Dreadful. What if kids started calling me that at school?

"He will sing and play piano, accompanied on violin by our own Jessie Garcia, a senior at Oakland High. How about that? I suspect this will be a special joy for us and the Lord."

The man was pouring it on thick. I wasn't sure if I should wave, grin or just look serious as I stepped down from the bleachers, winding between the other choir members, working toward the piano, my maroon polyester robe over jeans and my Sunday best white button-down shirt. I decided to concentrate on not tripping.

"You go, Abel!" Sadie shouted. Scattered whistles from the choir.

Old Mr. Thurgood, a real giant, stepped away from the piano and gave me a hug—he was nearly two feet taller—then found a chair on the other side of the stage.

Jessie came out a side door, dressed in a long black skirt and a puff-sleeved white blouse. She and I had practiced this a dozen times. We nodded to each other.

I adjusted my seat at the piano upward and there were a couple of laughs since it took so long. I turned off the microphone, didn't need it. I moved my fingers over the keyboard, downloading the music in my head, calming myself, and glanced up. Mr. Thurgood was grinning at me, nodding, offering a thumbs up, granting me his special permission to pound on his keyboard. His lips seemed wider than his face. The room was silent or as silent as most audiences get, a few coughs, someone blowing their nose, a baby crying, shushes but mostly the mood was expectant.

I glanced up at Mama in the top row of the choir. She was already tearing up. Not helpful. She was another star performer, her voice rich and soaring. These were all her friends. Mama started me singing seriously at three and piano at six. I loved making an audience gasp in joy. My Mexican dad sang too, mostly country and Mexican love songs. I dipped my head acknowledging Mama. She brought her hand to her mouth and did a sudden intake of breath. It sounded like she suppressed a sob.

"You go, sister," someone hollered out. This was a vocal congregation, very supportive of its members.

Then I looked over to my dad, who rarely came here, sitting in the first pew, watching me. A silent nod. No pressure.

Shit. Let me not mess up.

I wasn't much into the religion part of church, so much just didn't make sense. But I loved to sing and be part of a choir; everyone so talented, each challenging the other to do their best. We

9

comforted those who messed up. I was confident enough in my talent to reinterpret a song, to try and punch it into a new dimension. I didn't always play safe with my singing.

I began the intro to "You Raise Me Up." A great emotional piece. Or could be. It sounded a lot like "Danny Boy," sweet but soft and to me a bit dull. There was plenty of space to own it and I was cheeky and competitive. I was willing to take risks, particularly after Sadie's performance. I wanted to lift the rafters, shock and bring joy. Even if I flopped, the choir would have my back if not my parents, and we could have a good laugh.

My voice had serious volume and a wide range. Thank you God for making it drop last year, among other things. *When I am down*, the lyrics began. I'd heard a lot of singers do it. Josh Grobin did an amazing job. I wanted it more emotional, more range. *Il Divo* was good but still too subdued for today. I wanted a blowout. *You raise me up*, I sang. To me it called for power and a couple of "ya-ya's" as Mama liked to call 'em: drop your voice, warble, power up higher and higher, punch through the octaves, looking up to God and glory. Great fun. *I am strong*, the verse went. Jessie came in behind me at different points. The choir trilled at others. I can stand on mountains. I rose to my feet, rising with my voice. *Walk on stormy seas*. Then back sitting, pushing more soul into my voice. *More than I can be*. Anytime I performed, I lived in my own world. *Lead me home*. I was standing again at the end, lost in my head. The congregation was on its feet. I heard and felt the foot rumble pounding louder, building.

Sadie whistled, two fingers in her mouth.

"*Yes, Abel!*" my dad shouted, his boots slapping the floor.

"*Abel, Abel!*" Mama screamed.

"*Ah-men, brother!*" A man's gruff voice.

"*Wonderful, sister!*" A woman on the balcony.

I thought I was going to rip a lip with my grin. I bowed then pointed at Jessie, who did a bow and pointed back at me, clapping.

The foot pounding went on and on, peaked, then silence as the pastor lowered his palms.

This was joy; the life I wanted.

Afterward there was a potluck. One of the reasons we came here. Not that we were hungry but Mama had a talent for spreading a half chicken over several meals. Dad could do the same with a pound of hamburger, and we had lots of vegetables from a nearby community garden. There was seafood today. I moved toward the shrimp and waited for Dad's favorite saying, a corny homily. It was usually delivered with a tickle attack when I was younger. It made me laugh but was also meant as a warning. *"Camarón que se duerme se lo lleva la corriente,"* he said, "The current will take any shrimp that falls asleep." We each took a shrimp, touched them together in a toast, swallowed and giggled, our own private joke. He often called me his little shrimp and hugged me. It made me feel special.

His Spanish was, as he called it, "middle school Gringo" despite his Mexican blood. He was brought here before his first birthday and his parents made him speak English at home so he'd fit in. Officially, he was a Dreamer, his immigration status mired in politics. We were a real mix of races and colors. Dad was light brown with dirty blond hair, unusual for his heritage but not uncommon. I was middle brown, copper hair and brown eyes. Mama was part Irish and African American, the darkest of the three of us. She gave music lessons and was a part time singer in a shmancy restaurant. Dad worked in construction. He also loved to read and took online courses from community college. I studied music along with school. Mama and a group of music teachers in East Bay, including Sadie, sort of adopted me and were a constant presence. They called themselves *The Posse.*

Music was fun, math, not so much. The dress code was a joy—what boy doesn't want to wear a collared shirt and tie? Of course, it was a Catholic school.

2.

"Hey, it's Captain Duracell!" Mitchell taunted me, as he did most days, this time as I entered St. Mary's Middle School. He and his three friends surrounded me, grabbing my tie, shoving me into a wall. *"Hey puto!"*

"What?" I demanded, tired of their harassment. Seventh grade was bad enough without the jerks. I tried to twist and get away. *"Leave me alone!"*

Mitchell was tall, a strong heavyset kid with pimples. He grabbed my neck in a choke hold and messed my hair "Hey, Duracell, your bunny battery all charged?" They giggled like it was funny but he wouldn't let me go.

"Knock it off!" I yelled, hoping it would attract attention.

He slapped my face repeatedly. "Oooh, Baby Copperboy is unhappy."

Three girls chuckled as they passed by.

Where's a nun when you need her?

I tried hitting him and got a fist in my gut. I gasped and they used the moment to twist an arm behind my back and started to undo my belt.

"No!" They'd pulled my pants down once in the hallway. It was humiliating.

Kids stopped to watch the show as I kicked and squirmed.

Sister Sandra stepped out of the front office and the assholes dropped me on the ground and sauntered away, all innocent.

"Stand up, Abel. What are you doing? Comb your hair and fix your tie. No sloppiness. You know the rules."

Boys wore white shirts and a regulation brown tie with lighter blue and white stripes. Girls had plaid skirts and white blouses.

I scurried to my locker, put my backpack inside and grabbed my history book for first period.

Sister Marcia was the teacher, a sweet natured woman, one of only three nuns in the school, all ancient. She seemed oblivious at times and rigid, starting with the Lord's Prayer, as she did every morning and we all did our parts, eyes not always closed, watching for trouble, spitballs hitting me or one of the other "losers" as we were called. She never seemed to see it. If we yelped when hit, she called us out.

"In the name of the Father, and the Son, and of the Holy Spirit."

Today we talked about the creation of the missions in California, particularly the work of Father Junipero Serra and the first one he built in San Diego. She explained how he helped the natives find Jesus and save their souls. She seemed sincere, even getting emotional and crossing herself talking about the selfless work of the early friars. She nodded to someone behind me who'd raised his hand.

"Yes, Jason."

I turned around to see him. He stood and his expression suggested he'd be a dick. "Isn't it true that Indians were treated as slaves by the missionaries? I read they were put in prison camps, beaten and died of all kinds of diseases we brought."

"Are you suggesting that Pope Francis did not know what he was doing when he made him a saint?" She crossed her arms and her fingers bounced angrily up and down on one bicep.

Jason sat down, hiding his smirk. He liked to rile her.

Third period was heaven: music class. It offered students in different grades the chance to study independently and as a group. Mr. Hitchens, a young Black teacher, played the saxophone and the half dozen students were all good on different instruments. There were enough private rooms for us to practice individually and we sometimes came together for jamming.

Spanish class was easy. I already knew enough to pass although I wasn't fully fluent. One boy in the class was struggling and likely to fail, made obvious when he was asked questions. Like today.

"Clyde," Mr. Smithers asked, "¿Cuál es el nombre de su calle?"

He stood, looking down, clearly embarrassed. Clyde was big, muscular and with a rugged outdoorsman face. Rumor had it that his dad was in prison.

"Yo no sé." His face flushed, he dropped back into his seat, looking down at his desk. He was a loner, never talked to anyone. I felt horrible for him. I'd experienced humiliation too, so many times.

At lunch, I saw him sitting alone at a table. I set my tray next to him.

His head shot up in surprise. "What do you want?" His voice was harsh.

"Okay if I join you?"

"Why?"

"I can help with Spanish if you like."

He watched me for a long time, his egg salad sandwich hovering partway to his mouth.

"Why?" His voice was softer; his expression confused.

"Seems like you could use some help. I'd be same as you except my dad's Mexican and we do some Spanish at home."

"You're serious?"

"Absolutamente."

We talked in broken Spanish for the rest of lunch and got together after school at a nearby coffee shop. He wasn't dumb. He was mad but I seemed to calm him. I told him to text or call if he had a question.

Over the next weeks, we started talking about our lives. His dad was in prison; his mom was a housekeeper. I told him about my family and music. Turned out he played guitar and sang, mostly country. I told him my dad did too. We went to his house to study and hear him play. He was so nervous it was precious. He strummed cords for a couple of minutes considering his options and then sang Garth Brooks' "The Thunder Rolls." Fabulous song and he did better than okay.

"That's great, Clyde. You have talent."

Clyde asked me to sing. That was fair, given all the pressure I gave him to do his thing. I knew I was good and didn't want to blow him away like I was bragging. It needed to be acapella. A tune had been banging non-stop in my head since I heard it on the radio. I sang a low drama version of "Memories" from *Cats*.

He stared at me when I finished, his mouth open. "My God, Abel, you're so good."

"You could be too with some help."

I talked to Mr. Hitchens the next day. He agreed to listen to Clyde and offer advice. The big hunk all but turned green when I suggested it at lunch. As the bell rang, he looked at me, scrunched his forehead and said, "*Está bien, lo haré.*"

He brought his guitar to school and we put it in Mr. Hitchens' office. After school, we got together and he played. The teacher asked questions about his training and invited him to meet the class and play. My new friend was stunned but thrilled. Clyde got excused from his third period history course and joined us. He was shy but everyone encouraged him and he played. Afterward we applauded and gushed. You could see him lift his head, proud of the feedback.

The teacher whispered into my ear, "You did good, Abel."

"Clyde," Mr. Hitchens said. "We'd love to have you as a member of the class. Interested?"

His face reached a new height of scarlet. "I...I'd like that."

We continued our collaboration on Spanish and he was improving. One day the teacher asked him a question. He stood and gave the right answer.

"*Muy bien hecho,*" Mr. Smithers responded with a smile and nod.

Clyde sat down, grinning. He turned to me and offered a thumbs up. He gave me a bear hug after class.

"Thanks. People seem afraid of me. Yet you came right up. That means a lot. Add in the music class. This is cool."

School felt fun. I'd started arriving earlier to avoid the assholes waiting to torment certain boys. I tried to avoid normal lay-in-wait sites. Sometimes the long way around was the shortest route.

Math class was a horror. Ms. Pisinski was not a nun but could have been. She spent more time teaching the evils of masturbation than the multiplication tables. She never blushed; but we did. It was never clear how they were related, but one minute it was why 12x12=144 and then she slipped in the evils of spilled seed. Everyone immediately stared at their desktops. When another lecture started on the horrors of pre-marital sex, we tried not to giggle which guaranteed an angry reprimand. There was much speculation out of class on whether she was a virgin but I thought such talk was mean-spirited. She was a nice person even if a bit obsessed about sex.

We were late getting out of class one day, not unusual, and headed to lunch.

Mitchell and his buddies were waiting for me around the corner. I ran right into them.

"Why the rush Captain Duracell?" He grabbed me in a head-lock. His friends gathered around, laughing. Other students watched as they walked by.

"Pants the Mex," one of his buddies suggested.

"Let me go, assholes!" I yelled, thrashing wildly. They kicked my feet and pulled me to the floor.

"What the fuck!" one of the slugs yelled. He'd just got slammed headfirst into a locker, inches from my face. I heard punches. He cried out and fell to the floor.

Next, Mitchel's head was yanked back and he let me go. As the creep tried to turn, he took a fist to his face and then another, held by his hair. A punch to his gut. He was shoved face first into the wall and took another pounding to his back. He fell to the floor screaming, his face covered in blood.

It was Clyde.

He grabbed another open-mouthed, shocked hoodlum by his shirt and delivered a series of punches to his stomach. The guy vomited over the jerk already groaning on the ground. The fourth guy ran off.

"Come on, assholes. Fight me!" He swung a fist at Mitchell and the goon cried out and rolled to his side. "If you ever mess with Abel or anybody else, you get me back in your face! You butt wipes understand?"

He stomped his foot by Mitchell's head. "Answer me! Or do you want another knuckle sandwich?"

"Okay! Okay! I get it."

I flashed on King Kong swinging his fist and roaring in triumph after he defeated the Tyrannosaurus rex in that movie from the thirties.

"Clean up this mess!" Clyde roared.

The three got onto their knees. He kicked one in the butt.

"Take off your shirt, Mitchell, and wipe up the vomit."

Mitchell did so, his arms shaking.

"You two, clean the floor good or I'll make you lick it clean."

They did.

Students watching the take down clapped, whistled and took videos.

The three scrambled to get up and ran down the hall as Clyde helped me up.

Sister Sandra stepped out of a classroom. "What's going on?"

Clyde flashed her the thumbs up all is well sign.

I put my arm around Clyde's waist as we walked to lunch. His arm was around my shoulder.

"I hate bullies," he said.

"Can you say that in Spanish?"

We both laughed.

++++

I came home from school on Thursday a little down but pleased with the videos of Mitchell's takedown making the rounds. He and his buddies took the long way around me and ran when they saw Clyde.

How should I know the value of *pi*? Math today was talking about decimals in one breath and then how Jesus wanted us to remain virgins until marriage. I loved civics and social studies, history, and even science classes where we looked into a microscope and entered whole new magical worlds.

Strangely, both of my parents were home. Dad looked upset, his face tight, eyes red. I sat beside him on the sofa and put a hand on his shoulder.

"What's wrong?"

We hugged for a minute then he nudged me back, offering a tight smile. "Not now, please, Abel."

They talked a bunch of nothing at dinner. I never knew the weather was so fascinating for them or the new sewer lines being installed in our street. I tried to get them to open up and then my mother turned to me: "So how is your math class?" I just looked down at my plate, fresh corn, sliced tomatoes and a thin slice of grilled chicken. That was always my warning to be quiet. Talking about math was embarrassing and I never said why. I was not going to say anything bad about a nun. This must be something bad about Dad. She was trying to protect him.

When we finished dinner, as I collected plates and took them to the sink, I whispered to my father, "Please tell me."

Dad's voice was just as soft. "The union training program lost its funding. I'm out of work." He struggled to get it out.

I rushed to him and knelt, my forehead pressed to his chest. "I love you, Dad. We're *The Trio*," our secret name for the three of us. "We'll survive."

Later, I overheard them talking. Employers demanded a green card if you had a certain look, Dad said, and didn't want to hear about the Dreamer promise.

A week later, when I came home, they were packing. "We have to move," Mama said, her voice worn, tired, eyes bloodshot.

"Today."

We hauled stuff to a friends' garage, not that we had that much, and started couch surfing, a night here, a week there. My father sometimes slept in his truck to be near a potential job and be first in line for work. Or maybe there was no place for him. Being upbeat was tough. I tried to only cry in private.

I dropped out of Catholic school and enrolled in a free public one. Mid-semester. Not all credits transferred. I knew no one and making friends as the new brown kid was a challenge.

One family we stayed with, from church, had a boy about my age in my new school. We didn't talk. I'd tried to be friendly but he was upset to share his room with me. He told everyone I was homeless. I pretended I didn't hear the gossip, kids making fun of me.

Mom brought home an old hoodie sweatshirt because I needed something warmer. It had a cartoon of an eagle on the back. Kind of cool.

At school, a boy yelled so everyone could hear:

"Hey, Copperboy! You look good in that old rag. I donated it to the Salvation Army!" Sometimes it was better to be cold.

I signed up for the music program, thinking it might be like what I had at Catholic school. Mr. Dunkirk—a middle aged man who looked like Frank Zappa, the famous old rocker with long black hair, a huge mustache and a thick patch of hair under his lower lip—announced that our purpose was to learn to play well enough to form a marching band. No piano or singing. For most of the students, they had little background in music. He suggested I learn drums or the flute. "Woodwinds it is," I told him. So, piano and singing would only be with *The Posse* and the church.

I did my best to be invisible during the eighth grade. For several months we lived in a family shelter in San Francisco. When we timed out, meaning stayed too long, the manager contacted a non-profit doing free tents to the homeless. We got one and pitched it near Civic Center with a score of other homeless. At least we were hidden away, mostly, only a few people walking by and gawking. The city has no public toilets, maybe politicians figure homeless don't need to use such facilities or don't care. The Main Library became a lifesaver. People there looked at us like we were gross and lazy. It was humiliating. Both my parents worked or were job hunting; I was in school. It turned out the library hired their own social worker and I was approached by this woman one day while I was doing homework. She was sweet and respectful. She seemed to understand and cared. She helped find us space in another family shelter. I kissed her cheek; she gave me the biggest grin.

My dad found work here and there. They insisted I not get a job but focus on school, a place I didn't want to be. Then, the summer before the ninth grade, near my fifteenth birthday, the union program got funded. Dad went back to work with a meaningful income. We moved into a tiny apartment in Antioch. It felt like a palace. Just us, *The Trio*.

Yet another school. I was held back a year, a total downer, which messed up what kids thought of me. It also complicated what I thought of myself. I would be fifteen in a class of fourteen-year-olds. Kids would see me as a loser, "*the Mexican.*" Mama argued with the man in the admissions office but he just brushed her off. She went to the principal who did the same. Maybe repeating math without lectures on masturbation would make it easier to understand.

"Hi, my name's Abel." I was standing next to two students waiting for the assembly room doors to open. They looked approachable. And I was desperate.

"I'm Bryan Winter," the boy responded with a smile. "This is my sister, Elizabeth. Yeah, we're twins." They invited me over to their place after school, my first potential friends in this school. She was pretty with long black hair in a flip, a freckled face with bright red lipstick. She pulled me into her bedroom, closed the door, grabbed each side of my head and smashed her lips against mine, pushing in her tongue. I'd never kissed anyone. This was messy and very cool. She had us both naked in under two minutes, with confusion but considerable enthusiasm on my part. She sucked my dick, cooing over its size, introduced me to the joys of female breasts, taught me how to put on a rubber and we did it.

Somehow this was not how I imagined losing my virginity. Preconceived adolescent notions could be wonderfully wrong. Who needed to wait for marriage? A loss of some good years. I giggled while we were doing it, imagining Sister Teresa's face if she knew. For the next month, it was sex every afternoon. Bryan just laughed about it. She said I'd get a "B+ in orgasm" but was pissed I never took her out or bought her anything. Like I had any money. I thought it was a good grade considering my experience.

"We're done!" She announced it to me in a crowded corridor at school and sashayed over to another guy, all fancy in expensive clothes, and took his arm. So, he apparently had money, no mention about his dick or if he got a better letter grade. I was dumped.

Bryan gave me a hug. "This will pass, bro. Come over after school and we can talk." He was a year younger than me but we were in the same grade. He liked that I was older.

We sat on the edge of his bed that afternoon and yakked about homework, teachers and our football team. Then he changed the subject.

"I think you're the most beautiful boy in school, Copperhead." He ran his fingers through my hair and kissed me.

I pulled back. "What the fuck?"

He smiled, all cocky, nodding as if he knew a deep secret.

I liked his grin, then I grew one too. Somehow I felt turned on. I pulled his mouth back to mine.

Why not experiment like I did with my music? This was so much better than the flute.

What was it with this family? We fucked that afternoon with him giving me the lowdown on boy to boy. He was very physical, clearly enthusiastic and vocal. Best…he loved to bottom.

"How'd you know I wouldn't get mad? I was fucking your sister."

"Ahhh! So gross! I *do not* want *any* details, ever! But how did I know about you? Queer boys have a special mojo on spotting other queer boys. The way you move your butt was a giveaway."

I slapped his chest. Not very hard and kissed him.

I did it with him at first in part to piss off Elizabeth which it did, then continued because I liked Bryan, the sex was amazing. We became inseparable. Homework was always a team effort. We were competitive in working out, playing soccer and helping organize a garage band. I was on keyboard; he did drums. As ninth graders, we played Junior Prom!

One great year.

Dad bought me a beat up electric keyboard so I could practice at home and use it with the band. Put on the headsets at home and no one could hear me hit the ivory. Pretend ivory.

In the summer before tenth grade, at the ripe old age of seventeen, I practiced several hours a day, same for sex with Bryan. We decided research was important, watching porn to learn new positions, finding inspiration. We tried lots of kinky stuff. He topped me a couple of times but we both decided it was less fun. Friends knew we were dating, including our parents. His sister made that announcement.

"Make sure you're careful, Abel," my dad told me in private after Elizabeth slipped a snarky tell-all letter to my parents under the door. "It's great you've made a connection with a good kid. I like Bryan. Your mother and I were young, as you know. Sixteen and seventeen. Look how amazing that turned out. We had you." He looked at me, smiling and remembering. Then came back, more playful. "Now, I'll admit the brother/sister angle is a little unique but, what the heck." We were sitting at the kitchen table. "How about your classmates?"

Best not to mention racial slurs. "A few call us fags but most don't care. We're not the only gays at school. Some kids actually think the brother/sister angle is kinda hot."

Dad punched my shoulder and laughed. I knew both my parents disapproved of what Elizabeth had done. I overheard them talking. "I don't like tattletales," Mama said, "Abel's a good kid."

They had my back, always.

Life was difficult but we were still *The Trio*. The exciting new developments were changes in my body. Dad's genes were key as his muscular physique slowly replaced my skinny kid body. Just as big time, I grew five inches in height during the ninth and tenth grades, escaped my pimples to clear olive skin and kept growing and growing in an especially cool place that I could never mention to my parents. But Bryan noticed and grinned a lot.

++++

My boyfriend often came over after school and this was one of those days. We'd do homework and mess around if my parents were gone. No such luck today. I was in the living room practicing a new song when the doorbell rang.

"Hold on, Bryan!" I hollered, pulling off my headset. I swung open the door.

There stood a woman, dressed in khaki pants and shirt. Behind her was a man dressed in all black, a pistol on his hip like from a war movie.

"We're here to see your father." She smiled, her voice friendly. "I have some papers for him. May we come in?"

"What? Ah, sure, I guess." I moved back and they walked inside. Four other men, apparently hiding on each side of the door, dressed like the first one, stepped into the room as well.

"What?"

"Where is your father, honey?"

"What is this?" I began to tremble. "Who are you?"

"We need to see him."

I knew this was bad and had no idea what to do. "He's not here; he's at work."

"We know he's here. Please get him." She smiled again, reaching out and touching my shoulder, all friendly.

My parents came out of their bedroom and stopped. The look on their faces made it obvious I'd fucked up big time.

"We're with Immigration and Customs Enforcement. I'm agent Joanne McClure." She held out a badge and took it back before I could read it. "We have a warrant for your arrest and deportation," she informed my dad. "You have ten minutes to gather what you need and we'll take you into custody. You can file an appeal, then you will be deported to Mexico."

"No! No! He's my dad! Get out!" I hollered, my arms stretched wide, trying to protect him.

Dad stood there, clearly in shock.

The men moved quickly, shoving me aside, grabbing him, knocking him to the floor, pulling his arms back, three guys on him, and put on handcuffs. He resisted at first and took several punches, the men looked like they were having a good time.

I slammed a fist into one of them and got two hits to my gut. I dropped down. Mama screamed at them and slapped the guy. He shoved her down and kicked me.

"Please don't hurt my wife and baby!" Dad begged, sounding broken.

"Stand back or you'll be arrested!" the woman yelled at me and Mama, the sweet stuff gone.

One man pulled a gun. He had a smug look.

My dad was dragged away. His eyes were wide, mouth open.

The woman gave us a card with the address for the detention center. She actually smiled. "Good day."

We followed as he was dragged down the stairs and shoved into a van. One man walked backward to keep us at a distance, a hand on his holster.

I cried. The world had ended. How could this be America?

Over the next weeks we called our congressman and the news-papers. Our pastor did the same. A story ran about an ICE sweep, mentioning my father. The newspaper editorialized against such raids. The young man at the congressional office said he would look into it and offered us hope and prayers. The ACLU provided advice and a lawyer.

When we visited Dad, held behind chain link fencing in a warehouse, he seemed defeated. He was kept in a cage with a doz-en other men. There were other families, some with young children sobbing or just staring at nothing. We were caught within the system. Politicians were playing with our lives, exploiting the defenseless, trolling for votes, not caring about the human impact. There was no exit, his appeal failed. We brought him a small duffle with clothes and some cash hidden in a camouflaged pouch we sewed inside. Our finances were in freefall but he needed money to survive once he was back in Mexico, a country he left as a baby and didn't know or remember.

"I love you, Dad." My last words to him. I reached my fingers through the wire fencing and touched his face. My father was pale and thin after two months of confinement. He cried when his fingers touched my cheek, his thumb running over my lips. His tears tore me apart. The guards came; took him out in shackles.

Across the cage, he turned his head. *"I love you, Shrimp Boy. Dare to dream. Beware the currents."* The guards yanked him through the doorway. *"I love you Raven!"* he shouted and was gone.

I sat on a bench weeping until Mama said, "Be strong, son. Time to go."

I decided I needed to understand government and be able to do something to bring him back. A new focus for school, next to music.

I got a job as a night janitor in an office building. Paid under the table, less than minimum wage. Mama started a second job as a bar waitress, singing for tips. It was always tight on making rent. The church helped some. Secondhand shops and community food services became part of our lives.

The three of us Skyped every Sunday he could score a computer in a library, church or some non-profit. Dad liked the idea of me studying government if I kept up my music. He was having a hard time in Mexico City. No family there. Employers didn't believe he was Mexican or Mexican enough in view of his Americanized Spanish, light skin and dark blond hair. They mostly gave him a pass. Some called him "pochos," slang meaning rotten fruit. I overheard that one time when my parents were talking and didn't know I could hear. Yet he always worked at being upbeat on our calls even though his life there must have been beating him down. He did find occasional clean-up work on construction sites. We managed to send him a small amount each month, experimenting with different options, but all of them had charges even though their ads claimed they didn't.

I thought about him all the time, trying not to obsess. The memories were so good. Dad and I talking music. Helping me with reading as a boy, teaching me the joy of great novels, telling me stories about our grandparents. But the day he was taken from us by a fucked-up immigration system haunted me. I tried not to be bitter. America was a good place, I knew it was, but it went off track sometimes, policies derailed by politicians seeking to gain power by inciting hate. Insecure people looking for others to put down. Mama and I traded memories. That was soothing.

All this seemed to ramp up the romantic image I had of my parents, remembering them singing, watching them dance. Mama was definitely Beyoncé, I decided, because of her looks and voice, and Dad absolutely Enrique Iglesias, at least his face and movements even if his voice was country, like Johnny Cash. Teachers said I was just as talented. Even though I wanted to think it was true, I didn't believe it. I wanted to be like them. Was I a mama's boy as some kids teased? Maybe. I loved my family. No shame in that.

Bryan and I remained tight. He was so supportive. Without him, without all of them, life would be unimaginable.

++++

Despite all this, my parents wanted me to go to college. My grades were not the best in high school. Too many worries and distractions, too many holes in my records that limited scholarships and grants. If I did go to college, I wanted to be in the big city yet near Mama so I could help. We were a team and my income, small as it was, helped pay the jerk-off landlord.

Community college just didn't have the depth of musical training I needed. The two regular college options: The University of San Francisco and S.F. State. The former was a Jesuit school and I'd had enough of Catholic schools. I remembered the priest who tried to grab my butt and the math teacher offering a higher grade for a kiss. State seemed to have a better program for voice and piano at half the price.

With advice from my posse of music teachers, Mama and Sadie from choir, I submitted a tape my senior year with four songs from their requirements list. It must have been good enough because I was invited to audition in person with the possibility of a full scholarship. I'd thought it was a joke when I got their new three-song list, not just eclectic but with a range few singers could handle.

Mama cautioned, "Nothing good is easy, Abel. Know that God made you just as you are."

Worse, bad things grabbed you when you weren't paying attention. Just like Dad warned.

In my bedroom, I hummed Gloria Gaynor's glorious anthem "I Will Survive." Always uplifting. I needed to add it to my *repertoire*, a cool term Sadie taught me to spell correctly and said using it was not pretentious even if it sounded French. Which, apparently, it was.

3.

This was the day.

Shrimp Boy, as my dad still called me, was up before dawn. I was now a few days shy of nineteen and the term didn't fit anymore.

Mama had a teaching lesson with an eighth grade boy who really wasn't much interested in piano. But the pay was good, all that mattered. We debated what I should wear to the audition and decided on my black jeans, a pale green shirt and my one and only dark blue sports coat. I polished my one pair of black leather shoes. I even shaved, not that you could see my beard line unless the light was just so.

"This makes you look respectful," she said, "...that you take the audition seriously."

She left and I put on my headset and ran through the music, singing in whisper tones so I wouldn't piss off grumpy old Mrs. Olanda next door. She was a perpetually unhappy woman always looking for a fight and my singing set her off. I tried baking her chocolate chip cookies once. She took them but was still mean. When I heard her front door close, I tore off my headset and cranked up the volume like I was on stage.

Our apartment in Antioch was on the far side of the Bay from the university. I decided to leave ninety minutes early, the extra time to tour the campus.

It was an easy bus ride to the BART station which would take me to San Francisco. I always liked trains and today I felt all grown up in my sports coat, getting on the rail car like a young businessman headed to work, maybe a high paying tech job. I was reading a BART brochure as we headed into the bay tunnel, 135 feet beneath the surface.

It came to a stop. "Congestion at Embarcadero Station," an announcer informed us. We inched ahead for forty-five minutes.

I ran to MUNI as soon as we pulled into the Embarcadero. It headed out within ten minutes. Twenty minutes later, passing by some fabulous Victorian buildings, we came to a stop in front of the Duboce tunnel. We sat there for a long time as the driver inspected something outside the car. Eventually he announced there was a mechanical failure and we needed to transfer. I ran to the Castro station eight blocks away. It took twenty minutes but a train came. Not the right one but it got me closer. I called the contact number I had and got voicemail, explaining I'd be late. I tried texting but it was rejected. Must be a landline phone. Public transportation was glorious when it worked.

The campus was larger than I expected, even knowing the enrollment was about seven times my high school. It was crammed into the edge of the city, not ivy league beautiful but a friendly kind of utilitarian. Hundreds of students hurried across the central plaza, like Christmas shoppers at a mall.

"Excuse me, do you know where the Malrick Theatre is?"

The young woman I asked answered as she kept walking. "Sorry. Never heard of it."

Five more students gave the same response.

I asked a hunky blond man in a tank top.

"Never heard of it but I can show you the way to my dorm room."

I tripped and stared at him, wondering if I heard him right.

He laughed, blew me a kiss and continued on.

I stopped at two kiosks that had campus maps. No listing for the theatre. I found the Music Department. Went there to find all the doors were locked. I tried the number again and got voicemail. "How is this possible?" I asked no one. Had I written it down wrong? State was being generous in arranging this audition just for me. I couldn't afford to skip a day's pay on my summer job because Mama and I were struggling. So the Music Department had set up a special solo recital. I was already over an hour late.

I kept walking, feeling I had to keep going then realized I was back where I started, at the plaza. My brain fogged. I began to shake, panicked I'd messed up and dad's little Shrimp Boy was drifting away.

I collapsed against a brick wall, sliding down till my butt hit the sidewalk, sensing the rough texture pulling the fabric of my sports coat, not wanting it to rip but helpless to save it. I wrapped my arms around my legs, forehead rubbing my knees, determined not to cry. I'd been practicing for weeks and was ready. I had dreams but never seemed to get a break. Everything was too much. A pile on.

"Need some help?" A woman's voice interrupted my self-pity stupor. I looked up and my mental state must have been obvious, given her expression. She squatted down and patted my knee as I straightened up. "It can't be that bad."

"It is. Couldn't be worse." I shrugged, embarrassed, lips pressed tight, knowing I looked ridiculous. Her voice was warm and concerned, a distinguished older woman, dressed in slacks and tight knit blue sweater, gray hair in a neat bun. Her glasses popped—so huge and intensely purple I wanted to reach out and confirm they were real.

"Are you lost?"

"Yes, ma'am. I'm a dufus. I was supposed to have an audition with the Music Department. But it was hell day on BART and MUNI. Now that I'm here, no one's been able to direct me and the map makes no sense."

"Who's handling it?"

"Mrs. Thompson. I left her a voicemail and tried to text but never heard back."

"Oh, Sally? Let me give her a call. I have her private number. This is Memorial Day weekend, remember. Everything closes early."

I stared. Was she an angel? Mama was big on religion and claimed they existed on earth. I didn't believe it and just smiled when she made the claim.

"Sally? This is Ruth Schultz. I have a very frazzled and lost young man who is supposed to be doing an audition for you. Something about BART and MUNI and a bad campus map." She listened and laughed. "Uh huh. Great." She clicked off the phone. "She'll meet us at the theater. Her office is next to it."

"Us?"

"Absolutely. I'm going to take you there. Let's go."

"Thank you, ma'am. That's really generous of you." Did I sense the current? Maybe.

We walked at a fast clip past three buildings, her heels clicking as we went up a set of concrete stairs and into a hallway. The double doors were open.

"*Malrick Theater.* That's the name I was given. But nobody ever heard of it and it's not in the campus directory."

"Now I understand. This was just renamed for a big donor last week. Music staff knows but probably no one else yet and updating the campus map is low priority."

We stepped inside; the room was huge, mostly in shadows, lights low. I'd never performed in this kind of space. A large stage curved outward into the audience. Two levels of seats. Maybe 800 below and a big balcony. Just one occupant.

A blond woman, maybe fifty and dressed in a blue skirt and blouse, glasses on a jeweled chain around her neck, walked up to us. She was smiling, no trace of irritation. "Abel Torres, I presume." She put out her hand. "I'm Sally Thompson. I understand about the trains. I thought maybe you changed your mind about us. Glad you didn't. Ready?"

We shook. I smiled, not exactly my cool best. "May I have a

minute to warm up?"

"Absolutely."

I stepped down the aisle, starting some deep breathing to keep from fainting, doing scales in a low voice. This was it. I'd become a *cause célèbre* for my teacher posse. They were waiting for my call. "This may help," Ms. Schultz said, stepping closer and handing me a white cloth handkerchief. "You look a little damp. You can keep it." Her smile was warm and sympathetic, her eyes crinkled like she was on my side.

I did a quick mop of my forehead. "Thank you again, ma'am."

"A student saying ma'am. Don't you love it?" she said.

Mrs. Thompson smiled in agreement. "I have water up front. Do you have your music?"

I pulled around my shoulder bag and handed her a thumb drive.

"May I sit in?" Ms. Schultz asked.

"Fine with me. How about you, Abel?"

"I'd be honored, ma'am."

We walked to the edge of the stage. She handed me a water bottle. My reaction suggested I'd never seen one like it, which was true. "Push the green button on the side and the spout unlocks. I don't know what the blue button does. Take a minute and I'll chat with Ruth. There's no problem, no rush. Get your head in the space." She picked up the file and the two women stepped away. They talked quietly.

I drank, feeling silly but better, pouring some water on the handkerchief and wiping my face. My knees cracked as I bent down, breathing deep, trying to calm my nerves. Stage fright was not an issue anymore, yet my future was on the line. This wasn't a game, performing with friends in high school, church or parties. In this kind of space, I did feel like a shrimp. But I also sensed the current pushing me higher.

I was told they'd videotape my audition for evaluation. The sound booth about halfway back in the auditorium was likely where the camera was waiting. I spotted stairs to the side of the stage and walked over and up. The admission rules said I had to sing in several languages and styles: Baroque, Romantic, contemporary. I did that in the original demo tape. Then I got this list at the end of my senior year with songs that seemed mostly outside their guidelines and were difficult because of range and expectations of a teenager not trained in the classics.

I'd also submitted an application to the Political Science department because I wanted a dual major. I'd written an essay about my life and why I wanted to study politics. An official letter said I was accepted to the university and the poli-sci department would consider a full scholarship if Music did the same. Without them, I couldn't afford school and high rents living in San Francisco. Even with that, I'd need work to help my mom.

I tapped a finger on the microphone attached to a stand at the front. It was live. Three spotlights clicked on and I jumped. No added pressure.

Both women returned. Ms. Schultz sat in a chair in the second row. Mrs. Thompson sat in the first, taking my thumb drive and inserting it into a tablet on the table. One was a sugary piece from a 1950s Broadway musical. The second was one of the greatest songs in opera by Puccini, in Italian. The third was equally ridiculous, a pop song made famous by one of the best female vocalists of all time. I was expected to handle them. My vocal team had worked so hard to make me ready. Now it came down to this, the next twenty minutes. What could go wrong?

I heard the orchestral introduction to *Carousel*. When I received the letter, I had to look up the song. It was originally sung by a mature woman at a reasonable pitch.

Lifting the mic from the stand, a useful prop for absorbing and dramatizing my energy, I began "You'll Never Walk Alone." It was meant to be inspirational and I found mine. I imagined being with my father the last time I saw him.

All that ran through my mind, the mic in one hand, sometimes both, building my emotions to match the lyrics. Have hope in your heart. When I finished and the music ended, I looked out, gesturing to the empty seats, seeking energy from the applause, then down to my audience of two who said nothing. I really wasn't expecting them to since auditions were not a show. Still, it was not a confidence builder.

"Nice," Mrs. Thompson finally said. "Rest a moment and nod when you're ready for the second song."

I picked up the water container and took another drink, watching the women talking while I ran the next lyrics through my head. It seemed strange not being at a piano when I sang, like I was missing my best friend. Almost naked to just stand there alone on stage. But this was acceptable. I loved music and these songs were beautiful if difficult. At least I could say I did my best.

"I'm ready."

The orchestra began the lead in to "Nessun Dorma," one of the most distinctive and beloved songs in opera. Pavarotti sang the most famous version and I clearly was not in his universe. The lyrics were in Italian, one of the department requirements. I had power and range but opera required special training in using the chest. I just didn't have it. At least not yet and opera was not my intended musical direction. My coaches suggested I take some artistic adjustments to fit my voice and I did, hoping it was still respectful to the original. Poise was important in performance work and this was a test, in part to see if I had the confidence and guts to complete it and not run off the stage. I knew I could handle most any range from baritone to countertenor, the highest male voice short of falsetto. The song was muscular but the English translation was weak, kind of sappy, about love for a princess. The music began, and I imagined what my mother went through that day in the jail cell with her beloved husband taken away. I began in my best tenor, rising high into the climax. I felt their last kiss, almost tasted it, love lost and the promise to be together again. I felt depleted as I finished, bowing, dropping to one knee, exhausted.

"Thank you, Abel. A unique and powerful interpretation. Please take a few minutes and rest your voice. These pieces can challenge your throat."

From her comments I hoped for the best. Unique was not always positive; I'd once used the word to describe eating fermented kimchi so as not to embarrass a friend's mom. I stood, sipped more water and wiped my face, walking around the stage, doing more knee bends, a series of stretches, breathing deep to bring enough oxygen to my brain and build strength. I returned to the microphone.

"I'm ready for the third piece, ma'am."

I'd studied two versions of this, the famous one by Whitney Houston. Another by Dolly Parton, the actual writer. I'd perform Whitney's version, so pure and powerful, about love lost. An adult male singing Ms. Houston. That was almost ridiculous but I had no choice and I'd studied YouTube tapes of other boys and men who succeeded. My mom sang it beautifully and gave me tips. It was at times even beyond countertenor, and I'd need to reach into falsetto, an old friend. I nodded and the introduction began. I'd take my muse from its movie origin: *The Bodyguard*. About a great singer, Whitney, who falls in love with her chief of security, Kevin Costner, and they must separate. It was a tearjerker film and song. Perfect inspiration. As the music rose, I began to sing "I Will Always Love You." My version was different than hers but I could relate to the lyrics, giving me power. When I finished, another bow then I returned the mic to the stand. The lights clicked off. Whoever was in the control booth was ready to go home.

"Very well done, Abel," the teacher said. "I'll share the tape with staff. You have a unique talent. I know these three songs were a tiger pit. You did well. I hope it works for you."

I hurried off stage and Mrs. Thompson shook my hand.

"Let me also congratulate you, Abel," Ms. Schultz, said offering hers. "I feel lucky to have found you leaning against that garden wall. Your voice is amazing."

"Thanks again ma'am for rescuing me. And my gratitude to both of you for your help and understanding." I smiled and exited the theater, headed for MUNI. I might not hear back from the department for a month.

I texted *The Posse*:

Abel: I did it! She said I was good! Thank you for everything.

35

Sadie Wilkins, my favorite choir member, texted back.

Sadie: Halleluiah!

Now the waiting. Was I good enough?

Tomorrow my janitorial company had scored me a shift working in the laundry room of an East Bay Marriott. The music of spinning dryers; the joy of finally achieving minimum wage; the feeling, the hope, the current was at my back.

4.

Mama had a weird sense of humor when she named me Abel. Abel Torres. A quirky choice but better than Cain.

"Abel," she told me often, "when you hear criticism about faith or the color of your skin, know it's Satan's work. Same when it deals with wonderful gay boys like you." Kind of a mixed message. When I was in Catholic school, Sister Mary was her best friend, an old-fashioned teacher who slapped a mean ruler. No talking. No questions about sex. As if a thirteen-year-old thought of anything else. They conspired to make sure I was a righteous boy.

Mom is a talented musician and an inspiration. Her name is Raven Torres. So cool. When she performs in church, everyone loves her. On the other hand, when she did her magic at the restaurant, people drank, chewed their food, clinked silverware, talked, yelled at their children, coughed and sometimes belched.

After high school graduation in May, I lost Bryan. He moved to Chicago for college on scholarship. He was living with a cousin and exploring his new city. More than my dick felt lost although that was certainly part of it. We talked and texted daily for the first few weeks, laughing, telling stories, then less often and now, not much. He was slow to return my calls and kind of vague when he did. This was love?

Ideally, for any sort of college education I needed a tuition waiver plus full room and board. A letter arrived from the university less than a week after the audition. I was admitted as a dual major, Music and Political Science. A full scholarship to cover all tuition, room and board, books and materials! I'd still need to make some money for personal expenses and to help Mama and my dad. At least I now had a chance at success.

I texted my posse:

> *Abel: I got accepted! FULL SCHOLARSHIP! Without all your help, this could not have happened. I am so grateful. Thank you!*

++++

I was given space in an architecturally challenged dorm, fifth floor. Out the front window, a dazzling view of another room across the hall; out the back, if you stood on the bed, the quad was laid out in all its glory. It was a Junior Suite because it had its own bathroom, an upgrade I'd not expected. Best of all, my very own male roommate, my first potential friend on campus. I just stared when I opened the door, watching him hang a large oil painting.

"You like?" He pointed to the life size, intensely detailed portrait of a naked man, long hair flowing, standing on a giant clamshell. "Of course you do. You may call me Renoir." He stretched out his hand. "Close your mouth. No, I'm not related to Paul Wesley in *Vampire Diaries.*"

But he did look something like the hot, non-human Stefan Salvatore, only shorter, younger, less smoldering, with curly hair and a bit of a girly attitude. As we talked, turned out he was an art major, a painter, and from what I saw of his work—he shared a dozen paintings leaning against the wall—major talented, like what you might see in a museum. When I asked if he styled himself after any particular artist, he put his hands on his hips and frowned. "I am unique," he declared, lifting his chin, and gave me a list of painters he admired. I just nodded like I appreciated their work, but I'd never heard of any of them.

Our rectangular room was concrete block on two walls, plaster on the others, all painted an odd shade of light blue. Two single beds at one end, a built-in desk at the other with two office style wheeled chairs, two plywood wardrobes, two sets of drawers with bookshelves above. Everything was clean but scratched and gouged as only guys might do. Not elegant but it worked as long as we were loose and friendly. Renoir seemed cool and likely gay. Not that he was exactly girly.

During the next weeks, the Political Science department assigned a faculty advisor, a smart man and so gracious he startled me at first. Dr. Amos Baldwin. Everybody called him Dr. Amos. He was Black, maybe fifty, a little gray at his temples. We hit it off, clicking over politics, music and our mixed-race identities. He sometimes invited me to his home for dinner. His wife Alma was just as gracious and a fine cook. Afterward he and I would just talk. I told him I was gay and shared my family situation. Dr. Amos took a genuine interest which made me feel special.

Then there was my new part time job.

"Keep the damn dirty dish cart out of sight, kid," my restaurant boss barked at me. *"I won't tell you again."* Most of the staff was nice at the pissy South of Market seafood restaurant, but always a few jerks were wanting to show their power. I worked weekends as a dishwasher. The entry had a huge aquarium full of exotic fish. Diners could pick the one they wanted to eat. Mostly raw. It seemed like murder; I couldn't watch. The menu also specialized in questionable food species like sea slugs and urchins. I always brought a sandwich for my break.

In early fall, I was back in Dr. Amos's house feeling lost, my emotions taking over.

"My mom is going to be evicted and I don't know what to do!" I blurted it out without fully considering my words. "My dad's been roughed up twice in the horrid neighborhood he lives in. Police don't care without a bribe." I only knew about these by overhearing conversations I shouldn't be listening to. I needed to talk to someone, someone who was older who might help offset my sense of guilt for not being able to help, and to offer some magical words to make my pain stop. I felt my eyes start to water. I couldn't lose it in front of this smart and compassionate man.

"Sorry." There were no magical words, obviously, but I was so tied into knots I thought my sanity was in a dangerous state. Mama on the street and me in a warm dorm room! The twenty-five months since my father was taken away had not dimmed my emotions over that day. Now this. Somehow the idea of staying in college to study abstract ideas seemed an indulgence, selfish. I pulled out a tissue to wipe my eyes and nose. "I'm really sorry."

Dr. Amos looked momentarily startled and then concerned. We were sitting next to each other on the sofa. He reached over and pulled me to him, my face in the crook of his neck, one arm around me, his hand stroking my hair. "I'm so sorry, Abel. You never need to apologize for expressing your feelings. Certainly not to me. You clearly love your family and it's commendable."

"It's not your problem. I shouldn't be trying to burden you." I sat up straight and looked at him. It was humiliating to be like this. "You and your wife are always so nice. I'm just exhausted trying to figure out how a son helps his mother and father when he has so little to offer. Maybe I just need someone to tell me it'll all work out."

He asked about her situation; I gave him the short version: "Her restaurant building failed an inspection—maybe because the owner didn't have the cash to make under the table payments to the inspector—so he was forced to close for earthquake retrofitting and plumbing upgrades. Now she's mixing part time work as a waitress and singing for tips in a bar. I told her I was going to quit college and get a full-time job. She gave me 'the look' and shook a finger in my face. We cried and prayed together. But prayers don't pay the rent. Dad shares a room with a bunch of strangers in a horrible neighborhood."

He listened quietly, often nodding, his eyes compassionate.

"There are always options, Abel. Let's explore some." He bit his lower lip and looked down, working out just what to say.

"Your mother's right, Abel, under no circumstance should you quit school! You're a fine student and this is the pathway to your future, not working at dead end jobs." Dr. Amos's tone was adamant as we sat in his living room sipping iced tea. "Alma and I have some money set aside. Pay me back when you can. Or, not. We want to help you and your parents."

Nobody was ever that kind without wanting something. It took a moment of just staring at him to regain my wits and understand what he was genuinely offering. He was serious, an honest act of generosity.

"That's a wonderful offer Dr. Amos, and I'm blown away." I started to tear up again. "Sorry. But mother and I can't accept charity."

"Not charity. Just helping a friend, a student I admire and believe in. An investment in your future. We could make it a loan."

How was I lucky enough to get assigned a man like this, someone so concerned and generous with his time and resources? But no. A loan was the same as charity—Dr. Amos would be in his grave by the time I could pay it back.

"Thank you. I'm deeply moved and grateful, humbled that you would care so much about me. But I can't. Dad always said we needed to earn our way." I wiped my eyes and pulled myself together. Was I nuts turning him down? What were my alternatives for Mama? How could I help my dad? Why did I have to be so proud?

"All right. I understand why that's important. I know pride when I see it. Those are some of the reasons I admire you and want you to succeed. So how else can you help your parents? And yourself too. I know it's not easy for you."

"My father's too white looking. Weird, huh? Mama's looking for more work. I can't take more hours at the restaurant without dropping classes." And going crazy.

"How can I help in a way you'd accept?"

"Do you know anyone who needs a restaurant or casino

lounge singer/pianist or a first rate carpenter in Mexico City? Or who pays more for a guy with my kind of awesome dishwashing and janitorial skills?" I laughed just so I wouldn't get maudlin, and leaned back on the sofa. "Not very promising."

"I suspect you're more talented than you know. You told me about being in a choir, singing with your mother, playing piano, a boy band. I was the professor who read your essay for admission and financial aid. I asked the chairman to appoint me as your advisor and approve the scholarship. Your life's been difficult but you persevered and have the skills to fly. How do you see yourself?"

I had no idea he'd seen my submission. Instructions for it required candor and I gave it: homelessness, being held back a year, kids bullying because of our poverty, being gay, being mixed race, mocking my mom and dad, the humiliation. INS agents at the door, a gun drawn, dragging my father off in handcuffs. Saying goodbye to him. I wrote about our struggle to survive financially; working nights in high school while trying to keep up my grades. Learning the value of secondhand stores and food banks. Losing my shame through the power of music, the absolute joy of playing and singing, and the wonderful teachers who took an interest in me. I wrote about my family performing together, the thrill of being able to bring an audience to its feet with my voice and piano, the elation of my church congregation shouting hallelujahs as I sang about Jesus and love. I wrote about loving another boy and the happiness it brought, someone who accepted me as I was and not having to pretend. I wanted to understand politics, particularly as it related to changing the nation's laws on immigration. Making sure that Black lives mattered. I dreamed of having a good life, a respectable one, bringing pride to my parents and friends, in music, politics, my respect for others, and offering help to those who needed it. Maybe run for office.

"I turn twenty this summer," I told Dr. Amos. "I can't even be in a bar much less work in one. There's thousands of boy bands and singers, mostly unemployed. Yeah, some people think I'm good. My parents are very musical; we played and sang together at home and parties. Dad liked country; Mama liked love songs. I was a church favorite as a little boy."

"I can imagine you breaking hearts as a six-year-old. Forgive me if I'm blunt with some of my questions. You're handsome and could be a model. Olive skin. Copper hair. Piercing brown eyes. Athletic. Great build, I suspect, based on seeing you in a T-shirt. Do you date? That may be a consideration for what I may suggest."

Did he need glasses? "I've had a boyfriend since sophomore year in high school. We love each other very much but he moved to Chicago for school at the beginning of summer. We mostly text now." I shrugged; my love life was kind of pathetic. I didn't know when we'd see each other because airplane tickets were expensive. A boyfriend next to you in a warm bed wasn't quite the same as one two thousand miles and two time zones away. I last saw him when he came back on break, the sex was good but something was different. "Between my brilliant restaurant career, school, studying, working out, practicing keyboard and voice, spending a few hours a week with Mama, I have no time for love."

"You're more aware of the world than many students your age," he told me, "perhaps because of your interest in political science or just a natural curiosity about life. What you've had to endure to survive gives you a rare insight into the underside of reality. I admire you for it. You don't walk around in a headset and staring at your phone. You engage easily in conversation. You listen and respond. You're polite and well spoken. You smile, look people in the eye and appear interested in what they have to say. Trust me, connecting with people is a very rare talent." He was trying hard to lift my spirits. "It's really useful if you want to be a candidate for office."

I appreciated his rosy words but my future seemed bleak and right now I had to save my parents.

He leaned forward, elbows on knees, and steepled his fingers, looking deep in thought. "All combined, that leads me to a possible option. I'm feeling a bit conflicted on whether I should even mention this."

He seemed to be looking through me, trying to understand my soul. That's what it felt like, his eyes looking into mine but searching inside. I held my breath.

"I've an old friend in a certain business. He's a good man. We were roommates at Stanford and we've remained close for over two decades. He saved my life once, pulling me out of a car wreck. Let me say his business is not for the shy, judgmental or faint of heart."

"What? What is it?" I'd do almost anything to help my parents. Picturing my mother on the street, honestly, was there really anything I wouldn't do?

"What would you say if I told you my acquaintance might be able to help you earn a thousand dollars or more a week with three hours of work, mostly of an evening or perhaps a weekend afternoon. It should give you cash to help your parents. It would also be best if hidden from public view. Not something for your resume."

"I get paid under the table at the restaurant." What could possibly pay that kind of money? Did he want me to do porn or be a porn model? Or sell drugs? No. There was no way he saw me as someone who'd do that kind of work. Who'd pay to see a video of my butt?

"Not quite the same. What I'm going to suggest really has a Part A and Part B." He shook his head and smiled. Maybe an inside joke. "Or it might be better to say part C and B2B." Now he grinned. He took a sip of iced tea and looked at me hard, his brain obviously continuing to churn, making a decision. I could see it all in his face. "This seems to be your situation: limited options, an aversion to accepting offers of financial help either as a gift or loan and an immediate need for income. I'm going to take a risk with our friendship and mention something both conventional and way out there. This would be best kept between us, as friends, whether you want to proceed or not. Fair?"

"Please. I want to know my options and I can keep a secret. I trust you."

"I know you're a movie and old time TV buff. Ever see *American Gigolo?*"

"Yeah, in film history class. Richard Gere is hot and dates rich women older than his mother. He's self-absorbed and into fancy cars and sexy exercise routines. I found it hard to like him. But he does make money and has great clothes."

"Ouch. That's a film I loved when it first came out."

"No. Are you suggesting…suggesting I sell my…*ass?*" Holy shit! He wants to be my pimp. What did I just blurt out? "Sorry about my language." Mama always insisted I be polite no matter the situation, never use profanity and doing sir and ma'am with people older than me. But I wanted to scream my disappointment at Dr. Amos.

Studying my face, he held up both hands. "It's not what you may think. Remember this has two parts. I am proposing Part C. Sometimes a rich older woman might just like company, to show off an attractive young man at the opera or an art gallery opening. Or, an older gay man. An escort for companionship—that's the Part C—or to impress her or his friends. No sex. It's perfectly fine to limit this work to just such activities. That's all I'm suggesting. The pay is less with this option but it's still good money, far better than your restaurant work, and you meet some lovely people. My friend has several such companion escorts. Other times—that's the Part B2B—different set of customers. In Boy-2-Boy there would likely be sex but only if you're interested and agreeable. Compensation is extraordinary because the clientele is high end, the talent extraordinary. Discretion is key."

I just looked at him. *High end* sounded like a sexual position. I remembered the old bar in San Francisco called the *End Up*. What about Bryan?

"Let me be frank," he continued. "I detest prostitution when anyone is forced or exploited. Yet philosophically I have no problem with the idea of sex work. In this case that would be the second option. I don't think there are any moral questions about escorting lonely men or women to social events. Yet, being paid for sex is very different. I am not suggesting you do that without really understanding the dimensions of it and making sure you're comfortable."

This was both fascinating and appalling. But I wanted to

know more. "So this friend has a business with two parts, companions for old people and sex with younger ones. I've been paid to perform at private parties—singing—so I can understand part C. Can you talk more about B2B?"

"Of course. Based on our conversations, I take it you've had at least two sexual partners, one of each sex?"

"Yes." His question was blunt and intrusive, but I'd agreed to listen. I did tell it all in a late-night confessional with him weeks ago.

"True or false? You're comfortable with sex, very physical and maybe even experimental."

Not like any true/false test I'd ever taken. What did I have to lose being truthful? A weird discussion to have with a professor. But we were talking about my financial needs. I didn't sense he was hitting on me or trying to exploit me. So, he was really searching for a way to help, something perhaps outside polite society.

"Ahhh, true. Elisabeth was a little prim once we were in bed. Not sure how to say it. She was just kind of there. Bryan liked it anyway imaginable. We watched gay Internet sites, tried many of the positions. Not everything—there are limits." I blushed. "I can't believe I'm saying this to you."

"Honesty is good."

"Hard to imagine anyone paying for me to do either plan."

"Are you open to an initial meeting? No commitments. Explore the options. Or reject them both. If nothing else, you might just find it interesting. You may be surprised about the dimensions. You're a resourceful young man and may find opportunities beyond just the financial income. Those who use the service are often well-known and well-connected people you're not likely to meet otherwise. That's why discretion is so important. If you don't want to do it, say so and that ends it."

It was just a meeting. Why say no?

"Okay. I'm curious. Like you promised, no commitments, I'll just listen and ask questions." No downside to meeting and talking, right? Right now I could use a taste of adventure.

"Excellent. Now something needs to happen before that meeting. Take a deep breath, exhale, wait for me to finish before you explode. I'm going to be blunt. Here's my assessment, arguably superficial, dealing entirely with the outside of you, not the remarkable young man inside." He smiled, likely responding to the wide-eyed look on my face.

"You need to look the part. You carry yourself in a refined manner that's at odds with your current external appearance. Your hair's a knotted bramble. Your eyebrows resemble Cheetos. Your beard—it's spotty and scruffy. Some might consider your clothes…Salvation Army chic. No offense. I'm talking business image here and salability beyond the college campus. Make a few changes and get the big bucks."

Nobody had ever said anything like that to me. My mouth was agape. Should I be angry or insulted? He was being honest. I really had no time to worry about clothes or grooming. "A barbershop isn't in my budget anymore." I sounded the way I felt, defensive and upset. Did I really look like that? Why didn't Mama or Renoir say anything? Maybe I should thank him. "Nobody cares about my appearance washing dishes or in class. Sure, I've been to the Salvation Army outlet. They're better than Goodwill." Some truths were humiliating to admit. Being money-challenged and looking poor shouldn't be, but it was, today, with him.

"I want people to see the real you: handsome, sophisticated, talented, vibrant, exciting. For what I'm suggesting, you need a haircut, shave, some stylish clothes and, just as important, an upbeat attitude, a sense of exploration. I know it's inside you. I'll pay for it. Please accept that part of the deal. It's an investment, call it speculation. If you elect to back away, no problem, my loss isn't all that much. If you make lots of money, you can pay me back. Deal?"

"Are you going to do an Anne Hathaway on me like in *Princess Diaries*?"

"Yes. But we won't pluck your eyebrows."

We both laughed. "I trust you, Dr. Amos." I was grateful and scared. "There's no prince under this mop, but I'm more than a little jumpy about this."

Escorting some rich older woman to the theater seemed fine. Selling my body for someone to fuck seemed immoral and gross. Or was it? Maybe not. What if I thought the guy was cute and wanted to do it even without money? Was it moral to do nothing to help my parents when I had an option that might save them? What if my dad was killed or injured? Dr. Amos wasn't suggesting Plan B2B. Still, some guy I didn't know paying to touch me…was I this desperate? Maybe. I felt a little like I was living in *Les Misérables*. I needed to be practical. One step at a time. I'd read that prostitution is legal in some countries, like Germany. In one state a 12-year-old girl can marry a 14-year-old boy with parents' permission. Where's the morality in that? For guys my age, if there is no coercion, then isn't it a victimless crime? Consensual sex is legal for adults. If two single people have sex, some religions consider it a sin. Probably not the view of most young people I know. Some religions are obsessed about the sex act and seem to use it as a means of clerical control, as a way for men to rule women. Yet the government doesn't care if two people over a certain age have sex. It only cares if sex is coerced or money changes hands. I remember one priest screaming about the immorality of prostitution and homosexuality then later cornering boys for sex saying God wanted it to happen. Yes, morality can be a game used by some for self-advantage. Would the good—helping save my family—exceed any harm? Yes, absolutely. My thought process may be a little clogged but my obligation to my parents was unambiguous.

Of course, it was possible no one would want to pay to use me. Now that would be embarrassing.

"I'm open to try this and promise to pay you back from my fabulous new job if it happens. If not, I'll find a way to reimburse you even if it takes a while. I just don't want charity."

5.

After my much too early Thursday morning class, Dr. Amos took me to an upscale beauty salon on Maiden Lane. A man named Jonny, maybe forty, likely gay, examined me as Dr. Amos explained what he wanted. The conversation was about me but not including me. As if I weren't sitting right there.

"Make his hair long enough so he looks sexy and hip, maximizing the copper. Short enough that with gel he can part it and appear very law firm chic."

"Yes, lots of possibilities with hair this thick and with that unique color. What about a fade style, long on the top, then fading down to very short at the sideburn?"

"I like that look but with some alterations. It may be popular now with guys his age, but I want it a little different. No whitewalls. Shorter on the sides is good but long enough to comb. Give him a shave with a straight razor so he can experience how smooth skin can get. Find a hair product that will pop his remarkable color."

"What about the caterpillars?"

"Yes, trim and shape the eyebrows but keep it masculine."

"No plucking," I added. But they seemed to ignore me.

"Thank you for this opportunity," Jonny said, biting his lower lip and running his fingers through my hair. "Amazing. Give me an hour. No, make it two."

++++

Jonny was concentrating, his tongue sticking out as he trimmed and shaved me. I'd never experienced a straight razor coursing over my throat. His hands seemed steady but I still squeezed the arms on my chair. He kept repeating under his breath variations of "I know there's a gorgeous man under all this." He'd look at me like an artist sees a blank canvas, then step back, examine my head before moving close to trim a hair or two, and pronounce: "There."

I heard Dr. Amos before I saw him. "Who is this handsome clean-cut stylish man?"

Again, it was as if I weren't present.

"You like?" Jonny said, glowing. "I love a challenge." He touched my hair and ran his fingers down my jaw. "Baby skin."

"Yes, I like the look. You deserve your reputation."

I peered into the mirror. My eyebrows were under control. My hair was shorter on the sides, several inches long at the crown. There was no part in this version, just swirling hair. He'd used a light gel and brushed my hair up and back. He then ran his fingers through it, making it more windblown. It seemed to flop naturally, giving me something of a rogue teen demeanor, perfect for manning controls on the Millennium Falcon. Maybe the new Hans Solo. Yes, I liked the look.

"Here are two different gels," Jonny said, handing a jar and a tube to Dr. Amos, not me. "This is what he has on there now, light and soft. This other is stronger and can be used when you want that stylish hard-hold lawyer look. Both have the same chemical ingredients that will make the copper explode."

I really understood how Anne Hathaway felt in front of Julie Andrews, Queen of whatever country that was in the movie.

Dr. Amos paid and we left. "A salesman at Watkins Men's

Clothiers is standing by with options."

"That's a really expensive place."

"Great clothes can earn their price and they'll tailor one outfit for you to wear tonight. Only the best to highlight your special charms."

I'd already given him my key measurements. Renoir had helped me after I told him my grandma wanted to sew me something for Christmas. "Lucky you," he'd replied.

I thought about Julia Roberts in *Pretty Woman*, one of my favorite hanky movies. And Richard Gere. Oh yes. I bit my lip. I'd do either of them. It might have been cheaper for Dr. Amos just to pay Mama's rent. I'd pay him back in full someday. Somehow.

He continued: "After the fitting, I'll take you back to your dorm. Tonight's outfit will be delivered to you there, the rest tomorrow. I'll pick you up at five-thirty for an early dinner before we meet my friend to offer an evaluation of your prospects. Wear your new clothes and clean underwear."

Clean underwear?

6.

I read the message twice. I'd been dumped by text.

Bryan: Abel…I need to tell you that I met someone.
Can we still be friends?

A few words and a relationship was over. It took a while to process. Finally I typed:

Abel: I love you Bryan. I always will.

His reply:

Bryan: You're amazing. So talented and perfect. How could I ever not have loved you?

Past tense. Maybe we'd been too confident, or I was, all puffed up with testosterone and dreams. I should've known real love couldn't be so easy. I closed my eyes and the tears ran. I could see him, taste him and all the things we did together. Despite all the promise in all those songs, I guess high school love didn't really count.

Suddenly, my ass hit the linoleum floor, my chair collapsing and slamming behind me, hitting a wall. I let the pain roll through my tailbone. Sitting on the floor, I slipped a hand under my ass and rubbed. I started laughing. So perfect that one object of Bryan's fascination with me also just got dumped, flipped off by a cheap office chair.

Lover. I thought it meant if you loved someone, they were the center of your life and sex was a celebration. Naïve, that was me. We'd had some great times experimenting, getting to know our bodies, practicing techniques, learning about each other. We did much outside the bedroom. I wanted a relationship like my parents, two people who loved and supported each other. I knew it was possible with male/male couples. My parents had been supportive of my time with Bryan.

I guess it became one sided or I just didn't understand how it all worked. It had seemed perfect and certainly convenient before he moved. Maybe love was on a timer. I climbed to my feet and groaned, feeling old, and went to my bed, flopping on my back, staring at the lovely water-stained sound board ceiling.

My brain was scrolling scenes of our time together, so many memories. That's what the relationship was, memories. Now I needed to move on and appreciate what we had. Maybe this formal breakup was best, and given what I was considering, a sign. It was hard to imagine God wanted me to be a whore. I'd need to think about that. Another time. Still, I needed to keep my sanity. One less thing to feel guilty about.

Part of growing up was moving on. And being polite when you do. Mama was very strict about being "mannerly" and respectful even if you felt otherwise. Bryan and I always treated each other with kindness. People already had enough guilt in their lives. I would be cautious with my heart in the future. Not sure about my dick. They may be separate.

We were just two horny teenage boys who respected each other and had awesome sex. But apparently not love. I wondered what it would be like when I found it, if it existed, how different it might be. I wanted to believe I would someday experience the real thing, just like in all the love songs.

I rolled onto my side and cried.

++++

The house was on Russian Hill nestled between some of the most expensive real estate in San Francisco. Dr. Amos stopped in front of a driveway on what was obviously the back side of the multi-level home on a steep hill. Its beige stucco exterior had decorative columns up the sides, fancy molding at the roof line supported by a row of inverted scroll corbels and just below that were terra cotta panels of twisted vines. Quite a show. Likely remodeled several times over the decades but keeping the fancy good parts. I loved architecture and once wanted to pursue it but now I was into politics and music. Actually, what didn't I want to be? Everything seemed so interesting and possible at one time or another. Except being a mathematician.

I was nervous about our purpose but anxious to see inside. Dr. Amos texted and the garage door opened revealing two cars and an empty slot. He parked his 1985 black Mercedes between a Tesla and an old forest green Bentley. The door closed.

"I want to cover some things with you before we go in." He picked up his phone and began texting. "I told him to give us ten minutes."

Dr. Amos explained— "He will at some point ask about your interest in B2B. If you want to know more about the option, don't be embarrassed and don't be shocked when Dirksen asks to see your physique."

Did that mean naked? He wasn't exactly clear just saying the man would be interested in all aspects of my personality and talents and this one was important. Was my bubble butt one of my talents? I tried looking at this as a fact gathering adventure for a short and funny story in Creative Writing class. Otherwise, it was just too humiliating.

"Does Dirksen have a last name?"

"His full name is Dirksen J. Horvath. I owe you some additional detail on his background beyond his being close friends with me. He was an investor in the biotech industry, a talented rainmaker, his connections pulling in a wide net of investors. He made many millions. Unfortunately, he got sloppy and said too much about a new start up stock offering and tangled with the SEC which accused him of insider trading. But their case was weak; he cut a deal. No charges were filed and he agreed not to work in the industry again. He accepted a multi-million-dollar severance from his firm. He knows many rich gay and straight men through various board and volunteer connections, multi-talented men who might be in need of extra income. He runs a class operation, a serious business but he doesn't do it for money for a reason he may or may not want to disclose. It's very personal. No drugged-out or underage kids. He treats everyone well, protects them, no exploitation and men only."

"Is he gay?"

"Bisexual. He dated men and women in college. He had a male lover for over a decade who died of leukemia. He likes partners near his own age."

"You make him sound like a saint."

"Hardly an angel. But a good man. He recruited me to join him on a non-profit board to help people addicted to fentanyl and opioids. He had great empathy for them, ashamed of his industry being complicit in the deaths of hundreds of thousands of people. He raised stunning amounts of money. He's also very funny, often at his own expense. An interesting sidebar—his grandfather was Apache. Some good stories. I really admire the guy, as you can tell, and I personally have no problems with what he does now because he's honest and caring."

"Sort of like Miss Kitty in *Gunsmoke*."

"You're fixated on old time television," he said with a laugh. "Sheriff Dillon never said she was mistress of a house of ill repute."

"No, but it was implied." She'd played a role, upbeat, responsible, a social façade. Maybe that's what I'd have to do if I joined this operation. "Mr. Horvath sounds like a man I want to meet."

We got out of the car and went to an elaborately carved wooden door. Dr. Amos said, running a hand over it, "He had this made based on ancient Celtic art from around 1000 B.C. I think these interlocking circles stand for eternity. Amazing isn't it?"

"It's beautiful. A little surreal for an interior garage door."

"He likes his art. He hired a master craftsman in need of work to carve the door and helped him find more commissions. He believes those with great artistic skills need to be supported. Prepare yourself."

I heard footsteps. The door opened.

"Amos!" A man in dark blue leisure pants, Birkenstocks and a *Karate Kid*-inspired jacket: black with wide white trim. What was it called? The man stepped out and grabbed my friend in a tight hug, kissing each cheek which was not easy given their difference in height. But he went up on tiptoes. Then he turned to me.

"I love your *Karategi*, sir." I hoped I got the name right. I kind of slurred the word in case I got my letters mixed up.

"Well, well. This beautiful young man knows about karate. I don't actually do hand to hand combat, much too vicious. But I do like the look. Makes me seem a little bit fierce, don't you think?" He turned his head to profile and pursed his lips. It made me grin at him being so silly. His voice was soothing, a slightly higher pitch than mine. He was about five foot five, shaved head, shiny on top. His face was round and there was something about him that drew you in, warmth in his eyes and posture, humor and something else, maybe a shadow of tragedy. He had great dimples. Hard not to like the guy.

"Dirksen, this is Abel Torres, my student I told you about."

"Lovely," he said. I put out my hand and we shook. "Let's go inside so we can talk, and I can get a better look and learn more."

The interior was a bright mix of old and new. High vaulted ceilings, maybe fourteen feet and obviously lovingly protected and restored. I was captivated by the long cracks and texture in the thick wood beams, the crystal chandeliers and wall sconces with flickering electronic candlelight. The furniture was in light colors, the walls were cream with original artwork. A painting of Andy Warhol by Andy Warhol. A few feet away was a huge painting with several sketches of Jesus with some motorcycles and Warhol.

I walked up and looked at the signature.

Dirksen said, "It's a template Warhol made for a work which is now in a museum. What surprises people about Warhol is that he was a devout Catholic and volunteered at homeless shelters. His mother was very religious."

"Thank you for that background," I said. "I had no idea." I walked to another painting of a dark-haired woman in front of some kind of green leaves.

"Frida Kahlo," he said. "One of my favorites."

The view was panoramic; wrap around floor-to-ceiling windows showed Coit Tower, Saints Peter and Paul Cathedral in North Beach and the Bay Bridge with its lights dancing in vertical lines. I zoned out.

"This way, guys."

He led us into what might be called a den. Floor-to-ceiling walnut shelves filled with hundreds of books and tchotchkes, a leather sofa and two chairs facing it. On a pedestal was the head of a giant eagle, its beak open and deadly. I walked over and touched it. Maybe bronze.

"Abel, have a seat," Dr. Amos said. I took the small sofa, facing both men who sat in armchairs. I felt like I was on display. I guess I was.

A man with neatly combed gray hair, wearing a dark suit, maybe in his sixties, said in a deep voice from the doorway: "Gentlemen. What is your pleasure?" He cast a single glance over me.

"Oh, Walter, thank you. These are my special guests, Professor Amos and his student Abel Torres who might be interested in working with us. What do you think?"

"Very acceptable, sir." The man showed no emotion. "What type of refreshment?"

"That new Cabernet is divine," Dirksen said. Dr. Amos nodded agreement. "And you Abel?"

"I'll have the same."

"How old are you, Abel?"

"Twenty." Almost. Really, he has a butler?

"He'll have a Diet Coke. No wayward activities in this house!"

I almost choked, stifling a laugh.

Dirksen picked up a clipboard and handed it to me. "Take a look and answer this questionnaire so I can get a fuller understanding of your talents and interests."

They talked about mutual friends for several minutes and I tuned out, focusing on a painting behind Dirksen, the Virgin Mary holding baby Jesus. It had a Renaissance look, wide gold leaf frame like an archway, and a very unhappy looking Mary in the center. Of course, having to bear a kid without even the excitement of intercourse might be one reason. Convincing people you were a virgin while holding your baby would also be a challenge. Talk about difficult babies! Tiny Jesus was not so tiny and, being held close to his mom's fully clothed bosom, looked like he was forty, a little self-righteous, lifting up one hand with two fingers extended, either for benediction or a Cub Scout salute.

"Abel! The questionnaire!" Dirksen said.

"Sorry." His tone and twinkle made me smile. The questionnaire was at least a dozen pages, single spaced with room for comments. Not what I expected. There were general questions about interests ranging from opera, ballroom dancing, politics, history, the symphony, ballet, art, swimming, horseback riding, golf and others. A long list of options on talents. They must reflect the interests of his clientele.

"Can you play a musical instrument?" *Yes.*

"Can you do ballroom dancing? *Yes.* I wrote. *My parents are very musical and love to dance. They even got into some contests and won trophies. They taught me and I used to dance with Mama. She was so good. We continued after my dad was deported. It helped lift her spirits.*

"Indicate the kinds of dancing you can do well." *I'm half Latin, what do you think?*

"Salsa." *Yes. A favorite.*

"Fox trot?" *Yes. Kind of 1940s but okay for a slower routine.*

"Bachata?" *Yes. But boring. Lots of hip movement.*

"The Swing?" *Yes. Fabulous, great music, almost jitterbug at times from the 1920s.*

Mama said I was good, but she's my mother. Also, the dance teacher at school, a more neutral source.

"Are you comfortable around older people?" *Define old?*

"Do you have any tattoos?" *No, my skin is pure but not untouched.*

On it went. Then there was the last section. It was what I feared. This was marked Plan B2B. "If you are open to having romantic contacts, please answer the following."

Should I answer or not? Sure, see where it goes.

"Do you enjoy having sex." *My time with Bryan was wild. So, yeah.*

"Do you prefer men or women for sex." *A male preference.*

"If men, do you enjoy anal intercourse? Top, bottom or versatile?" *Whatever.*

Then a list of sexual positions and actions. Some, sure. Some, no, no! There were a few terms I didn't understand and suspected I didn't want to. People really did some of these things to each other? I'd look them up on the Internet just in case. I handed the clipboard back to him and they stopped talking.

"The last part covers quite a range," I said. "Frankly, I don't understand all of the sex stuff. Not sure I want to take part in part B2B. I really don't want to do some options like bondage. It creeps me out." Although I did like it with Bryan. So, maybe.

"If it does bother you, then you don't have to do it," Dirksen said, matter of fact and reassuring. "My goal is to figure out your skill set, your talents, your interests, the things you'll do, things you might try, things that are a definite no. Consider this a talent agency and I'm a matchmaker. In Yiddish I might be called a *yenta* or even a *shadkhan,* although not for marriage making. My job is matching certain skills to fit certain paying customer needs. Will sex be part of every assignment in the second option? No. But some, yes. So, I need to understand your parameters. Given your age, rarely if ever will you be with men younger than you. I never deal with anyone under the age of consent. Men in their twenties or thirties are possible for you. You should have a willingness to be open and adventurous. You'll also have to deal with women but not for sex."

"Thanks for the explanation. I guess being a male prostitute is more complicated than I thought."

"That's a harsh term. You're an escort and I'm your business manager. Should we proceed with more detail on Plan B2B? I feel confident we could do well for you with being a companion. You are handsome and well spoken. Do you want to consider B2B? Up to you."

"Wow. If I say yes, that doesn't mean I have to proceed, right?"

"No. Don't do anything you don't want to do."

"All right. What do you need to know?"

"Actually, I need to have a look at you."

Dirksen's voice was warm and not what I expected for what I suspected he was about to ask. He was kind of a gay Miss Kitty in Dodge City.

"Okay."

"Please stand up."

I stood and faced him, my kneecaps twitching. I was in tight jeans, a pair of shoes called a Wolverine wingtip, more expensive than my entire wardrobe at home, a well fitted dark Armani sports jacket and a rich blue nailhead shirt with an open collar. I'd originally left one button open, but Dr. Amos had opened two more when he picked me up. I wasn't sure just what my demeanor should be. Different than being a dishwasher. Maybe I needed to start perfecting my breezy whore mask.

"Please turn around." Then, "Please take off the jacket and put it on the sofa. Face me again."

Dirksen watched me from his seat. "All right, please take off your shirt."

My mouth opened and I looked to my professor. He nodded. So, I took off my shirt and placed it on the coat.

Dirksen got up and walked over to me. He ran his hand down my chest. "Great pecs, firm, hairless and washboard abs. You'll be very popular." He stepped back and sat. "OK, strip to your underwear."

"Professor…" I looked to him.

"Go ahead. Consider it an audition for a new play."

So, I peeled down to my black *2(x)ist* shorts. A third the price at Nordstrom's Rack.

"Nice. Please, turn around."

It was embarrassing but I thought I was handling it pretty well.

"Excellent. Great bum. And basket. All right. Please take them off."

"Ahmm. I'm not comfortable doing that," I said, feeling myself blush. Although people would laugh about this in my short story.

"Nonsense," Dirksen said. "I need to know your assets if I'm going to sell them. Potential clients often ask for physical details."

"Don't do anything you're uncomfortable with," Dr. Amos said solemnly. "Do you want me to leave?"

"I'm cool with you being here. Okay, maybe you can close your eyes. But I really don't want to take off my shorts."

"It's all right," he said in his most reassuring bass voice. "Imagine you're Daniel Radcliffe stepping out on stage in *Equus*."

Dr. Amos turned his head and I pulled my shorts down and just stood there, focusing on the face of the not so happy Baby Jesus.

"Very nice," Dirksen said, squeezing his chin. "It will be very popular."

He was talking about my dick, not me. But, yeah, I liked it too.

"You're beautiful—athletic young adult male perfection. You can put your clothes back on. You should know that we sell fantasies and that's often greater than what hangs between your legs. Sometimes it's just about charm and good listening."

"I'm very nervous about doing this."

"That adds to the fantasy. Let me explain. When I got out of finance, I decided to create a business unlike other high-end operations. Have you heard of the Manhattan Madam?"

"A woman who ran a major prostitution ring. Big name clients. She got busted."

"She got too big and careless. It was mostly men wanting women. Gay men have a different view of sex. At least that's my observation. I decided to deal only with a gay clientele and also be open to non-sexual engagements, such as accompanying wealthy men or women to events and parties. It's a small service company. Clients and talent are thoroughly vetted. You'll get a health screening. We know your background. Dr. Amos vouches for your character. We'll do a criminal search. Anyone we set you up with will feel confident the relationship will not be revealed and that you're healthy. On the other side, I also require proof that our clients have no STDs. We can arrange private testing here. We also use a private investigator to research all of my customers and frankly turn down a few. It actually gives clients confidence that we value their health and safety."

"I don't think I'll have any problem with a blood test. I assume I can insist on rubbers?"

"Absolutely use protection. If a customer tries to do something that puts you at risk, walk away. My rules are very clear. I'll back you up."

"How many men do you have in your stable?"

"Funny. Welcome to the barn. I have a list of about fifty men. Early twenties up to sixty. Some only do companionship and most do both. All with interesting backgrounds. Professional men, also teachers, athletes. I know them all, many are personal friends. I don't make a match unless I think it will have a high probability of success not only for the physical romance angle but also the conversation, additional activities like art shows or ballroom dancing. I want to make connections that generate repeat customers and talent anxious for doing it again. All the clients are very rich."

"Are you going to tell him about Randall?" Dr. Amos asked in almost a whisper.

Dirksen seemed surprised and downcast. He was quiet, gathering his thoughts and began so softly I had to lean in.

"My nephew was twenty-two, handsome, just out of college. Police investigators told me he was meeting men online for money. A few hundred dollars. I had no idea he was desperate. Randall lost his life because pride kept him from asking for help. It motivated me to make it safer for men like him as best I can. Everyone in my talent pool has a career but sometimes they need extra funds and are open to this kind of work. I make sure they get that in a safe environment."

"I'm sorry." What a horrible experience. "May I ask if you ever have problems with law enforcement?"

"A fair question. They leave me alone. It's completely discreet. Away from moralists and reporters looking for sensation. I'm a big donor to several law enforcement charities. I also have a few good friends in that line of work and we sometimes help each other out."

It was all overwhelming. "Dr. Amos says you're a standup kind of man. I trust him completely."

"I'm pleased to take you on as a client if you're willing. Just companionship or B2B?"

"Frankly, I need money for my family. I'm open to both although a bit wobbly on the second option." My knees were shaking as I spoke.

"Great. We'll start with a non-sexual assignment to see if you're comfortable. Given your unique and handsome charms, you can expect very good money. Many of my models make two thousand dollars or more for a single booking. Big tips are common. If we can talk later this week, I'll share more details after I read your questionnaire. If we proceed, I'll need to take some photos. With your clothes on. Fair?"

"Yes, sir." Had I just agreed to be a prostitute?

My brain was swamped with years of religious school guilt and platitudes. Prostitutes were in the Bible. Mary Magdalene was said to be a reformed prostitute who hung with Jesus and, according to the Gospel of John, Jesus appeared to her alone after the Resurrection. Quite a statement. Maybe they were dating. The whore thing didn't seem to bother the Son of God. Of course the Bible was also full of evil, sometimes promoting it—like genocide, murder and infanticide. Mostly Old Testament. Jesus being seen with whores pissed off the Pharisees, a group of small-minded businessmen and religious figures Jesus called greedy and wicked, his main adversaries in Judea. They were very weird about sex, silly, railing against thinking about it, even avoiding touching their penises when taking a leak, according to some stories. I'll bet that led to some stinky robes. Even brushing against a woman accidently was a horror. I thought about one former high level male politician, a Vice President no less, who reportedly refused to be in a room alone with a female. I bit my lip to keep from laughing. What would Jesus think should he return? When he returned? Would such modern-day Pharisees condemn him? Likely, but who cared? Sex was a human need. Why was a simple transaction between two consenting adults considered a crime? We'd just legalized marijuana so why not prostitution? Early San Francisco had been famous for its fancy brothels and feather hatted madams. In rural Nevada, brothels were legal in most counties and apparently well run or at least tolerated. If they didn't have clients, they wouldn't exist. I'd seen stories of hookers riding in Nevada Day parades. Of course, I was in California. The challenge was making sure consent was freely given. My head seemed to be in a loop debating my new career.

I'd seen street prostitutes and we had several in the congregation. One was a member of the choir, a nice woman named Deidre who was trying to deal with her drug addiction. She told me about abuse by pimps—drugs, beatings, rape. Was Dirksen a pimp? By definition, yes. But not like any I'd heard about. Was he for real? A good guy managing whores? Is that what I would be?

One step at a time. I had to go into this with caution. I had my pride. If he needed a photo, just my face. I'd run if Dirksen was not a man of his word. I wasn't exactly a sheltered teenager, having been homeless and often living in rough neighborhoods.

"Abel! Abel!"

"Oh, sorry, I got lost in my head."

"Welcome aboard," Dirksen said standing, and offering his hand. The man was stunningly matter of fact about his business yet amusing and practical. I was feeling humiliated baring my booty to a stranger. He took out his wallet and handed me five one hundred-dollar bills. All crisp. "An advance in case you need some cash." He sat down and I just stared at the money in my hand. "I'll deduct it from future earnings so you can relax about accepting it." Had Dr. Amos suggested this?

"Please sit back down." He flipped through my pages of answers, sometimes smiling, then looked at me. "One more test to help determine the type of client best suited to your skills. Imagine I'm a semi-handsome, forty something rich snooty gay tech exec who thinks he's God's gift—actually most are like that—and you're meeting at a fancy cocktail party. Tell me about yourself in a way that intrigues him."

It was going to be a long evening.

++++

The ride home was quiet until we reached my dorm. Dr. Amos was giving me space which was nice. There was no way I could make big bucks without sex. If so, was I reduced to a commodity? I had my advance. Five hundred dollars was more than I made in a month. Despite all assurances, what if I was expected to fuck old women? Or, old men? What if I couldn't get hard?

"Would Dirksen be my pimp?" I asked.

"Not the right term. He said manager and I would add friend. He's a good person in an old and stigmatized business. You heard his story. His people are class acts and his clients rich, urbane and discreet."

"I'm not sure urbane fits for me. Have you seen the old movie, *Down and Out in Beverly Hills?*" I asked. "Nick Nolte is a bum who gets cleaned up and dressed in nice clothes by a rich couple, Bette Midler and Richard Dreyfuss. I feel kind of like him."

"Bad comparison. This is a way to protect your family and set aside some cash while you're meeting influential people who could be helpful in your career. Play the angles."

"My new career as an upscale prostitute." My voice was calm. I wasn't insulted or angry. I wouldn't miss the fish tank murders, grease traps or dishwater hands. I was just trying to get my head around it. Everything was a tradeoff. I'd be selling access to my body to help two other bodies I loved and wanted to save. Was that bad?

"Stay positive. See each client not as someone to service but as someone you might enjoy. Find something you like, physically or intellectually, and go for it. Never forget you're a young man with much to offer."

Like my big dick. I wished I believed him. He was my college advisor. How would I explain these fancy clothes to Renoir? Or, Mama?

7.

Renoir wasn't in our dorm room when I got home around eleven. I hoped he was all right. Maybe we needed to set up a pact, just a text, so we knew each of us was safe. Or was that too much like a parent would do? What did college guys do?

I stuffed the new outfit at my end of the closet and pulled the sliding door closed. Then I crashed, dreaming of Julia Roberts in downtown LA walking the streets. When I got up with the alarm the next morning, Renoir was still not back. He'd had a coffee date with some guy he'd met in the Student Union. He must have gotten lucky. I didn't want to think of alternatives.

I fussed forever with my new hairstyle, using light gel and struggling with a disobedient curl. I gave up, my hair would do what it wanted.

European History, Modern Politics and Advanced Music Theory later, I grabbed a ham sandwich and headed back to my room. My new look seemed to be drawing glances from other students. I hoped they were positive.

Renoir was waiting. He stood as soon as I opened the door, pointing at the stack of fancy suit bags and boxes lying on my bed.

"You had a special delivery this morning. Three *expensive* sports coats, a dozen *expensive* shirts, an *expensive* dark suit, some *expensive* shoes and a few other *expensive* things like bags of new underwear and socks. Notice that they're all *expensive.*" He walked up to me and touched my errant curl. "Look at your hair! All styled like a Calvin Klein model. You shaved! What's going on, my broke and beautiful *'I'm not dating anyone'* friend? Did you land a *sugar daddy?*"

He put his hands on his hips, cocked his head, squinted, and tightened his lips. Pale skin with freckles and a mop of curly brown hair. Sort of adorable and very much the younger, cattier brother of the TV vampire. He was eighteen but looked younger. "Tell me right this minute!"

Renoir was a good friend and we confided everything. "Can I look at what they delivered and put it away?" I needed time to think.

"Five minutes."

My brain churned with possibilities as I examined and hung my new clothes in the closet and over-stuffed drawers. Yes, all new underwear, no more Goodwill castoffs. I looked forward to discarding the worst of my pre-whore wardrobe. I was the one who was going to have clothes to donate! Renoir looked irritated. I really needed advice. Could working for Dirksen really be good or would it ruin me? I was scared, clasping my hands tight to keep from shaking.

I gestured to our beds. He sat, legs tight together, hands folded on his lap, chin up, his lower lip pressed out in a pout. Very theatrical. I sat directly across from him, just three feet away. Dorm rooms are not spacious.

"Well? Your best friend is waiting." His voice trilled on the last word. Normally that would make me laugh. His tone so serious it was playful. Would it still be if I was honest? I needed candid feedback. I was preparing to do something that could ruin my reputation, even put me physically at risk. At the same time, it might also solve my family's money problems. I loved my parents and wanted to help even if they might be appalled if they knew my plan.

"You know my financial situation. My mom will be evicted. An older man, a good friend, very sophisticated, offered to give me money, no strings, but I said no. I just won't be a charity boy. So, he said he knew someone who ran a business for handsome men escorting rich men and women, like at the opera or dancing."

His mouth dropped open. "You mean a prostitute?"

I needed to ignore him. "So yesterday my friend took me to a hairstyle salon, they gave me a fancy haircut and shave. Then I went to a men's store and was fitted for various jackets and shirts. My friend paid for all of it, a gift to help me but I intend to pay him back. I need to look sophisticated. I got some tight new jeans, a beautiful shirt, a sport coat and shoes to wear for a meeting last night."

"Unbelievable."

I avoided looking at him. "The man I met was very nice. A stunning home on Russian Hill. He was funny. He…he needed to see my body, so I took off my clothes."

"Fuck!"

I had to keep going or I couldn't talk. "He said not all my assignments would require that. He liked my dick."

"Who doesn't?"

"Don't be rude. I might just do companionship assignments like taking a grandma to the opera, no sex. Or, for more money and if I was willing, sex. He said I could make two grand a week, likely more, for just a few hours work in a single night. So, it wouldn't interfere much with school and I could help my parents. Please give me advice. You know I trust you."

I bent over, elbows to knees, hands to face. "Renoir, I'm really scared." Was the money he gave me an advance on owning my sex life?

He moved over, sitting beside me, and put an arm around me. "I did not see this coming. Can you do this one baby step at a time till you evaluate the ick factor?"

"That's what he said."

"You know, for a pre-famous portrait artist, I'm a practical, down-to-earth guy. I say proceed cautiously if you're sure you can step away, see where it leads. But even a few weeks at that level of pay could do what you need to do for your family, at least short term." He pulled me tight to his shoulder. "I really do admire your love for your parents. Compared to mine who haven't talked to me since I came out last year as gay and a supporter of Black Lives Matter. As you know, I'm not sure which one was the most offensive."

I wrapped my arms around him. "I'm sorry about them. Thanks, Renoir."

"Since I've been so helpful now and will be in the future, can I do a nude painting of you for my Art Anatomy project? The new you, not the old one."

"Will it include my dick?"

"Did Michelangelo include one on David?"

++++

My coming out was a cocktail party at Dirksen's mansion a week later. All coats and ties, at least for the talent and staff. Dr. Amos went with me to show support and to visit with Dirksen.

I met some of the talent before the party started. About a dozen men, different races. I was the youngest by about five years and the oldest were up into their forties. A poet, a high school math teacher, a fencing instructor, a professional ballroom dancer. All knockout handsome or compelling or both. I talked with one sci-fi author with the sharp angular face of Mr. Spock. Him I'd date. He told me he made more from his Dirksen engagements than his books and thought it was enjoyable and gave him ideas for his writing. All of us looked well built in our sports coats and jeans. They were all friendly and charming. For this kind of money we had to be. But I couldn't compete with their depth of education and skill in conversation and flirting.

Dirksen had invited some elected officials, men and women, neighbors and assorted society types. Dr. Amos mixed well with the politicians, talking policy and upcoming elections. Clients were here too but, like the talent, hidden in the larger diverse group. No funny business, just talking, having a good time. It wasn't as if you could walk up and say, "Hi, I'm Abel and I'm a whore. Do you want to rent me?"

Walter, all dressed up in a tux, brought me cranberry juice on the rocks. "Thank you," I said and grabbed a mushroom stuffed with crab from a passing tray. The waiter was a sassy looking white side-walled brunet. He was grinning at me. Did I know him? Did I want to?

I talked to some congressman—Ted I think his name was. Or Thom. My political science background gave us a lot to talk about. You would've thought I was fascinating but the way he looked at me and occasionally touched my hand and shoulder suggested he found me compelling in other ways. He wasn't exactly creepy, just at the outer edge of friendliness.

The background music was very soft and extremely boring, lulling my senses. A man who looked like Kermit the Frog kept staring at me. No way. I didn't see Dr. Amos anywhere. I noticed a beautiful grand piano in one corner of the room. I walked over and lifted the cover on the keyboard. I was on whore tryout but what the heck? I sat down, adjusted the stool. Very softly, I did a long riff leading to one of my favorites and maybe appropriate here. I began the melody thinking about Sam at that bar in Casablanca when Humphrey Bogart asks him to sing one of the great love songs of all time.

I began to sing, "As Time Goes By."

There were maybe a hundred and fifty people at the party and all of them seemed to turn and look at me; some converged around the piano. Dr. Amos emerged from the crowd and gave me a thumbs up. No one was loud, just some whispering as they stared at me, sometimes glancing at each other and then back at me. I upped my volume as if on request. When I finished, there was loud applause. The Muzak had been turned off.

Dirksen stepped through the crowd. From beside me he announced, "In case you've not met him yet, this is Abel Torres, a university student with a bright future." Quietly he said, "Go ahead and perform some of your favorites. Make them love you. This is perfect marketing."

I sang an old favorite, Paul Simon's "The Sound of Silence," always so emotional and bold. Hello darkness, yes, I'd been there many times. It was as if the audience was frozen in place while I sang.

An elderly man using a cane came up after I finished. "Have you ever watched Andrea Bocelli sing 'O Solo Mio?' I suspect you have the voice."

"Yes, sir. Many times. He has such a beautiful instrument. I know the song well. I used to practice it with my high school voice coach to stretch my boundaries, although I did take some liberties. Are you sure you want..."

"Please. Too much modesty. I suspect you're better than you think. Have confidence."

I smiled and hoped I'd prove him right. The version I did in school was in both Italian and English, not Bocelli's rendition. It was a beautiful piece, a great powerful melody, usually performed with a string orchestra. I started the introduction, thinking about the sun upon my lover's face as I stood below his window. I remembered the first time I kissed Bryan Winter, the look in his eyes. I got lost in the lyrics as I always did, throwing my head back, full tenor and falsetto on key notes. When I finished there was quiet for a moment and then robust applause. Several women were tearful, a few men too. Connecting with an audience was a high.

"I knew you could do it. Congratulations." The old man shook my hand.

Walter brought me a glass of water. As I sipped, an older woman, tall, wrinkled and schoolmarm severe with a red scarf around her neck, stepped to the side of the piano. People made way for her, whoever she was. She looked somewhat familiar to me but I couldn't place her.

"That was beautiful, young man. Your first song made me think of another about time passing and hungering for the touch of a loved one. By any chance, do you know 'Unchained Melody?'"

"Wow. Yes, ma'am I do. I performed it in high school and my dad sings it. But I'm not one of the Righteous Brothers." It was featured in the movie *Ghost*, a favorite of mine. Patrick Swayze and Demi Moore were so perfect and the song a magical fit.

"Please."

Dirksen raised an eyebrow and glared. No doubt about his view. I tried not to smile.

I took a breath and started the introductory passage to establish the melody and give my mind time to cue it up. I began to sing, dropping my register for this opening section, the way my dad liked to do, high volume.

The lyrics about needing a lover's touch were maximum romantic. As always, I thought of Bryan, my muse, my lover lost, and was absorbed in our passion and the power of the music, the words and Bryan in my arms. I could feel his breath on my neck. My love, my darling. My eyes were damp, thank goodness I didn't need to read the music. My voice soared. God speed your love. When I finished, I bowed from the bench. The applause was almost deafening. There were even a few whistles.

The woman had tears in her eyes as she hugged me. "Thank you, Abel. That was my late husband's favorite. You did it beautifully. Who needs an orchestra when you can play like you just did? What a voice!" She kissed my cheek and stepped back through the crowd.

So it continued for the next half hour, people suggesting titles and I did my best to sing them, having to reject those I didn't know. It made me feel important. I understood why Mama liked to perform. Even as a toddler I was surrounded by music. Thank you, Mama.

I noticed the pouty looking brunet waiter watching me with intensity. I checked to make sure my shirt was buttoned and my fly zipped. I looked back at him, still staring, and lowered my head to hide the flush on my face.

"Let's give this man a hand," Dirksen said, clapping. "Let him get back to mingling. I know you'll want to talk with him. Thank you, Abel. Beautiful."

As people turned and got back to the party, Dirksen leaned over. "I had no idea you could perform like this. Why didn't I know this about you?"

"Singing wasn't on your questionnaire."

"I guess it's not one of the skills my customers generally clamor for. Senator Wiseling loved it."

"No wonder I recognized her. You mean that woman's Amanda Wiseling, our United States Senator?"

"Indeed."

"And the name of the waiter who is staring at me?"

"His name is Zachary and he's not a paying customer. Focus!"

++++

"So how was the cocktail party?" Renoir swiveled around in his chair as soon as I walked into our room."

"It was fun to talk politics with some elected officials. I sang some songs at the piano."

"Naked?"

I laughed. "By the way, last week I gave my mother your number in case of emergency. She asked for it."

"Oh, Raven is such a lovely woman."

"You call my mother Raven?"

"She insists. So delightful. I wish I could call her Mom. Mine's still not talking to me."

I stared at my roommate. He looked so pleased with himself I wanted to do something to wipe off that grin.

"Don't give me that look. She and I've been texting all week. She wanted to try out the number to see if she got it right. We started going back and forth."

"What are you telling my mother?"

"You mean about you whoring around, not picking up your underwear, snoring, dirty sinks, soap scum on the shower door? Was there something you wanted to keep secret?"

++++

Dirksen called later that night. Renoir had left to meet with some friends which made it easier to talk.

"Abel, you're a hit! Four people approached me about your availability. Three men and one woman."

"C or B2B? Are any of them cute?"

"Cute is not the right question. Focus on one C and the rest B2B. Only if you want to do it. Just say no if you have concerns. Your singing, by the way, was magical and romantic. A great marketing boost to the Copperhead brand. Because of your voice and looks, compensation will rock. If you want to proceed, one potential client is the CEO of NetLine. Very rich. He was the skinny thirty-something with a buzz cut. Better looking than your average self-besotted techie billionaire. You might not even have to fuck him. He'd like to show you off at a party. Senator Wiseling also wants to use your services."

"What? She knows what I am? Or, or what I will be? I'm not having sex with her! She's as old as my late grandma!"

"Never say never. She knows and doesn't care. So, a C assignment. She just wants you to attend a party she's giving, play a bit, be charming, flirt with some of the guests, help lower the average age in attendance. I give her a discounted rate even though she has a large event budget. Lots of political types and you study polisci. Ask all the questions you want answers to about campaigns, government, anything political. You'll net fifteen hundred under the table in maybe three hours. Cash."

"Why do politicians attend your party?"

"My campaign contributions, fundraisers. I've raised millions and my parties are entertaining. Beautiful people like you attend. You've met part of the crew. Another item, switching topics, get in the habit of being a good listener. Charm everyone like you're doing. I'll explain soon."

"What about the brunet waiter?"

"Priorities, Abel, priorities!"

8.

Dirksen said I could bring a guest, someone young, to the Senator's cocktail party in Presidio Terrace, home to lots of old money, apparently. I mentioned it to Renoir and he pushed me onto the bed and tickled me until I said he could go. I was going to ask him anyway.

Lyft dropped us off at the Senator's home, a Georgian brick townhouse with a classically columned portico. A formal garden with lots of boxwood hedges. White wisteria hung from one edge of the porch. In the yard fragrant star jasmine covered an archway over a stone bench.

Renoir was in full artistic drag: tan riding pants—bulging at the hips and tight to the knee—highly polished black riding boots covering most of his calves, a matador inspired black shirt and vest with lots of sequins, reflective gold and silver threads. Also a few tassels. It emphasized his basket which was impressive, the padding subtle. Attached to his belt was a riding crop. An electric lime scarf wrapped around his neck completed the look. Who was I to judge an artist? Besides, it would be entertaining to see how people reacted. I was dressed much like I'd been at Dirksen's except for wearing a striped tie.

"Glad you kept it simple," I teased Renoir as we went toward the house. "Where's your cape in case we encounter a bull?"

"You're being disrespectful. An artist needs to make a statement and stand out. You know, I think Haight Street Costumes is superior to Salvation Army for this kind of quality."

"Who can argue with the result? Trust me, you stand out."

He slapped my shoulder.

A guard at the front door, smiling at Renoir's attire, checked us off a list and we were welcomed inside. A small band was playing quietly somewhere in the crowd of maybe two hundred people gathered mostly in a grand ballroom but also smaller rooms to the side. Most people seemed twice our combined age or older. A lot older. Fancy cocktail dresses. Numerous tuxedos. Pearl armies surrounding female necks. A few open shirts on old guys with big bellies trying to look cool. Servers everywhere. A carved ice eagle, maybe seven feet high, stood behind a bar on a table. The handsome brunet from Dirksen's party stopped, blew me a kiss and kept moving with his tray of hors d'oeuvres. I remember that word being on a spelling test in high school. Got it wrong.

Senator Wiseling spotted me and worked her way over. She gave me a hug and air kisses. I did the same back as if we were old friends. An odd tribal custom for a kid from the exurbs. I introduced her to Renoir and said he was my roommate at SF State.

"Are you a jockey?"

"No ma'am."

"A matador?"

"No ma'am."

"Do you sing?"

"No, ma'am, I paint."

"Houses?"

"Canvases."

She introduced us to so many people I lost track of their names. She was doing all this for me as if I were somebody, but I was being paid. Although technically I was still in my pre-whore period, she knew what I was. She was my first customer. A half dozen men held my hand too long as we shook. One ran a finger across my palm. I just smiled and counted quietly in my head to keep from screaming. Did all these men know my new line of work? How?

A few came onto Renoir. "Did you want to take my pulse?" he asked one guy who quickly pulled away from his handshake and disappeared in the crowd. He grinned in triumph and I bit my lower lip to keep from giggling. Not appropriate if I was on display.

I recognized some names and titles but only from class discussions and reading the news. An assemblyman here, a supervisor there. I spotted Governor Bowfield, a sprightly red-headed woman known to be into Harleys and fringed buckskin jackets. She reminded me of the late Governor of Texas, Ann Richards. In twelfth grade I did a paper on Ms. Richards, who'd made headlines saying of the first President Bush: *"He can't help it; he was born with a silver foot in his mouth."* Governor Bowfield also had a touch of Annie Oakley. The senator took us over to her and I suddenly wished I'd peed earlier. *The governor!*

"A poli-sci major," the governor said, and extended her hand. She was smaller than I expected but shook hands like a lumberjack or at least how I imagined a lumberjack might shake. "Excellent choice of study, young man. We need more people your age interested in politics."

"Thank you, ma'am. I'm honored to meet you." I decided to take the opportunity to do some politicking, thinking of my dad. "Thank you for protecting immigrant rights. My dad was a Dreamer and got deported. I know the bill was controversial, but you were righteous."

"Righteous is not something I get called very often," she said quietly. "Thank you. I'm so sorry about your dad…"

Other people approached her, pushing past us, so I wandered away, smiling and nodding in response to stares. Twenty minutes later the band took a break. A waiter tapped my shoulder and pointed to the senator, signaling me to follow her to the grand piano. As I approached, the hot brunet waiter pushed a card into my coat pocket and kept walking. Someone clinked a knife on a glass to get everyone to quiet down.

"Friends," the senator addressed the crowd, "welcome to my home. As you know, I am always looking for exceptional young talent. Abel Torres is nineteen but almost twenty, he assures me, a political science and music major at S.F. State. He has agreed to grace us with a few songs. I heard him at a party a week ago when he played a request of mine. Here's a reprise. Abel."

She pointed at me and I smiled and sat, a little nervous, which was always good. I took a breath, held it and exhaled before I played and sang, "Unchained Melody." As I finished, Senator Wiseling came up behind me and put a hand on my shoulder. I could see her reflection in a mirror, holding a handkerchief, dabbing away a tear. She had provided a play list through Dirksen, so I went through a half dozen songs, all less stressful until I spotted the governor headed my way, people moving to give her room.

"By any chance, do you know Johnny Cash's 'Ring of Fire?'"

Why not something easy? My dad used to sing it and I sometimes joined him and played accompaniment. But my vocal cords were years of heavy drinking shy of Cash's voice. I'd look like a fool if I tried to do an imitation. Singing the song of a legend is dangerous unless you're an Elvis impersonator. I had to be playful with it, serious enough to do him justice, but a bit sassy, with my own personality and a bit more theatrical. Using a piano instead of guitars and trumpets gave you more room to innovate.

"I'm no Johnny," I began.

"I don't expect you to be."

More deep breathing while I closed my eyes to see his face in concert videos and find my own voice. Love burning. Wild desire. Down, down. Sex. I sang with gusto, given the title, enjoying it, losing myself again. Throwing my head back, rising off the seat, pounding the keys. Even the opening word, "Oh," needed to be dragged out forever to do it right. Over the top even for one of the great singer's greatest performances.

I was still afloat when the song ended and I sat back down. It took a moment to return to the room and applause. I'd persevered despite the butterflies. The governor took my hand. "Well done. Not Johnny but you have your own distinctive style and a lot of spunk. You did good. Real good. Thank you, Abel."

Renoir told me afterward, adding a hug, "Fuck man, I didn't know you could play and sing like that."

The rich tech CEO, Ted something, or Bill, or maybe Chuck was there again. He said we were booked the following Tuesday, low key, no drama, as if he were giving an assignment to one of his staff members. So romantic.

"Nice," I said, "looking forward to it." Some advance warning from Dirksen would have been good. I hoped he'd give me a bio. From the guy's leer, this would be more intense than singing Johnny Cash.

As the party wound down, we said our goodbyes to the senator and walked down the front steps.

"Abel!" a woman's voice called after me. I turned and the governor, flanked by six armed guards in black with holsters, moved towards us. They looked dangerous. And hot. I carried a copy of my birth certificate in my wallet as a safety precaution. Mama insisted. Proof I was born here.

"Want a ride back to your dorm?"

"You're kidding? Absolutely! Wow!"

She looked pleased.

We walked up to a silver four-door Maserati. A Quattroporte, read a little emblem. The driver's door was opened by an officer and she slid in. The front passenger door opened, and I was nudged inside. Renoir got in the back seat, sitting between two sizzling young guards. He was entering the gay rapture.

The fucking Governor of California was personally driving us home! I was in the seat next to her! Could I possibly explain to Mama how this happened? I noticed black SUVs pull in front and behind as we moved into traffic. The governor liked to drive. Of course. She didn't speak, I didn't speak; we simply exchanged smiles when she dropped us off.

Back in our room, Renoir showed me a business card he got from one of the guards. He grabbed me and lifted me off the floor.

"What just happened? I can't believe it! A date! Call the brunet!"

I pulled the card from my pocket. Zachary O'Brien. With phone and email numbers. It said Special Events under his name. He was likely still cleaning up at the party. I sent a text—

Abel: Hi. Want to get together and talk?

—and then had second thoughts. The guy was searing. Did I want a hookup? Wasn't that what I had with Bryan, a convenient hook-up anytime relationship? Could I date and be in my new line of work? Would Zachary be appalled if he knew? I should figure it out before we meet. And not mention it to Dirksen.

His reply came seconds later.

Zachary: YES!

He included a photo of himself shirtless at the beach.

Yes, indeed.

I'd only been with one other guy in my life. There were plenty of other opportunities but I was a one-man guy, Bryan. At least that's how I saw myself, just like lyrics in pop music reaffirmed. I missed the sex but had so many issues in my life that maybe that one wasn't prime, at least not right now. Still, see where this goes.

Maybe I could pretend any prostitution gigs were done in an alternative dimension, a bit like visiting Narnia, found only through the back of the magic wardrobe. My first adventure might be with Peter, he was cute. Or Asian. No, that would be kinky; the author claimed the lion was Jesus. If I did it, theoretically, would Mama be more upset that I had sex with Asian or that he paid me to do it? Would that be an existential question?

9.

Zachary

Talk about first impressions!

People were gossiping about Abel as he moved through the party. Who was he, people whispered...Lots of crazy speculation. Zachary listened quietly as he served champagne and crab puffs. When the copper-haired beauty started singing, everyone could stare and gawk without feeling guilty. People seemed rapt, enchanted by the voice, amazed at his mastery of the piano, admiring such a clean cut, well dressed young man. That, or wanting to fuck him. It was a Dirksen Horvath party, after all. Always something edgy and unstated.

Now the event was over. Picking up one dirty long-stemmed wine glass after another, many edged with lipstick, tiny plates dripping with colorful sauces, and dainty forks, all carefully counted and boxed for a trip back to the caterer for washing. Cleaning all counters, tabletops and floors, searching all the secret places guests might stuff things. The glamorous work of a society party waiter, hired for our good looks, tight bodies, deft maneuvers to keep from knocking into drunken guests, the ability to deflect amorous advances and gropes without giving offense. We were an elite tribe, eye candy desperate enough to spend nights earning just over minimum wage, dreaming about huge tips.

Zach was doing his professional best when he heard a text ding on his phone. He shrieked, certain it was Abel. It was.

He debated including a photo when he texted back. Was he being too forward? The guy seemed a little conservative. Zach knew his own physique was muscular given the stares and propositions he got at the gym and when he went out dancing. He took special pride in his abs. He was bigger than Abel, but not a huge difference. He wanted to make sure Abel knew more about him while not being too forward. How you communicate is important. He seemed interested and Zach wanted to ramp it up. So he selected a nice beach shot, hair appropriately windblown, pectorals perfect in the sun with just enough shadow to make them pop. A casual snapshot posed but looking candid.

Ding. It was done.

Tonight was the second time he'd seen him. His golden brown skin, that craggy copper hair, his trim yet muscular build obvious in his tailored jacket and jeans celebrating a perfect bubble butt. His face was handsome yet still boyish. All this sang to him. When Abel sang, Zach lost it. He'd never heard such a voice: powerful, soaring, rich, perfect diction and so sexy. It was like the guy didn't know what a total package he was. That made him even more special. Zach had been with a lot of guys but never seen one so exciting. He knew nothing about him but wanted to learn. He'd taken a chance and given him his card. And the man responded.

Improbably, Abel might be an escort, one of many beautiful men on Dirksen's team. But he seemed too innocent and pure, maybe a little lost. At the first party he came with an older black man, likely a teacher by his tweedy look, so he might be a student checking out how the rich live. You're reading too much into first impressions, he told himself. So what if he was a prostitute? He would just be getting paid for what Zach did for free. If he was on Dirksen's team it would be Dirksen who would approach a client. He only dealt with very rich men. Not in Zach's league. But, Abel

Torres was interested in him, two guys attracted to each other.

His life was finally coming together. His first year in law school was all he'd hoped it would be, yes, thanks to his own efforts, also to professors who mentored him, calling him exceptional. Plus scholarships. He could see himself as a lawyer, almost taste it, standing up in court, defending the powerless. He'd been rescued from the streets by someone who cared and helped him regain his life, self-confidence and, just as important, self-respect. His parents, physically abusive, disowned him when he came out to them. A homeless teenager, humiliated, desperate, he did odd jobs for little money, sometimes trading sex for food or a place to sleep. Perhaps most painful: friends who were part of his parents' evangelical church turned their backs on him.

Zach remembered sitting on a sidewalk in the Tenderloin about a year after he started street life, a sign at his feet asking for help, his face as filthy as his clothes, desperately hungry when a guy he knew in high school came by and saw him. His name was Dillon. He'd bullied Zach all ninth and tenth grades. He smiled and held out a twenty dollar bill. Zach reached for it and Dillon pulled it back.

"First, ya gotta suck my dick," he'd said.

Zach did.

Survival played hell with pride. At least this time it got burgers for Zach and a friend who lived in a camp under a freeway overpass. Dignity was overrated when you were hungry and homeless.

Now he lived in student housing. He didn't think he looked hardscrabble. But we see ourselves as we want to. Abel said he just wanted coffee and to talk. He must have liked what he saw.

Anything to spend time with him.

Abel was so elegant. He could be a model. Pricey haircut, designer clothes, perfect complexion, moving with grace, like a dancer. Maybe he was rich. He looked like it. Hopefully, if he was, he wouldn't think he was too good for someone like Zach. He was smitten which was ridiculous because all they'd done was exchange glances. Sometimes you think you know for sure, something in the exchange.

On the streets, not long after Dillon ripped apart what was left of his sense of worth, there was an attack on the encampment. A boy, his friend, was murdered. Police took him in for questioning. They called a queer homeless center and an adult volunteer named Titus came and saved his life. Temporary housing was the first step to renewal. Permanent housing followed, again thanks to the center and adults who cared. He promised to never let Titus down. He'd helped him get back his lost education, Pell grants, scholarships and into college. They'd not seen each other in a long time. Not sure why. He wanted Titus to be proud of him should they ever meet again.

"We don't pay you to daydream!" Zach's supervisor snapped from across the room.

"Sorry." Just another hundred glasses and dessert plates to go. Without this job life would be tough. He had scholarships but needed books and everything outside school.

Dirksen only dealt with a high society clientele and his parties paid much better than minimum wages. At these events there were tips split between the help. Dirksen was a generous tipper; everyone wanted to work his gigs. He was friendly, real down to earth for a millionaire. He treated him like an equal and made him believe he was.

Zach had watched Abel walk to the piano at the first party and sit down, testing the keys. He looked a bit timid, starting quiet and building as people turned and smiled. The song for the senator was a knockout. He was going places.

Abel at least had enough interest to ask Zach to coffee. He felt his face flush just thinking about him. What would he wear?

Later, sitting at his desk in his miniscule student apartment, Zach opened his book on federal tax law. There was a test tomorrow and while the Internal Revenue Tax Code didn't stare back at him with brown eyes and luxuriant lips, it was his life now.

Abel Torres was a dream.

10.

The CEO texted he was four minutes out and I needed to meet him on the sidewalk near my dorm. I picked up my black cashmere Zegna sports coat, rubbing it over my cheek, so soft. Under it I wore a sage-colored silk shirt. I opened two buttons.

"Do three," Renoir suggested. "Does he pay your pimp in advance in case something goes wrong?"

"You're not helping."

"Remember Julia Roberts never kissed her tricks." He sloppy smooched my cheek. "Fucking good luck!" Then he laughed. "Wipe off the side of your face."

Thirty-two-years-old, a CEO, a Dartmouth undergrad but never finished. Developed some kind of gadget to enhance videos and a new gizmo on data mining. Worth about a billion dollars. In his photo he was boyish, with frameless glasses and wearing a suit with red tie. Yeah. The shirt neck was too big. I couldn't see his teeth in the photo. He had a flattop, very 1950. I kind of remembered him from the party but there were several clones. Apparently, he was there with his brother who spotted me and agreed I was perfect for what they wanted. I needed to approach this as a new adventure, something to learn from, and always with a sense of humor, keeping any giggles silent until back in the dorm.

I raced down the stairs and reached the street just as a black town car pulled up. The rear door opened. I saw Chuck Markus. Did I call him Chuck? Or Mr. Markus? He scooted across the backseat and I slipped inside and closed the door.

"Here is a copy of your non-disclosure contract with your… employer," he said with great elocution. Maybe proper whore protocol was what they taught at Dartmouth. "Do you understand that nothing we do or say can be disclosed to anyone without my permission?"

What a way to start a date. "Yes, Mr. Markus. Dirksen was very clear." I hoped his bedroom manner, should it come too that, was a little more romantic and not a dick killer.

"Good. Call me Chuck. At this event, you'll frequently put your arm through mine and look up at me, a bit of awe and infatuation in your eyes. You're posing as my boyfriend and people need to believe it. Be demure, even a little bashful, if anyone asks you about our relationship. You can whisper, 'It's the sex' if you want. I want people I work with, and this is a mostly work party, to see a new side of me."

"That's all?"

"People think all I do is work. They see me as sexless. I want to look like a human being to them, not a robot. A handsome young man fawning over me is a good start."

I was a fawner.

"Did you review your music?"

"Yes, I practiced and am ready when called, sir!"

"Knock it off. You're in love with me, remember?"

How could I not be?

"Ms. Johnson, our event planner, an *I Love Lucy* redhead, will announce that my 'special friend,' that's you, wants to sing a song in my honor. You'll go to the piano and call me over. Announce something like: 'This is for the hottest man in the room'" As you play you'll frequently look at me. Afterward, we'll mingle for thirty minutes then go to my penthouse."

Moving this guy from robot to human would take some work. He'd mentioned one of my favorite ancient comedy shows. That was a plus. I tried to look at his teeth in the darkness of the car. They seemed even and white. Did I want my tongue to venture into that cavern? Dr. Amos said to find something special about my dates and focus on that. Everyone has something unique. This guy had a billion of them. Maybe I would find something else when we got to the party.

We took an elevator to the fortieth floor of a building I'd seen before, South of Market, many colors, odd little fake balconies and cupcake embellishments, like the architect was a twelve-year-old and the builder cheap and with bad taste. But we were not here for the architecture and no one wanted my opinion. Just to see my face and adoring eyes. But probably no drool.

A classical guitarist was playing in the back of a crowded room with a domed ceiling and amazing views. She was good, a nice rich sound. Maybe a hundred people, most of the women beautifully dressed; most of the guys in T-shirts and tennis shoes. My date at least had on a sportscoat but he did wear some kind of odd canvas shoes. So, his dress style was not his special quality. I put my arm through his, leaned my head briefly toward his shoulder as people turned to us. And sighed.

As we walked around the room, I got a chance to see his teeth. He laughed at something someone said, a bit of a fake laugh, and I could see his tongue and lower teeth. His mouth looked okay. Renoir would appreciate I was following his advice. Someone brought us champagne flutes. Mine held sparkling water. Not sure about his. "This is my special friend, Abel," he said introducing me to most everyone. "I call him Copperhead." I moved to his right side so I could shake hands and hold him at the same time. At one point someone had something important to say about a work project and he turned away, immediately lost in technical minutia. Not a turn on. Two twenty-something women came up to me.

"So, what's he like?"

Now, I could take this a number of ways. I motioned for them to join me in a huddle. I whispered, dropping my voice into a scorching growl: *"So big! So hard! So wild! So amazing!"* I thought that might get me a big tip.

They giggled and hurried away, holding the blazing secret that would burn their lips if they didn't pass it on and on. The story should make it around the room in about twelve minutes and likely bear no relationship to what I told them. I read somewhere about how quick naughty gossip spreads and mutates.

Eventually my boyfriend for the night came back and we continued our journey. At one point, I turned my head and gave him a kiss on the cheek. He grinned and pulled me close for a light kiss on the mouth. No tongue. No spit. Thank God I was okay with his teeth.

Eventually, the *I Love Lucy* unnatural redhead announced a special treat. "May I have your attention. Chuck's 'special man' wants to sing him a song. Abel Torres. Known as Copperhead."

There was polite applause as I went to the piano.

The version my Mama liked was by Nat King Cole. But the Andy Williams take was gooier. It won an Academy Award for best song in the 1950s so there must be some merit.

"Chuck, my beautiful man, please come closer." There were a few awes from his co-workers and applause.

He walked to the side of the piano. We briefly interlaced fingers. Then I began to play, opting for a butch sound, pegging my voice closer to baritone than tenor, looking into his eyes. They were likely his best feature, kind of gray, so concentrate on them.

I sang "Love is a Many Splendored Thing" with enough syrup to make Andy proud. Two lovers kissed. Our fingers touched. The morning mist. I had a good time. We did a bit of that for show after I finished. I wanted to make sure he got his money's worth.

The billionaire lived in the penthouse of the Millennium Tower, also known as the leaning tower of San Francisco, a 58-story quasi-boondoggle. Experts claimed it was safe. I continued to stay in character, holding his arm in the car and across the entry to the elevator, nodding at the guards.

Once we got inside, he suddenly lost his CEOishness and

seemed frozen. We were just standing by the opening to his living room and its dramatic views everywhere. I wasn't sure what to do. Hoping a distraction might help, I walked over to look out the windows.

"So amazing, Chuck." I could see the Transamerica Pyramid, the Bay Bridge, Oakland across the bay. I turned back to him; he stood rooted, unchanged, fiddling with his hands, nervous and not hiding it. I walked over and put my hands on his shoulders.

"Is there something wrong?"

He glanced briefly at my face and looked away. Then it hit me. This rich guy, demanding in his office world, cocky, was not experienced in the many splendored thing.

"I did sign the non-disclosure form and I will tell no one." My voice was soft and sincere. And hopefully honest. "Please trust me." I pulled his head to me and brought my lips to his. He didn't open his mouth.

"I…I've never been with anyone." His voice was a squeak.

Now I found that something I'd been searching for, something I liked. He was a virgin! I wanted to be his first and introduce him to the good side of love. Slow and sensual? Hot and pounding? How did I handle this? I took his hand. "Let's go into your bedroom and get to know each other."

He was quiet as he led me to the room. It was large, every inch decorated by some designer, a giant four poster bed, all steel and sleek. The walls were a dark green with a lighter trim. Lots of recessed lighting. I found the switch and turned the rheostat to low, a nice soft mood. The desk, chair, a dresser, all had the silver metallic look, a little cold for my taste. Of course, I was used to second-hand furniture. We walked to the side of the bed. I tossed back the comforter, turned and put my hand behind his neck, kissing his cheek.

This was my first real test. Catholic guilt was pounded into me in grammar school. But so much of that is bullshit. I agreed to make myself available to a select number of wealthy men so I can save my family. If I handle this with respect I should be respected in return. This man, attractive and lacking some social skills, seemed like he had promise. I just needed to help him grow and find ways to open his life to the joy of sexuality. So, no guilt.

"It's cool with me to be your first guy to have sex with. I feel honored. You know you're a good-looking guy, don't you?"

He blushed and looked down. "Uhmm, thanks." His voice was a nervous whisper.

"May I take your coat and shirt off? Here, I'll remove mine first."

Chuck licked his lips and I took that as assent. I placed my jacket on a chair, unbuttoned my shirt and let it fall to the floor. His eyes widened examining my bare chest. I slid off his sports coat and placed it over mine. When I started unbuttoning his shirt, he swallowed and put a closed hand to his mouth, breathing rapidly. I pulled the garment open and then undid the cuffs. I rubbed my hands on my pants to warm them then put both palms on his chest, exploring his pecs and pushing his shirt back off his shoulders. He pulled out of the sleeves and it dropped to the floor.

I took each of his hands and pressed them against my chest. "Feel free to inspect," I said and kissed his neck, running my thumb over a nipple. His breath caught. He hadn't moved his hands so I put mine around his wrists and slid them around my chest. An odd squeak and he continued on his own without my help.

He ran his hands up and down my sides, squeezed my arms, raced fingertips over my abs. For the first time his lips lifted at the corners, a smile struggling to emerge. I needed to protect him, make sure that together we could move past his fears and enjoy God's gifts.

I kissed his chin and nose, lowering my lips to his. I licked and opened but his mouth was drawn tight. "It's all right. Please let me kiss you." I pushed again and he opened his mouth. "Maybe some tongue?"

We started slow and tentative, building his confidence. He began getting more aggressive and I returned it with matching urgency. After several minutes, we pulled away, both of us breathing heavily.

"Nice," I said. "You taste good." I stepped back and kicked off my shoes, pulled off my socks. "Is it all right if I take off my pants?"

He responded with a tight nod.

"It's going to be so good." I removed my jeans, rolled them up and tossed them next to my shirt.

His eyes were fixated on my shorts. I moved to him and touched his belt.

"May I help you with this?"

He bit his lower lip and made a noise I took as consent. I undid the belt, unbuttoned his Armani slim fit denims and pulled down the zipper. I stooped down and removed his shoes and socks. He voluntarily lifted one leg and I pulled the pants off. He then lifted the other. We were both looking at each other wearing only our shorts. Mine black *2(x)ists* and his white Diesel boxers. Too bad they couldn't get the brand logo larger, looking at the billboard of a name.

I stood and embraced him, kissing the side of his face and moved in for a kiss. He put his arms around me on his own and pressed tight, still trembling. This was a huge step for him. He was so vulnerable. I wanted to do this right.

With both of us panting, I pulled back and asked him to lie on the bed. He did, but tight against the edge.

"Can you scoot over so I can sit next to you?"

He moved and I sat, running my hands over his chest, leaning down and sucking a nipple, moving a hand down and touching his shorts. His breath caught again.

"You're a very sexy man. Is it all right if I continue?"

"Please," he whispered.

He was still soft, likely from nerves. As I rubbed him, he lengthened.

"May I remove your shorts?" I didn't want to spook him by being aggressive. I had experience with this kind of situation only with Bryan, and I was remembering how I first was with him. But Bryan and I were often wild, cavorting like we were sex starved teenagers, which we were. I had to learn patience and practice consent with this man. I stood, he lifted up, and I pulled them down and returned to my perch, picking a spot by his knees.

I picked up his dick with one hand rubbing my thumb up and over his slit, fondling his balls with the other. His knees were trembling. The man was scared but wanted this.

"May I?" His head nodded ever so slightly. I moved my mouth just above his pubic hair. He smelled of sandalwood soap. I picked up his cock, impressive and appealing, then put it in my mouth, licking the head, enjoying his sudden groan and jerk. I wrapped my mouth around his full length and sucked, enjoying the clean woodsy smell with a touch of vanilla. He quickly stiffened and I added my hand, stroking him, then sucking again. I picked up the pace and, without warning, he ejaculated with a shout, just missing my face. It splashed on his stomach and I rubbed and sucked again. It was a huge load.

I ran a finger through a puddle and raised it to my mouth, his eyes fixated. I put on my tongue and groaned in pleasure. "Delicious. Like whipped cream and strawberries." I scooped some more with my finger and brought it to his lips. "Check it out." He opened his mouth and sucked. It tasted like the two men I had tried, myself and Bryan, but less salty. I wasn't sure where the strawberry comparison came from, maybe that improv drama class I took in high school.

"It does taste good. I never realized that before."

I swirled the rest around his stomach and licked my fingers, his eyes watching each movement of my tongue. I knew he was going to pay me a lot of money but I wanted to do this for him, build his confidence.

He touched the back of my head, his face open and in awe. "Thank you."

I moved to his side, my smile all teeth. I was happy for him.

"I've dreamed of this for so long." His voice seemed restricted, words shyly emerging.

"Let me get a towel."

His gaze was curious as I wiped his stomach and dick with a warm, damp wash cloth. Another first.

"Sit up." I moved against the headboard and invited him to put his head in my lap. He looked like a naughty schoolboy, turned on his side and put his cheek against my crotch, a hand rubbing against my balls. I stroked his hair. His eyes closed and it sounded like a purr. We stayed like that for several minutes.

"My brother was right about you. Handsome and kind."

"Thank you. I should thank him. I'm just pleased you enjoyed this. I certainly did. This is just a tiny part of gay sex. So much more to explore and enjoy."

"Will you teach me?"

"I'd like that." We were silent for a while. I wanted to understand more about him. "May I ask what kept you from being with another man? Certainly not your looks."

"I was being a self-obsessed nerd. Every guy I knew, gay or straight, bragged about doing it. I think I was fifteen when I invited a boy I liked to my bedroom to do homework. I made a move and he laughed, saying I was a sick joke and left. After that I just focused on my studies. I thought of my tech product my senior year and it consumed me through my junior year of college when I launched my business. It's been my entire life ever since. At some point everyone you know has partners and assumes you're active. How do you approach someone at thirty as a virgin? I was too mortified. Being rich made me even more cautious. My brother knows all about me and pushed me to meet you. He thought you were handsome and real. I'm so glad he did."

"I'm really happy he did, too."

"Now, may I reciprocate?"

I gently moved his head and I stood, stepping back a pace. "Do you want to see more?"

"Yes, please." He rolled on his side, up on his elbow and stared, waiting for the performance.

I pulled off my underwear, lifted up my package and offered a sly grin.

"*Oh, God!*" he cried out, rolling out of bed onto his knees.

It startled me before I relaxed and realized this was excellent for both of us for multiple reasons. So much for slow and sensual.

"Oh, yeah! That's great! Please be careful! Please, watch your teeth. Oh, so good!"

He had officially emerged from his sexual prison. This wasn't bad for my first real date as a man for hire. I felt I was doing something important that would change his life. Open up new possibilities.

As I watched, my brain wandered, as it often did, and a favorite old television theme song squirreled through my head. *Have Gun Will Travel* was a 1950s series about a fast gun for hire in the wild west. My dick was my gun. I started to laugh and caught myself, realizing where I was. I needed to maintain my suave facade. And make sure I showed him the respect he deserved.

"Yeah man. So good! Ouch! Be careful!"

11.

Getting home so late made the alarm more irritating than usual. I made it to my first two classes and headed back to the dorm. My brain felt like it was about to explode, my head pounding. Too much happening for this teenager. Maybe I could unload at lunch with Renoir.

I opened the door and there was my mother, sitting with Renoir, laughing about something.

"Close your mouth," she said, standing and walking up to me with arms spread.

I tossed my backpack on my bed and stepped into the embrace. "I...I didn't know you were coming to the City." She was dressed in a light blue blouse and darker slacks. Simple but elegant on her.

"Renoir invited me for a campus tour. I've been curious. All those wonderful buildings and such landscaping. Such a nice campus. I also brought a small hamper for your dirty clothes. Renoir said you needed one."

Renoir had a very satisfied grin as he walked up to us. A hamper?

"Let me tell you," he said, "my ratings are skyrocketing, strolling around with Raven. I had several people text me wanting to know if she was Beyonce or her sister. I replied 'I'm not at liberty to respond.'"

Mama laughed and put her arm over his shoulder and mine. "Such sweet boys. Where's lunch?"

++++

"What'd you do to the guy?" Dirksen asked, sitting in his kitchen. "I think he's in love with you." He opened a pouch and handed me a bundle of cash. "He gave me the total fee—*your two thousand plus a two-thousand-dollar tip!*" He reached into a separate pouch. "Here's fifteen hundred from the Senator."

"I sang to him." I looked at the money for about three seconds before reaching out and taking it. More money than I'd ever held. And it was mine. "He liked my dick."

"Obviously. He wants to hire you again for a party later this month. I think before that, just dinner at his penthouse. Don't fall in love. You're a working professional and it could get in the way. Of course, if you actually loved him, then go for it."

I liked Chuck after we worked through some attitude issues but could not imagine loving him and any amount of wealth wouldn't change me. "No danger of that." Looking at all the money raised a question. "Do they pay you in cash?"

"No, generally not. Clients transfer money into a special account. I keep cash here in my safe. Makes it more fun."

"That makes sense." But I had a second reason for coming here. "Can I ask you for a favor? Maybe some advice?"

"Of course." His elbows were on the arm of the chair, fingers knitted together, his face open, waiting, interested.

"I took this assignment to save Mama from eviction and get some money to my dad. Could you help me? I have no idea how to set something up. It would need to be anonymous. They can't know I did it because I just…I can't tell them how I got it."

"Do you have contact information?"

I pulled a piece of paper from my back pocket. "Here's the name of Mama's landlord with a phone number and addresses for her and Mr. Cumber. Maybe say you're a long-time admirer. Say you've seen her show. I listed the restaurant and bar she used to play at plus a few of her best songs. This is my father's address and his unreliable cell phone number in Mexico City. He lives in a rooming house, a bit chaotic, and here's the manager's number but probably no point in contacting him there. A better bet is the non-profit where he volunteers and gets services. Here's an address, number and the name of the executive director. The man used to live in the U.S. and is friends with my dad."

"He'll want to know the source, I suspect."

"Maybe make up a name of a charitable group I contacted, or maybe a philanthropist who attended a concert and I asked for help."

"How much for each?"

I handed him back the bundle. "Clear any back rent and pay it forward a month if there's enough and send what's left to my father. I have that other cash in my dorm room hidden under dirty underwear."

"Nothing for you?"

"You already paid me the advance." Now I could at least make a payment to Dr. Amos for the clothes and hairstyle, if he'd accept it. Also, maybe next time, paying back the five hundred to Dirksen.

There was a favor I wanted to broach. "I was thinking that one way I could explain my clothes and some spending money to my mother is if I had a real job, paid some taxes. Maybe it would be as an entertainer, what I seem to be doing in my three assignments so far. Is there a way you could hire me at some modest salary, do some IRS withholding, make me legit? Deduct what you pay me from my earnings plus any bookkeeping costs. If that's crazy or impossible just say so and I'll figure something else."

"Ingenious. I've never done this before for my talent but I do pay staff, like Walter. Let's do it." He reached out for my hand and we shook. "Congratulations, Copperhead, you're hired. I'll text you some kind of employment sheet so I have your tax info and Social Security number. Shall we say two hundred per event on the record and that you're doing, at least for pay purposes, two events a week."

"Thank you. That's perfect."

"Ooooh. Another idea. How about I include a clothing allowance since you're a performer? That could explain the fancy new Copperhead. I'll do that off the books."

"Wow. You're being really nice." I gave him a squeeze and he was ready for it. This would offer a smidgen of legitimacy for Mama and an explanation for friends at school. Not that I should really be ashamed, but I guess I was. That Pharisee disdain was hard to get out of my head.

"You deserve nice, Abel. Are you ready for more?"

"Sure." Back to business.

"This one is much more than just being hired as an escort, at least for me. Congressman Danny Wilder wants you. I think you met him at my party. Shorter than you, trim, clean shaven, thick, curly hair. Nice looking. About thirty-five, I think. Tries too hard to be cool. His politics are liberal as they must be in the Bay Area. He's having a small party of political types and wants to show you off and maybe if you're willing, have sex after."

I felt like a commodity but I needed the money now that I had a structure set up for my parents. "Is he rich? Your rates are kinda high for a politico."

"No, at least not publicly. He keeps a hidden and sizeable slush fund for particular needs. Let me write down his number and address. You can make arrangements. He's expecting your text."

"No problem. Do I have to fuck him?"

"Don't do anything you don't want to do. I promised you that and I meant it. Discretion is crucial to him. I suspect you can be *aggressive* and do what you want in private. That's what another team member told me. So, a little drama may make it easier. I'd like you to please him so much that he wants you as a regular client."

"Define *aggressive*."

"Dominate. See him as a sub. Take charge. Are you fine with that?"

"I can do that. It might make it easier." Bryan and I liked to role play.

"Also, pay attention to what you see and hear."

"What do you mean?"

"Dr. Amos says you're remarkably mature and composed for your age. He believes your values are admirable. That's my assessment as well. With this congressman, you may be in a position to overhear things or see documents that might be of interest to the FBI."

I blanched. "What?" *The FBI?*

"There's some evidence about the congressman being involved in questionable activities. For him, being with you is just a pay-to-play transaction. For you it might be more. A lot more. For your country. I've made arrangements for Agent Ramon Cortez to join us for lunch to explain. He's an old friend and we work together sometimes."

I had to digest this. Fuck the guy while I steal his secrets? This added a new dimension, making me a whore-plus. As I thought about it, I liked it; no, I was thrilled. My work was more than getting some guy off. It lifted much of my guilt. Could I be a male Mata Hari, like the Dutch courtesan who was a spy in World War I? Greta Garbo played her in a marvelous 1930s talkie.

Paladin, Paladin, Where do you roam?

"Abel! Abel!"

"Oh, sorry, I drifted off."

"Here's the congressman's number."

++++

Agent Ramon Cortez was stiff as I imagined an FBI agent to be and about my height, brown skin, clean shaven with tight curly black hair. Maybe late thirties. The three of us met in Dirksen's dining room.

He squeezed my hand hard and I did the same back. A lot of information is contained in how a man shakes hands. I was not going to come off as some wimp queer.

He smiled, sat and turned to Dirksen. "He's got a clean cut, athletic look. I can see why the congressman wants him. So his type."

Dirksen smiled and opened his napkin as two women brought out grilled salmon over a mushroom risotto.

"Thank you," I said. One woman smiled. I took a bite. I could get used to this.

"Complete secrecy if you undertake this assignment." The agent had the hard glare down pat. "Clear?"

"Clear. You have my word." I was startled by his gruffness but tried to hide it. "What am I looking for? What's my role?" This was exciting. An undercover man in both senses of the word.

"You'd be a secret government informant. He'd see you as a multi-talented professional with sexual skills. You'd be looking for evidence this man is selling out his government."

I set my fork down and leaned back, suddenly feeling some apprehension. This was real, this wasn't a game. "That…is…quite… an undertaking. I don't know much about the spy business. Nor the sex business."

"I'll take you through some FBI basics and a few tools. Discretion is a must. So is safety. Don't take risks. If he figures out what you're doing, no matter how good you are in bed, no telling what he might do. Or those around him. Am I clear?"

"Yes, sir."

"First, the easy stuff. When you're in his apartment, scope the layout. Check out the make and model of his cell phone. See if he has a landline. Also his computer make and where it's located. Listen to everything he says. That's what you first need to know if he has you back."

For the next two hours he walked me through how to plant listening devices, tap into his computer, examine mail and packages. Cortez told me to listen and ask questions in an innocent way. "If he meets with anyone, memorize how they look, face, body size, voice. Try for an introduction. Stay close enough to listen but without making him suspicious. Sex brings down walls. Use it as cover."

"What's he doing that brings in the FBI?"

"I'll give you a sense of the case but tell anyone and it's a federal crime. Understood?"

"Yes sir."

"We suspect he's using his position on the House Armed Services Committee to leak military secrets to Ukrainian agents working for Russia."

I just stared at the man. "My God." I laugh-grunted, feeling a bit hysterical.

"We found the body of one of our agents working on this in a pond in Virginia. I don't want to sugarcoat what we're asking from you."

"Trust me, you're not." I felt numb and frightened. I clasped my hands on either side of my nose, breathing deep, exhaling out my mouth. Man, I had better be one hell of a fuck. Paladin was not feeling as cocky.

"Now," the agent said, "I'd like to spend the next couple of hours on self-defense and even more important, how to be the aggressor. I want to see your strengths and where you need work. There'll be private training sessions with another agent. It may save your life."

"My dad and I used to box," I told him. "One of my gym teachers was really into gymnastics."

"Use the bedroom on the third floor," Dirksen said. "I've cleared the room and there's padding on the floor. Just in case, a first aid kit is in the adjoining bathroom."

12.

Zachary and I agreed to meet in a coffee shop in the Stonestown Galleria, not far from school. I had a couple of hours between an important music course, Fundamentals of Ear Training, then Native American History.

I got there first and, flush with cash and testosterone, ordered two low fat medium lattes and found a table. I felt good about what I wore, a T-shirt with a picture of a laughing Jesus. Mama bought it for me. It really accentuated my pecs, probably not her intent. Casual and simple. I squirmed on the seat, my body sore from being tossed around the room by Agent Cortez in my martial arts session. I had so much to learn. But I was curious and horny.

I was looking at the news feed, the latest depressing report from Washington, when I heard the tinkle of the door opening. He was in tight jeans and a trim blue shirt open halfway down. Strutting toward me, he was clearly made for seduction. I stood and struggled not to gawk.

"Say there, I'm looking for a dangerously handsome chap with copper hair. Have you seen him?"

I stepped around we embraced with more enthusiasm than what might be normal for a coffee date. "My friends call me Copperhead." I'd told him when we had exchanged texts that this was just a get to know you event. But seeing him made my dick jump. He kissed my neck, taking a slow, wet lick and sat, a self-satisfied grin in full force.

"I like your T-shirt, Copperhead, and your nickname. Your chest makes the Son of God very appealing. I'd like to kiss him."

"I like your shirt too. I'm glad your mama never taught you how to button." I could see the sharp cut of his pectorals. He opened another two buttons, spread the fabric and smiled. His teeth were perfect.

It turned out Zachary was also a college student, first year at U.C. Berkeley Law. He was twenty-two and single, working part time for a catering company that focused on the society set. I gave him selective highlights from my background, minus Dirksen. I was excited that we both had an interest in law.

"I love the way you sing, like a pro yet still so innocent and sexy."

"Thanks. My family is really into music. My mother's the one who's a pro. On your other point, I'm not exactly innocent and you can make your own judgments on sexy."

He extended one leg and touched mine, making his judgment clear. We each took a sip of coffee and stared at each other. I pushed my leg tight against his. Why couldn't this guy be rich and hire me rather than the congressman?

"So, Copperhead, how did you get invited to Dirksen's party?"

"My faculty advisor introduced us."

"Are you getting academic credits?"

"Law school humor, I assume?"

"Are you working for Dirksen, part of his stable?"

So, he suspects. Should I be honest and risk scaring him off? Who wanted to date a prostitute? I wasn't sure I would. Who said this would be dating? No point in wasting his time or mine if he was offended.

"I'm in a trial run to see if I can handle it. I need the money for my family and it's good so far. My first gig was at the senator's party. No sex, just showing me off, a young man to flirt and provide entertainment."

"Cool. I've no problems with it. Dirksen's really nice, also generous and forgiving, but you seem uncomfortable about it."

"I am." Was he really accepting of this? "Paying me for entertainment as the senator did, is cool. I've only had one actual date for pay with sex and another scheduled." Was I really confessing this to a stranger? "A rich tech executive wanted to show his team he had a boyfriend. I know they'll not always be so easy. That makes me nervous. Even a little afraid." There. I was truthful.

"Just so you know," Zachary said, "I've taken money from guys when I got kicked out of the house because I was gay. You do what you must to survive. No judgments from me."

"Uhmmm."

"Yes?"

"Do you want to go to my dorm room? My roommate's doing some kind of art project. I only have ninety minutes before my next class."

"I'll call a Lyft."

++++

"Renoir! What are you doing here?"

"I live here."

"*Please*! Can you go study somewhere for a couple of hours?"

"You're the waiter from the senator's party!" He looked gleeful. "I'm Renoir and I believe you're Zachary. I told him to call you so I should get some credit." They shook hands.

"Thanks for making the suggestion," Zachary said as Renoir picked up his shoulder bag, his face a full mischievous grin, and swept dramatically from the room.

I turned around and my guest had taken off his shirt and was kicking off his tennis shoes.

"You don't waste much time," I said, quickly stripping down to my shorts. Other than my paid assignments there had been no man in my life since Bryan. None before.

He pulled off his shorts and I just stared. He was a porn model come to life, already giving me a salute.

"Well?" he said pointing to my *2(x)ists*.

I pulled them off and watched his reaction.

His smile was pure lechery; his voice deep, each word slow. "Which bed is yours?"

I pointed to the one on the left. He grabbed my hand, pulling me tight against him, his tongue pushing into my mouth. He tasted like a peppermint Lifesaver. His hands ran up and down my back. I squeezed his ass just as he pulled me onto my bed.

"I know we don't have much time so maybe slow and sensual next time. You got a rubber and lube?"

"Yes! *Wait!* No! I mean yes, but can we slow down for half a minute?

"Sure. It was your invitation."

"Can we not go all the way this time? You're not a customer. You're a handsome man I'm starting to date, at least that's how I see this and hope you do too. Can we maybe explore our bodies, find release and save more for another time?"

"Abel, I'd be lying if I said I didn't want to fuck right now but you're a heartthrob and I'd be thrilled just to explore your body. With my tongue."

"I can live with that."

I skipped Native American History.

13.

I was a few minutes early when I got to Congressman Danny Wilder's condo by the Bay Bridge. I slipped fingers into my inside pocket to make sure the listening devices were ready if I had an opportunity. He'd left my name with the security guard so no problem getting in. I was about to knock when I heard yelling inside.

"You're an idiot!"

"There's plenty of money. You'll have more than you need."

"Fucking amateur. You're going to blow this!"

The door suddenly opened and a baby-faced man in a sports coat pushed me aside as he stomped away. I tried to memorize his features as I turned back and saw my evening's entertainment staring at me. The congressman seemed shocked.

"Is this a bad time, Mr. Wilder? We had an appointment, but I can come again when it's more convenient."

"No. No, come in. You're just what I need. Let me freshen up and put on a jacket. A car will pick us up in fifteen minutes."

An Apple Air sat on a desk in his bedroom. A Samsung Galaxy in a black silicone protective case. Panasonic on a land line.

Several framed pieces of art in the living room, possible sites for a device. I heard water running in the bathroom; I pulled out my rubber gloves, slipped them on and put an Apple logo sticker under his computer. A wireless device, undetectable at least to me, could pull data and send it out. The water turned off. I pulled off my gloves just as the bathroom door opened and he stepped out. I turned sideways, pretending I was looking at a photograph on the wall as I slipped the gloves into an inside pocket in my coat.

"A great photo, isn't it?" He walked up to me, putting his arm across my shoulder.

I leaned closer. "Looks like beach volleyball."

I sort of remembered him from the party and he did look like his photo in the FBI bio. He was thirty-eight, a three term Democrat, elected to the East Bay seat vacated by the death of his father. He was newly on the Financial Services and House Armed Services committees. Impressive assignments for a congressman with little seniority. He was also out as a gay man.

"We're going to a small party. You're my boy toy date. Most of the people here are LGBTQ. Smile, compliment people, agree when they compliment me, hold my arm and look adorable. Then we'll come back here and fuck. I paid for the night."

I was spending the night with him. Really? News to me. What were the odds that my first two gigs involved insecure men? Maybe that's who rented prostitutes.

He took a call. More yelling. *"No, there is not a problem."*

I texted Dirksen, "All night?" and he came right back. "Yes, he paid extra at the last minute. But only if you're comfortable doing it."

"No. I'm not alone," the congressman snapped. *"Not an issue. He's just a whore."*

I stared ahead like I didn't hear it, focused on the newsfeed on my phone. Do I go through with tonight, do what I was paid for and continue my FBI assignment? Did I just leave? Did I play dumb and cute, listening carefully and trying to understand what all this yelling was about and reporting to the FBI? The latter, of course, just as Dirksen and Agent Cortez suggested. This was for my country. So this sweet faced, dense young whore with a hot body and big dick would be a mesmerizing boy toy tonight. I was already forming ideas about it.

Paladin, Paladin... I hummed quietly while he continued arguing with somebody. I listened carefully.

++++

There were maybe twenty people at the party in some North Beach loft. The place's furnishings held the kind of bland modernism that was popular. I had no idea why; just another fad. Too bad it was in such a great old brick building. People came up to him almost immediately. A hot young man in a coat and narrow old-fashioned tie, so pure he was adorable, sort of like a Mormon-on-his-mission, approached me and introduced himself.

"Hi, I'm Alexander, the congressman's new assistant. Can I get you something?"

"Do you have cranberry juice?"

"My kind of drink."

I held onto Wilder's arm while he talked with an older woman, dressed too young, her breasts overflowing the push up bra and blouse. She was asking him questions about some upcoming political event. I dropped his arm and turned away. Alexander brought my drink and we talked. This was an internship for him. He wanted to know if I was dating the congressman.

"Short term only," I replied and watched him flush.

"I think I understand. Here's my card in case you want to talk about anything after you're finished with this, ah, engagement." He seemed to stumble over his last word.

"You're making some assumptions about me."

"Am I wrong?"

"I don't talk about such things in public."

"I think you're beautiful."

"Are you a Mormon?"

"How did you know?"

"Maybe I'll give you a call sometime." He could be a good

source of information. Or other uses. Was I really this jaded?

"Sweet."

The boring party finally over, back at his apartment—his official residence was in East Bay but he kept a party condo in San Francisco—Mr. Congressman swaggered into his bedroom, his ego insufferable from all the fawning compliments, the big stud. I followed. He opened a closet and started hanging up his clothes. "Put your clothes on the chair." His voice was flat and hard, almost brutish and certainly disrespectful. No matter. I did my usual, if you can call it that, standing in my black *2(x)ists*.

He turned around. Small dick; tiny balls. He struggled to pull off a very tight undershirt. Then, oh my, he had a paunch. I'd heard of compression undershirts. I wanted him to put it back on. Best to keep that a private yearning. Actually I had no problem with his figure, just that he should be more honest about it. Take pride in who you are. Maybe honesty was what this whole FBI thing was about.

"Take 'em off!"

I slowly pulled down my shorts and kicked them off. I lifted my package and let it back down. Another pose. His mouth opened; his gasp suggested he was a bit bedazzled. Perfect.

I fell into my role. I sauntered to him, Rhett Butler moving to Scarlett O'Hara in a BDSM remake, stopping inches from his face. My mask was confident, commanding.

"*On your knees, boy!*"

He looked at me, I squinted and slapped my hands on his shoulders, pressing down hard, taking control.

"*NOW!*"

He slowly dropped to the floor. I lifted out the prize and he opened his mouth. To get hard I imagined fucking Zachary. After a few minutes I pulled him up and pushed the congressman onto his bed, making sure he knew who was in charge.

I rubbed our dicks together. He groaned; I did too since it seemed appropriate although perhaps for different reasons. He tried to kiss me; I turned my head and blew into his ear. "So hot. I'm going to fuck your brains out." I was such a fine actor.

His face held a deer in the head lights quality as I leaned back, onto my knees, spreading his legs, spitting once, putting a finger inside. Then two. With my other hand I pumped his dick. Actually it just took a couple of fingers. It all seemed to work as he writhed and whimpered. I slipped on a rubber, squirted lube onto the appropriate places, lifted his legs and plunged in. He screamed, a good sound for him, and I held his legs high and tight, pounding this asshole's ass. He wasn't getting out of this.

I slapped his hand away from his dick. "Mine!" I yelled. Bryan and I saw this in a porn film once. I lifted his butt higher, pulled out, gave him a solid spanking, a dozen slaps, his cheeks now a dazzling red, and plunged back in. When I figured he'd have a hard time walking I ordered him to jack off. When he did, I came too, roaring as it hit. I pulled out and rolled on my back.

"Get a warm towel and clean me off!" Such a he-man. This was a scene Bryan and I watched in high school. *"What are you waiting for?"* Why was I thinking about Bryan?

I think he said, 'Yes sir," and did it. Being in character was fun. I thought about using a belt on his butt tomorrow, hopefully one with metal grommets to leave welts.

Paladin, Paladin…

++++

"What's your magic, Abel? Wilder seems like he's totally infatuated with you."

"Just my dick. Wasn't that the goal?"

"Whatever. We should talk. Can you come by? I have money and results from my bill paying duties."

"On my way."

Another two thousand dollars cash. With a five-hundred-dollar tip, and my first official week's paycheck for four hundred dollars less taxes. I slapped my hands together. Finally something in my bank account even if it was small. I sorted the money and handed him back five hundred. "That covers what you paid me. I'm grateful."

"You really don't have to do this."

"I want to pay my way. It's part of our agreement. And…it's important to me."

He smiled in a way that made me feel good. "How was the congressman?"

"He's a conceited jerk with a tiny cock and wears a girdle."

"Too much information. Anything else?"

"He had an argument with a man in his apartment. I was still outside. Something's about to happen but no details on what. A man said the congressman was an idiot and was going to blow it. Wilder yelled there was plenty of money for what they'd need. A baby-faced man, maybe thirty but looked fifteen, black hair, cute, stormed out of his apartment, and shoved me aside. He was slender, coat and tie, slight accent but don't know from where."

"Excellent. What else?"

I gave him details on the layout and phones; planting one bug.

"I used a belt on his ass this morning. He loved it and I was still inside him when he took a call. Was that keeping close enough to hear his conversations without arousing suspicion? Is that an approved FBI technique? I didn't stop but I did slow enough to listen. I heard two first names. I think they were Mick and Tonya." I laughed. "Sounds like a Bullwinkle cartoon. Oh, and he referred to me as 'just a whore' on one of his calls, 'not anyone to worry about.'"

"I concede he's a jerk. But a jerk who's powerful, perhaps corrupt and can afford you. But that's exactly how you want to be when others are around. If they don't think you're paying attention or not smart enough to understand what they're doing, it makes you invisible, like a mobster's babe."

"I guess I can be a babe. Babe with a penis."

"You're special in ways beyond your looks and attachments. The names you mentioned match ones I've heard before from Cortez. Useful. I believe it's the first direct connection between them. He'll call you later today. Are you ready to spend another evening with your favorite billionaire?"

"No problem. And the congressman? I am a whore-sleuth,

after all."

"That's the spirit. Chuck wants to go out with you day after tomorrow. Seven p.m. at his place. I think dinner and whatever happens after. We're working on a date for Representative Wilder."

"Maybe I'll take a paddle with holes for the politician."

"Lovely. I have several you can choose from."

"Great. What about the news on my parents?" The reason I was doing all this.

"The landlord's a dick, but money eases all things. He didn't care who I was, but he bought the 'smitten fan' line. Her back rent is paid and she's current. Maybe advance rent after another outing. Rents in Antioch are a lot more reasonable than San Francisco. About your father, I've a friend on the board of a non-profit called *GiveDirectly*, it sends money without a middleman to the extreme poor, in this case through that non-profit you mentioned in Mexico City. An intriguing new concept. He agreed to be a conduit for Mr. Torres. I got notification that your dad picked up a thousand dollars. My contact said he was crying when he realized this was for real. You did good, my friend. I'm proud of you."

I sat spellbound as he told me, absorbing the news, before I folded into my lap and broke down in tears.

14.

I'd heard of Black Sand Beach but had never been there. Our three vans took a road on the north side of the Golden Gate Bridge, and, at what seemed like the end of the road, we continued on a narrow splash of asphalt not much more than a wide path, no guardrails and cliffs on each side. A harrowing fifteen minutes later, we pulled into what was apparently a parking area in the rough, overlooking a steep decline.

The bridge was far to my left, the open ocean to the right, and straight ahead, across the mouth of the Golden Gate, was the western edge of San Francisco, Land's End, Baker Beach, Sea Cliff.

There were thirty of us, all members of Dirksen's talent team. Before we left, while we waited for the vans outside his home, I shook hands with everyone. Some I'd met, others were new. Too many names all at once. But the faces were startling. Many classically handsome yet others interesting, unique and appealing in different ways.

"For those who have not been here before," Walter, the ever-present butler, said "the trail is steep and not well maintained. Keep a sharp eye out for poison oak and watch your step. A catering crew will be coming shortly with refreshments and lunch. I think all of you know, except maybe Abel, this is a clothing optional beach."

"People go naked?" I coughed out, in shock.

Several of the men laughed. "Optional, Abel, optional."

"The water is freezing so be prepared," Ben Chan added. "It will definitely shrink your appeal." He sat next to me on the ride. He was in his thirties, knockout handsome, a scuba instructor, spoke three languages including Cantonese. An expert in Chinese philosophy, ancient art, exotic waters and fish. I felt like a dunce trying to talk with him. When I got flustered in conversation, he was very sweet, making me feel good about myself. That made him perfect for Dirksen.

"Why do you do this," I asked Ben.

"Are you kidding? The people I meet are interesting and the way Dirksen sets us up, I'm mostly with someone knowledgeable about my interests and we can talk and learn from each other. I also get to see private collections. The sex is usually enjoyable. Not every date I ever went on growing up was great but even bad consensual sex can be good. Don't you think?"

"I really don't know."

He looked at me kind of strange. I didn't want to say I only dated one guy. I wanted to maintain my whore cred. "And the money?"

"Yes, certainly. I make far more from Dirksen than I do from teaching scuba diving. He heard through the rumor mill that I was having serious issues about keeping my business afloat. He gave me this option. I was leery but after one assignment, I loved it."

When he looked down at his phone and answered a text, I glanced around and saw Walter was by himself. So I moved over and sat by him.

"Well, this is a surprise, young Abel."

"So how do you know Dirksen?" At his quizzical look I added, "I mean if it's okay to ask."

He laughed. "Of course. No secrets. My career was military

and I served with his father in a specialized unit. When Dirksen was old enough, he joined us. After one tour, he left and went into investing."

"So, how'd you end up as a butler?"

He smirked and squeezed the back of my neck. "When I got out, Dirksen offered me a job as a kind of office manager. The butler thing I do for my own entertainment, kind of a lark, and because he knows he can trust me with confidentiality. Any more questions?"

"No, sir. Thanks for filling me in."

Wandering down the narrow dirt path, and a stairway part of the way, was fun but at times challenging, particularly when a branch of poison oak stuck out over the trail and we had to squeeze around it. As we reached the beach, a giant baby-blue ship, *Maersk Line* in huge letters on the side, stacked with thousands of containers colored like a Rubik's Cube, passed by heading out to sea. The beach sand was black, maybe volcanic in origin, which seemed appropriate given the name. It was an unusually warm weekday and we were there mid-morning. Everyone took off their shoes and walked barefoot to the east end which I was told was the queer section.

Beach towels came out and were unfolded side by side on the sand. Dirksen stripped down to his boxers and donned what I assumed was a caftan, dark red and black. It fit him both physically and personality-wise. As I watched, every guy stripped naked.

Lying on my towel and pulling part of it over me, I discarded my Bermuda shorts and T-shirt and replaced them with my blue cotton swim trunks. Watching all the handsome men and great bodies, I felt intimidated. Even the older ones were hot. Could I get assigned guys like these?

"Come on, Abel," Britt Summers mocked me. "Take it off. No modesty here. Let's see it." The professional surfer, in his twenties, blond and perfect, was not going to let me keep on my trunks. He looked like an old-time teen idol.

"Abel! Abel! Abel!" he said and other joined the chant. Most of the guys were clapping, whistling for the new guy, part of team

building, I suspected. And fun.

I stood up, my face likely very red, and turned toward the cliff and pulled them down, letting them take in the back view.

"Turn around, pirouette, we want to see it all," Gus Martinez, on the next towel over, ordered. "Come on." He was Hispanic, dark curly hair, a fencing instructor, maybe forty.

I slowly turned around, lifted up my arms, took a muscle man pose, and waited for the reaction.

Whistles and laughter.

Two caterers arrived with baskets of wine, soft drinks and sandwiches. They went about their chores, taking no obvious notice of all these men standing around a folding table, naked, unselfconscious, picking up plates.

Dirksen made the rounds, making light conversation. I sat, enjoying the stunning view, arms around my knees. Several men stopped by to ask how I was handling all this. It was surreal to have five naked, beautiful, and mostly hung men standing around me. I could see why they were popular. All of them seemed smart, great conversationalists, helping this nervous kid feel welcome, and all of them very fond of Dirksen. I stood so I could just look at faces and avoid all other body parts.

I felt like this could be a new family for me. My whore brothers. No, not respectful enough; my gaggle of remarkable new friends.

"You sing great," an older man said in an Italian accent, strolling up to me. "I don't think we have formally met. I'm Matteo Renzi. I curate Medieval art at the DeYoung Museum."

I stared, my mouth open in shock. He looked like the Italian heartthrob, Raoul Bova, in my favorite romance movie of all time, *Under the Tuscan Sun*. When Bova kissed Diane Lane I always swooned and felt like I might again as we shook hands. Matteo's voice, the depth, the accent! I remembered his bio from what Dirksen gave me. He was sixty, into martial arts. How was it possible that a man who could be my grandfather was so sexual? I glanced at his dick. He was bigger than me! I felt myself start to stiffen and tried to hide it.

"Happens to all of us, Abel. Get used to it. This is quite a crew."

"I'm going to take a swim!"

++++

My phone rang on the way back to town. I looked at the name and bit my lip.

"Oh! Hi Mama."

Two of the men glanced at me and smiled. I turned and looked out the window.

"Just heading home from the beach. Out with some friends."

"Yes, friends are important. This weekend?"

"Sure. I can come Sunday."

"I love you too, Mama."

As I disconnected, someone grabbed me from the seat behind me, another swiveled around from the seat in front, and the guy beside me started giving me a knuckle grind on my head. They were laughing and eventually I did too. I felt like these were good friends. No, I probably would not introduce them to Mama.

15.

"Copperhead, did I ever tell you my reaction when I first heard your high school audition tape?" asked Dr. Benjamin Moss, Chairman of the Music Department and a phenomenal violinist. We were meeting in his office. I was surprised at the invitation. I'd only met him once at an event for freshmen. I was a nobody.

"No sir. I assumed somebody must have liked it because I got the chance to audition in person."

"After the voice instructor heard it, she shared it with me. I was in the back of the auditorium when you auditioned. Sally Thompson called me when she knew you were on your way."

"Did you create the song list? It was a challenge."

"Yes. I wanted to see how you'd handle a variety of types to test your range and potential. It was outside our normal options. I was blown away by your male interpretation of 'I Will Always Love You' from *The Bodyguard*. It's a challenge for any female pop singer much less a male."

"It was a stretch but I love the song and like to expand my range. Same with 'You'll Never Walk Alone' in a much lower key. I practiced for weeks in the soundproof study room with piano at my church. My mom and my music teacher contacted friends and I had a whole posse of advisors. All the songs were difficult but beautiful. Ms. Houston I'm not but I admire her and I gave it my best guy voice interpretation."

"Your voice is a remarkable instrument. My observation is your range potential is four octaves at least, five likely with a pure countertenor and an ability to handle falsetto with finesse. Few have that. Freddie Mercury could do it. You're gifted on piano—your professor shared a tape of your practice—and we'll continue to help you advance, but it's the nature of your voice, your physical capacity as well as your training that makes me think you could have a serious career. You also have a great natural presence when you perform. An audience relates to that, bonds with a performer. What are you working on now?"

I felt stunned by this kind of praise. A restaurant crooner's kid. I was a freshman. What did he just ask me?

He smiled, repeated, "What are you working on?"

"Sorry. Ms. Carville has me on 'Shallow' from *A Star is Born*. Such an emotional movie and song. Bradley Cooper and Lady Gaga were spectacular. Ms. Carville has me singing both parts as a stretch but it's great fun changing pitch, male to female and back. We skipped the duet. I think I'm a poor substitute but I love the music. We have a good time with it."

"Can you give me a few bars from wherever you like? Whatever feels natural."

"Yes, sir." I stood. You had to be ready to sing in all kinds of settings in this department and without embarrassment. Playing the piano at least required an instrument. So I performed the music in my head, eyes closed, feeling the beat, head bobbing, the words about longing for change, needing more. I thought about my dad in shackles. Desperate people I'd met in the homeless shelters. I'd lived it; I felt it, and hoped it transferred into my voice.

When I finished, I hesitated a moment before opening my eyes.

He was grinning. "Very nice. Powerful emotion. Heartfelt. Well done. Now, I want to share something we'll be announcing tomorrow. The Music and Drama departments are going to jointly produce a musical next spring with help from one of the big downtown theaters. Drama will assist, partnering with professionals and our department will provide the orchestra and hopefully many of the singers. It will be open competition." He paused. "We're still working out details with the unions but I'm hopeful."

"Great," I replied. "What's the musical?"

"A never-fails big ticket seller: *Les Misérables*. What do you think?"

"I've watched it a hundred times on TV. My mom took me to see a traveling Broadway version downtown when I was in high school. So powerful. Stunning music and lyrics. So much more than the typical musical. I really relate and cry every time I see it."

"One of our voice instructors will be advising the outside director on selection. I'd like you to audition."

"I've never done anything like this," I said dubiously. "Just band, choir and solo. What role did you have in mind?"

"Jean Valjean."

"Are you serious?" I lifted a few inches out of my chair. I felt oxygen escaping my brain. "The guy on PBS, the one they use for fundraising, he's like forty-something years old. He could be my father. I'm a freshman! I don't want to embarrass myself!"

"Makeup can do wonders on aging. You're older than most freshmen. Your voice has power and maturity. But you need to work on technique. I've a donor fund for special students. I'm assigning an additional coach from outside the school to work with you. Ms. Elenore Grimly, the former Met star. Do you know her?"

"Sure, I know of her. She's famous. But sir, holy shit! Sorry. You want me to perform 'Who Am I?' and…and 'One Day More'…I…I don't know what to say. 'Bring him Home' is so haunting. Valjean is the backbone of the musical, of the book." I felt like I was losing it. This was too much. "I don't have that kind of operatic voice. Or stage presence!" Or really the free time between school and being a whore spy.

"Yet!" He had a trust-me smile. "Have more confidence in yourself. Why do you think Ms. Carville has you studying 'Shallow?' It's why I included 'You'll Never Walk Alone' in your audi-

tion to test your range and confidence. Give it your best. 'Bring Him Home' is a mix of falsetto and chest voice. Challenge yourself. If Ms. Grimley and Ms. Carville say you're hopeless then I'll give you something easier. Maybe a slot in the chorus and you focus on poli-sci and pursue a political career."

He raised an eyebrow and smirked, so I knew he was mostly kidding.

++++

I felt submerged under heavy expectations. This was beyond reason. I could imagine how I would croak out the first versions while shaking on stage. Then there was the FBI sting. But there was a more important option tonight. I texted I was on my way.

The door flew open before I could knock.

Zachary was naked before God and neighbors. Not the least bit embarrassed. So much for talking about career goals. I looked around to make sure no one was looking out a window. What was he thinking? No, it was obvious.

++++

Afterward, I burst out into song, Marvin Gaye's magical, "Let's Get It On, Baby."

"Shut up!" some guy yelled from the next apartment, pounding on the wall.

"Wow," Zach said as we leaned against the headboard, holding each other. "Nobody has ever seduced me with song. I like it. Maybe not my neighbor. But screw him."

"This is actually post seduction. We already climaxed." I liked to show off sometimes. Actually, a lot. A little of Marvin's music seemed corny but perfect. Romantic. Zachary O'Brien had boyfriend potential. The physical part was amazing. Only going partway meant so much remaining. Now I wanted to get to know the man and not just his dick. I wanted to go slow and he wanted it all now.

Society in general would see my part-time work as loathsome. Should I even consider a romantic relationship? Dirksen warned against it, a distraction from my new line of work. For me, whatever you call my new profession, it was so far amusing, an adventure and considering the secret detective angle, maybe even important. I managed it as if it wasn't real life, at least intellectually. Just a performance and like in ancient Greek plays, I wore a mask. There was no coercion and I could turn anyone down. Neither of the guys I'd been with were disgusting physically or politically. They were interesting. Actually they were fascinating, people I would never otherwise have contact with. So that helped. Then there was the money. Catholic guilt be damned.

Yet, it was real. Agent Ramon, Walter and Dirksen made it clear I needed to be very cautious. I could get hurt. Even killed. This wasn't some movie role. How unfair to Zachary if we bonded as lovers and my body was found floating in a pond. Or, his.

Zach stroked my cheek and turned my head to face him. "Going slow is fine but challenging. I like you a lot and maybe we have something here and need to learn about each other, like you say."

He kissed me and continued: "Maybe my love life would've been more satisfying if I did more of a paint by numbers romance. Learning to appreciate each other in tiny bites seems like hope for our future, like we might really have something. No judgment from me on what you're doing to help your family. It says a lot about you. Not everyone would literally put their ass on the line." He started to laugh. "Sorry. I couldn't resist."

I punched his arm. *"Asshole!* I grew up in toxic Catholic guilt. Sex out of marriage is evil—according to the priest who was flirting with me. Here I am using my body for money, and with men. The nun who's a friend of my mother would faint if she knew."

"And your mom?"

"Working in a swanky restaurant and a casino lounge gives her a different world view. She actually joined PFLAG when I told her. She's working as a waitress now in a bar. If she knew I was the mysterious admirer paying her rent...I don't know. She loves me. But if she knew... We've been through so much together. We're pretty tight."

"Maybe someday I could meet her. In case you haven't figured it out, I like you."

I kissed his cheek, excited that he really wanted to take our relationship further, beyond just the sex. "I like you too."

"So, can we say we're dating? Not just a limited hookup or the friends with a modest benefits thing?"

His eyes were focused on mine. He needed me and that made me happy. My gut, certainly my dick, and maybe my heart, said we should explore possibilities.

He ran a finger over my cheek and in the most sincere, smarmy voice announced: "Every time I look at you my asshole feels hollow."

"That's dreadful! I thought we were being honest here."

"I read that in a porn novel and I've wanted to use it like forever. But never found the right guy. I think maybe now I have."

"Zachary O'Brien, if you're cool with what I'm doing for money, I would love to date you exclusively."

He swiveled around and sat on my lap. Also on my cock which was very appreciative.

"Zach, I thought we were going slow?"

16.

Chuck Markus wanted me to join him for dinner at his penthouse. An overnight. I suspected it would not be as simple as last time. I might have to do more than stand there and groan.

School had been endless this week, my mind felt drained. Two quizzes in political science. I'd been working out hard, practicing piano and voice. Two vocal coaches should be classified as a form of torture. Opera and pop are in different parts of the body. Now my date wanted yet another part. Not the right word. Zachary and I were dating. This guy Chuck was sweet, but I needed better terminology for process and the act. Rendezvous? Appointment? Consultation? Assignation? Trick? I'd ask my talent manager what term other crew members used.

This was a Thursday and Dirksen knew I had a nine o'clock class on Friday morning. I wore an open shirt and leather coat with jeans. I brought a small shoulder bag for overnight with my Dopp kit, a knit shirt, underwear and socks so I could head right to class.

The guard at the front desk called up and waved me through to the private elevator. My Internet search said the last time this unit sold it went for forty-five million. I didn't think I'd fuck my way to owning it. But I could appreciate it while I fucked. I knocked on the door and it was answered by a stranger.

"Hello," I said, "I'm here to see Chuck Markus."

"Yes, I know," he said, extending his hand. "I'm Reggie, his younger brother. Please come in. Can I take your jacket and bag?"

"Sure," I said, handing both to him. "Where is he?"

"Running a few minutes late. If it's okay, he invited me to join you both for dinner then I'll disappear into one of the guest-rooms. The cook is preparing dinner."

He laid the jacket and bag on a chair and walked to the bar. "Would you like a drink?"

"Just water is great or fruit juice." I didn't drink much anyway but Dirksen said I should never drink or take drugs when working so my wits were not impaired.

"Are you still in school?" He looked not much older than me. He had on a knit shirt that fit nicely, showing a solid physique, better than his brother. But the fuchsia color and orange stripes were startling. Was he an artist like Renoir?

"I'm working with an East Bay video crew and taking a few college classes. In case you're wondering, I'm twenty-one. How old are you?"

Dirksen said I should avoid being honest if there might be a problem, but I didn't see one here. I was legal for sexual consent. "I'm twenty. A freshman at S.F. State. I'm a dual major: poli-sci and music."

"You have an amazing voice."

"You've heard me?"

"I was at Dirksen's party with my brother. I told Chuck you'd be perfect. I asked Dirksen and he said who you were. I told him we wanted your services."

"That's right, Dirksen told me." I had to smile, it was too fun-ny. "You picked me out of the whore lineup. That makes me feel special." How did people know who was for rent? Did he get a secret flash card listing whore anatomy and skills? It was a bit hu-miliating but I kept my voice upbeat, sounding more ironic than upset. A man just a year older ordered me like a Starbucks. *I'd like a tall, extra foam whore with cinnamon.* Why was he here when I had a fuck assignation with his brother? No, fuck appointment was more accurate. This better not be a three-way.

"I didn't mean to insult you." He put out his hand again and I took it, not sure why he thought I was upset. "Please accept my apology. I just thought you were interesting—handsome and talented, someone special. I hoped you might be able to break my brother out of his shell, out of his head. Something about you suggests you can. Sorry. I probably said too much."

"No need to apologize. I like him. Thank you."

"He's a very special man."

"I hope I can meet your expectations and his."

The front door opened and Chuck came in carrying a backpack and seeming a bit out of sorts. "Sorry I'm late. So many problems with our new launch. But I think we got it fixed." He tossed his coat on the back of a chair and the bag on the seat. "Hi, Abel. I'm glad you met my brother."

He stepped up and gave me a quick platonic hug. I returned it; glad he was here. With him, I knew my role.

"Give me a minute to wash my face. Reggie, can you take our guest to the dining room?"

Dinner was perfect grilled halibut with a lemon butter sauce. And a piece of chocolate fudge pie with whipped cream. No one mentioned the reason I was here. I learned more about NetLine and its new contract with the Pentagon on cryptography, which I didn't fully understand but was fascinated to hear. Reggie's work on an earthquake documentary offered new insights into how the earth shifts. The brothers were both extremely bright and unpretentious. They asked me about school. It felt natural, like new friends sharing stories unless I thought about my real mission. Afterward, Reggie announced he was disappearing into his room for the night.

"Shall we?" I said to my own private billionaire as I stood and offered my hand. His expression shifted from easygoing entrepreneur full of passion for his work to a bashful man unsure what was going to happen next. I liked the guy, which certainly helped, and his virginity was endearing. I wanted to gently introduce him to the power and joy of sex. That was what his brother was hoping for.

As we stood in his bedroom, I pulled him to me, slowly running my hands over his body as I stripped him. His knees were shaking; he was petrified.

"I promise to be gentle."

"Sorry I'm so nervous."

"Believe me, I understand." I stripped naked, giving him a show, then pulled him into the bathroom, opening the glass door for the shower. I stepped inside, adjusting the water temperature, and reached out my hand for him to join me. His expression reminded me of a little boy about to do something naughty. I washed his back, soaped and rinsed his ass, his front side, and he giggled.

He gasped when I wrapped my hand around his dick and dropped to my knees. His cock responded to my sucking prowess and that seemed to relax him. It was enjoyable because I sensed he was a good man. I pulled his now hard dick forward and let it snap back to his stomach. He grinned, still the little boy marveling at what was happening.

We dried and I moved him to the bed, pulling back the covers. His eyes were fixated on my cock as I set out rubbers and lube. Laying with him, rubbing my chest over his, I moved to his side, enjoying his gasp. I kissed his cheek then lips. "You're beautiful," I whispered. "This'll be fun."

I had no interest in him romantically but I wanted to be a kind of Florence Nightingale whore. I licked and sucked down his neck, working to leave a red spot on his chest, something to surprise him and maybe a source of pride. I finally reached his cock and balls. He tasted good, clean with a scent of a woodsy soap. When my tongue worked over his hole, and slipped a finger inside, he screamed.

"Should I stop?"

"Oh, God, no. Please!"

I added a second finger, making certain to keep his dick entertained, and slipped on a rubber. I began a gentle penetration, holding his legs back, slow in for two inches, back out, slow in for three. He squirmed and whimpered as I reached full penetration, his cock at full attention, his breathing heavy. I rested, giving him time to adjust and kissed him until I started again, faster, deeper seeking his pleasure spot. He yelped when I found it and kept up the pressure. I did my best to make sure we came together.

This time he got the warm towel. We talked, laughed and took a nap.

Nearly two hours later we showered again. He was buoyant, clearly having found a new favorite activity. Like a kid with a new toy, he'd discovered his erogenous butt, the joys of dick and male tongue. I took delight in him, the billionaire issue paling in importance because I sensed he could become a new friend.

"I had no idea how good it could be. I hope you'll continue to be my teacher till I'm ready to fly."

"I'd like that very much."

He woke me up once in the night to do it again. Also before I left for class. Parts of my anatomy were a little sore but I was excited for him, happy to see him building confidence to find a real boyfriend. I didn't love the man but I respected him and was glad I could bring a new sense of joy into his life. Aside from the money, it seemed easier to justify what I was doing if I could attach some social good.

17.

After more music theory and an excruciating, often humiliating hour of bonehead math, I turned the key into my dorm room and Renoir shouted: *"Romeo, oh, Romeo!"*

The first thing I saw was a janitor's mop pail with several dozen red long-stemmed roses.

"I couldn't find a vase but found this in a utility closet. I know it takes away from the effect but still…three dozen roses. THREE DOZEN!"

"I assume you read the card."

"Of course, part of my role as your special advisor. Your billionaire friend is rather taken with you. Unfortunately, no hidden cash. Just flowers."

He handed me the cream-colored card:

> *I cannot thank you enough for freeing my heart and other body parts.*
> *Affectionately, Chuck*

"I think it's charming." My laugh was a mix of pride and embarrassment. "I'm helping him overcome his fear of intimacy."

"I'd think your dick would instill fear, not lessen it."

++++

"I think he wants to marry you," Dirksen said with a grin. We were in his kitchen, having a simple quiche and salad lunch. "You're some kind of magician with Mr. Markus."

"He's a really nice man. He actually brought his brother to get to know me. Very sweet."

"He's the one who booked you."

"So romantic. How many sex partners get selected by the brother?"

"Here's three thousand plus another two grand tip. How's that for romance?"

"I'm still staggered that people pay this kind of money." I tried to sound cool and relaxed but my heart pounded thinking about this poor kid from Antioch making this kind of cash. More dangerous—learning to depend on it.

"These are rich people. Money doesn't mean much. Supply and demand is part of the answer. Marketing. Fantasy. Once they fixate on you—well, there is only one Copperhead." He teased. "Oh, that hot cocoa skin…"

"Right. I'm one of a kind. You're trying too hard." I smiled, enjoying the praise even if I didn't fully believe it. I was a package. Why couldn't some of this have arrived earlier in my life?

He forked a last piece of crust and looked at me. "I hope you see me as a friend."

"Of course. I trust you as much as Dr. Amos." I'm glad I could say that. Our smiles felt warm and sincere. "Call me Copperhead. Most of my friends do."

"Thank you, Copperhead."

"Can you send two thousand more to my dad and put the balance into an account for me?" I suddenly felt like a banker, kind of cool. "I think my mom's still doing fine on the rent now. She's so happy, relieved. Mystified about the source, but…. My dad is thrilled with the money. He cried on our weekly Skype call. I guess it runs in the family."

"You bet. On to your next assignment: the sometimes charming, often smarmy Representative Danny Wilder wants more of your manly talents. I want to up your Snooping-In-the-Night skills."

"Bring it on."

"He doesn't gross you out or anything, does he?"

"Only when he takes off his shorts and girdle. I don't understand why he has to wrap his stomach in a ridiculously tight elastic crew neck. Kind of like a mummy. He's fine naked. I don't have to kiss him. It's like an out of body experience, like playing a role in a reality TV show. He seems into it and we also have great conversations about politics and government. For a poli-sci major it's fascinating. Insights I couldn't get from school. So, are we ready for my 007 role?"

"You're funny." He picked up a small cloth pouch. "Just for the record. I don't wear one. My body is naturally tight." He laughed, patting his stomach. "Agent Cortez says they're pulling some data from his computer. But he wants you to plant the others if you can."

"It shouldn't be a problem. Maybe tonight I can distract him with some bondage play."

"You are a true artist." He unzipped the pouch. "Here's an almost invisible mike made to look like a tree knot to put behind the headboard—by the edge for best results. You said it was dark walnut. This should be invisible even if he looks for one. The FBI can pick up conversations in bed or anywhere in his room. You can innocently lead him on about different topics as you whip him with the paddle."

"You just want to hear him scream."

"There is that."

I examined the device and the instructions.

"Agent Cortez wants you to look for items of interest. It might be his mail or something he leaves on his computer screen. Take a photo if you see something, then email it to your home computer and erase the photo. Just in case someone gets suspicious and checks your phone. But only when he's out of the room or otherwise distracted. Take no chances."

"These are not exactly hard-on inducing words."

"Yes, but you're barely past being a teenager."

I just smiled.

18.

I wore my new tuxedo on my next date with the congressman. Not that I had an old one. I'd never owned such a garment—thank you Dirksen—or worn one. In school we'd all rented cheap odd sized dinner jackets for prom. The description for my tux—MY TUX—was easier to take than the price tag: Tom Ford Windsor base peak-lapel. *Only* five grand. What the hell was a Windsor base peak-lapel? It felt like an angel was wrapping his wings around me in a way that accentuated my physique. I turned and examined my image in front of the mirror behind the door. Not bad.

I hoped I could eventually make enough money to reimburse Dirksen and fully pay back Dr. Amos. Best not to worry now.

The shoes were Paul Stuart, men's Heron leather loafers, only six hundred. Then there was the fancy shirt—which actually fit my neck size—and a bow tie which Renoir adjusted before I left. Walter had said no to a vest, I was to be traditional with a black silk cummerbund. He said they dated back to the 1850s and were worn by British military for dinner in India; often called crumb catchers but really to make the officer look a bit slimmer. Sort of like an exterior girdle. All perhaps useful in a cocktail party when you can't drink cocktails and you run out of things to talk about.

The event was an LGBTQ national fundraising organization, Equality America, honoring Congressman Danny Wilder at the Fairmont Hotel. The website listed various dignitaries including Senator Wiseling, so it was a bigger deal than he'd indicated. I gasped looking at the program. My name was listed as entertainment with the two songs I'd perform.

When we arrived, a combo was playing at the side of the room, long lines at the half dozen bars. Q's liked their liquor. Or, in my case, fruit juice. Lots of waitstaff but not my favorite one. Several elegantly dressed men flirted which was always reassuring if you felt as out of place as I did.

Wilder kept me on his arm for the first twenty minutes or so, to show me off. I looked up at him adoringly, per his instructions. When people started coming up to him, crowding around, I pulled away. Turning toward the stage, I saw Alexander, his hot Mormon intern, holding out a glass.

"Cranberry juice for my boss's handsome dude date." He grinned, giving special emphasis to *date*.

"Thank you," I replied, accepting it, taking a sip and raising my eyebrows. He was so innocent looking. I sensed it might be a façade.

"Is the piano on stage grand enough? For your recital, I mean."

"I'm not Kanye." I was startled at the size of the room. At least a hundred tables, ten seats at each, three giant screens, mounted television cameras. I'd been told it was an intimate event when I agreed to sing for him. Although I was surprised when I had to sign a release.

"A love song to your *date*?" He rolled his eyes.

"Don't make fun of me or your boss. He'll introduce me as his special friend and the two songs. Everyone will go, 'Ahhhh.' 'Over the Rainbow' was his choice. It's not the traditional movie version but we had fun with it in school. Eva Cassidy's interpretation is slower, soulful, lower key."

"Who's she?"

"A young singer who died of cancer in the nineties just as her career took off. It's haunting. The other piece is 'I Will Always Love You.' I gave the congressman a list of songs and he picked these two. So, what the fuck."

"Please don't swear."

"You're sensitive? You gave me your card to call you when I'm not fucking your boss. Really?"

"Does that mean you'll go out with me?"

"Can you sing?"

"No."

"Can you paint?"

"You mean on canvas? I've taken some classes."

"I'll be giving you a call."

During the event, the senator mentioned me in her remarks and said I was special, that I'd performed at her home at a recent party, adding, "Someday you can tell your friends you heard Abel Torres at this event, early in his stratospheric career." She pointed at me and I pointed back, humbled by her comments. "His fans, and I'm one, call him Copperhead. You can guess why."

After his unending talk, Rep. Wilder introduced me as his "special friend." Lots of "*Ahhhs*" and I went onstage to applause. He kissed my cheek, a few whistles, and I went to the piano.

It was good. I was good.

In the Uber back to the congressman's apartment, Wilder kept kissing me and I kept dodging his tongue. He thanked me for the songs. Lots of cell phones recording in the audience and the organization was videotaping the whole event for their website. I got a standing ovation...twice. People actually did a *Copperhead* chant at the end. Of course, applause from a queer audience for a Judy Garland song was almost a mandate in LGBTQ culture.

He opened the condo door and froze. Two men were standing, arms folded across their chests, in the shadows. Just one light on behind them, the drapes closed.

"Close the door." A man's voice.

The middle-aged men wore ill-fitting gray suits, the color of choice apparently with Russian criminals. Maybe the bulges were shoulder holsters. I needed to play it innocent, the dumb little piece of boy ass.

"What's up, Mik?"

Did I sense a quaver in the congressman's voice? So this was the guy in the Russian sleeper cell. Great. I looked at them and then away, then back, trying to sketch their faces in my head.

"We need to talk. What you wanna do with your boy toy?"

"He's cool. Just a pretty whore." He took off his jacket and handed it to me. I went to the hall closet and hung it up along with my own—too beautiful to drape over a chair—adding a touch of swish. The men watched. So I took off my tie, cummerbund and shirt as well, bare chested, and sauntered back to the congressman, a bit sultry, and kneeled at his feet, putting my head on his lap.

"Is this going to take long Daddy?" It also made it obvious I wasn't wearing a wire.

"Oh for fuck's sake!" Mik sneered.

"So, he loves my manhood. Like I said, we can say anything. He's no problem. What's happening?" The congressman stroked my hair. The paddle was coming out tonight. I closed my eyes and listened.

"We think somebody ID'd Clover. Tapped his phone. A hack at the bank might be tracing our funds. Hard to say at this point how many accounts were accessed, not just us."

Clover. The FBI had identified him from my description when I saw him leaving the congressman's apartment in a huff last week.

"Any idea who?"

"Could be rivals, partners are getting nervous, the feds. We need to figure out who."

I rubbed Wilder's crotch. He loved it and I thought it kept me in character.

He slapped my hand. "Later." He looked pleased being irresistible.

"Clover may need to go low key," the other man said with a slight accent. I wasn't sure from where but I tried to memorize the pronunciation of a couple of words. "We checked the line to your computer and it seems clean but be careful. Something may be in the works. The handoff's in ten days."

"All right," the congressman replied, pushing my head aside as he stood. I looked irritated as part of the act but was pleased I could get a better look at both men. "Daddy will be with you in a minute, sweetheart.".

I knew he'd be appropriately inane.

The men left. I followed Wilder into his bedroom and slipped off my clothes. He sat at his computer and logged into a bank account. I came up behind him and rubbed his shoulders and blew air into his ear. When he started to log out, I took his hand and pulled it behind his chair to my rising cock.

"I need to fuck you, Boy. *Now!*" I pulled him to his feet and stripped him before pushing him onto the bed. The welts were glorious.

After he fell asleep, I slipped out of bed and went to his computer. Using a Kleenex, I touched the mouse and the last image popped up. I picked up my cell phone and took a photo of the screen then forwarded it to my home computer and erased the original. I put the machine on *Sleep* and went to the bathroom to pee. It was lucky this was an overnight but not so great because I'd have to fuck him in the morning. I'd expected to be trembling when I did all this, but I felt calm. It was the sex I didn't enjoy. I'd call Dirksen and Ramon tomorrow.

I crawled into bed beside him and put a cold hand on his back. "Move over!"

++++

Ramon the FBI agent, a sketch artist named Abigail, and Simpson, a second agent, apparently a linguist, sat across from me in Dirksen's living room.

"The photo helps," Ramon said in his agent voice. "Now we just need to figure out what happens in ten days."

"Money for secrets," I suggested.

"A good possibility," he replied. "But what and where?"

"That was brilliant playing a love-sick submissive," Dirksen said, leaning against a door jamb. "He must have been thrilled, a beautiful young man stroking his ego."

"Can you listen to these various pronunciations and see if they match what you heard?" Agent Simpson then tried different slants to the same words I'd suggested.

"I think the second one," I said, feeling ignorant. I was so certain I'd memorized it last night. He nodded and made some notes.

"Your latte, Master Abel," Walter said, setting a small tray on the table beside the sofa. "I hope I did it right."

I picked it up and took a taste. "Perfect. You spoil me, Walter. So much better than Dirksen's. Maybe you can train him," I teased. I was becoming increasingly fond of the man. We'd started talking here and there. Trilingual, droll, and he seemed to like me.

"My pleasure, sir." He smiled and left the room. I was a whore and he called me sir. Did I make light of what I was doing to counter the embarrassment? Maybe. But Walter made me feel less conflicted.

Abigail came over to me, sat down and showed me her sketches of the two men. I suggested some changes. Finally, "Yes, that's close. Maybe a narrower nose on the guy on the left. On the other, push the hairline back a bit, thicker jowls."

"*Mother of Goodness!*" Walter said, walking back into the room, holding his iPad and laughing. "A friend just sent me a video. Abel's song is making the rounds: 'I Will Always Love You.' Equality America's promoting it as part of a fundraiser and it's getting picked up. Our own Copperhead." He set the iPad upright on the table and we all gathered around to watch.

I loved the fact that Walter never used swear words. *Mother of Goodness.* Perfect.

19.

Dirksen Horvath's tone was apologetic, not his usual mischievous persona. We were in his den, talking about a range of topics when he switched back to work. "I'd like to schedule a meeting with you and a possible new client in the next couple of days. Another assignment has developed and I apologize for it given your schedule, but this has big long-term implications."

"What's up whore master?" It popped out without thinking.

"That kind of language can get your butt smacked."

"I'm the dom, remember? Just ask my least favorite congressman."

"This one is different," he said, a smile back in his voice.

"So another Dirksen?"

"What?"

"A *Dirksen*, what I'm calling what I do for you. Distinctive, but the meaning obtuse except to those in the know."

He stared at me, shaking his head. "Oh, kids! Back on topic— I told a friend at the State Department about a call I got from a Saudi prince who owns a mansion and horse ranch in Woodside on the Peninsula, among a dozen such homes around the world.

That's where he's stashed his twenty-something-year-old nephew.

"Last month, somebody walked in on Ali sucking a busboy's dick at a big dinner banquet in Riyadh. So the uncle, Prince Ab-kar, flew him to California to control a possible scandal. This prince is high in the Saudi military establishment and the nephew, a Cambridge student, works in military intelligence. The busboy's been bought off and faces beheading if he leaks."

"I'll bet that got his attention. Such an opportunity, working with people who enjoy beheading. Do they know the congress-man's friends? Maybe they all trained together."

"Ali saw the videotape of you singing at the political event. Apparently it's been posted on various YouTube and chat sites. You have a growing fan club."

"I don't have time for Facebook or chat sites but, yeah, I know I'm out there."

"You have many admirers, thanks to your appearance at the political fundraiser. Plus, there are other tapes, likely when you were performing in music classes, iPhone videos from classmates. He told his uncle he wants you and the uncle used his sources to find me. He wants to keep the nephew happy and far away from Saudi Arabia. Ali is also a prince, by the way."

"Really? A prince? Rapunzel I'm not. Also I'm kinda busy. There must be some limit on how many guys I can service. Or want to service. You've many hot men in your stable."

"Some members of our crew deal with a dozen customers or more—not every week but periodically. It's all about schedul-ing. Not everyone demands constant attention. My diplomatic contact is convinced this could be a breakthrough in getting in-tel on Saudi leadership. The young prince is miserable living in Woodside. His only entertainment is riding thoroughbred horses and watching you on tape. He knows no one. He speaks excellent English but his personality is…"

"…a snooty prince?"

"A smart, frustrated, unhappy, well-connected, handsome, well-built snooty prince. The uncle is willing to pay a premium if it keeps Ali happy and out of Saudi Arabia."

"Define premium."

"So much for being too busy."

"Don't be snarky. How much?"

"Fifteen thousand for the first engagement. If Ali is smitten, as I assume he will be and apparently already is, then five thousand each time thereafter. Plus tips which could be generous."

I couldn't speak as I analyzed the offer: assuming two a week, if I could handle that volume, maybe four hours work. It would take me two years at the fish murder palace to make that. Or multiple congressional fucks. With my other work, Mama could get a nice apartment. Dad could go back to school. How could I handle three men, actually three customers and a budding boyfriend, and still go to school? How often can a twenty-year-old get hard? The answer is often. "What would I have to do?"

"If you're agreeable, you'd meet with the two princes here, talk with the younger one, get to know each other. Have sex if he wants *and* if you're willing. If you're not agreeable, I'll tell them no. Let's see where it goes. It's possible he won't like you once you meet. Chemistry is hard to predict."

"Would I still fuck the congressman?"

"Yes. At least I hope you will, given what may be at stake."

"Of course." He was almost Catholic in his guilt-tripping me, fuck the crooked pol to make America safer. "Can you send me information on the uncle and nephew? Maybe photos."

"I have them on my desk and will text them shortly. Someone from the State Department wants to talk to you in advance. You're a patriot."

"We 007 whores are special. So are you. I wonder how much of America's safety depends on gay dicks."

He smiled at me as he got up from his armchair. "I suspect that number is highly classified."

++++

"My apologies for being late." I extended my hand and the man ignored it, looking really pissed. He had a right to be; my vocal coach wouldn't let me go on time and I could hardly explain my appointment. I was twenty minutes late and had no way to reach him.

Instead of taking my hand, Edward Gobbins slowly rose from the plastic chair outside my dorm room and adjusted the gray striped tie on his button-down white shirt under a blue pinstriped suit. I suspected he'd gotten lots of looks on campus and people wondering why he was sitting in front of my room. I'd have to come up with something. I continued to hold out my hand. "I really am sorry." He took it and it was a soft shake but he was a diplomat and maybe that's how they did it. He was middle-aged with a funny mustache that covered his upper lip and cascaded over his mouth. It seemed so in contrast to his suit that maybe it was his unique form of diplomatic rebellion.

Once inside my room, I pulled a stack of books off Renoir's chair and offered it to him. He seemed to be making a judgment whether he would be better off standing. The chair was vintage, a few rips and stains. "It's dry so I think you're safe to sit."

He said nothing but sat, holding a leather briefcase in his lap. "My singing coach—"

He held up his palm. "Let's talk about Prince Abkar, young Prince Ali and the Saudi political establishment."

For the next hour, I listened and asked questions, glad to get this kind of detail. My meeting with the princely duo was already scheduled and I probably needed to let Zachary know but I really couldn't reveal the politics. Gobbins had sworn me to secrecy. This was a different kind of assignment and it intrigued me, a rare opportunity to study political science on an international stage, not to mention making a whole lot of money.

20.

There were five of us around the table in the Hungarian restaurant, a bit like the Russian mafia meets suburbia. The congressman was at his romantic normal, promising we'd have a brief dinner meeting so he could talk business and show me off before heading back to his place. Apparently one of the men was gay and "he'll be envious," apparently a good thing. I wasn't sure if I was supposed to be flattered or appalled. He instructed me to be gooey eyed toward him. Certainly easier than kissing.

The three men were in suits. One was in his twenties, dark hair and very attractive. He kept looking at me. I nodded and tried to ignore him. His name was Trevor. Never heard a last name. Clearly the queer one. The other two were in their sixties. Mik—who was at the congressman's apartment—and Tony, a new face and name. I concentrated on his features to consider how to describe him. A little like Jeb Bush. I looked up at Congressman Danny and sighed, per his instructions. I noticed Trevor hide a smirk behind his hand. He knew this was B.S. I gave him an irritated leave me alone glance. It only increased his fascination.

After the main course, I excused myself to use the bathroom.

Trevor did the same. He came up to the next urinal.

"You're adorable," he said.

"Thank you."

"And so obviously enamored. Do you want to get together?"

"I'm flattered but I'm with the congressman."

As we washed up at the sinks, he handed me a card. "I don't really know what your arrangement is with Representative Wilder, but if it's open or a one-off, I'd love to take you for a drink sometime."

"I'm underage."

"That's too funny."

I tossed a paper towel in the trash and he came within a few inches of my chest. "How about ice cream?"

This might fit in with my sleuthing role. I needed to think strategically. Lick his peppermint, so to speak, and gather information. His forcefulness was off putting, and I would have flipped him off under normal circumstances. So I told him, "Maybe we could meet and talk sometime, about what you do, what we have in common, maybe become friends."

Back in the congressman's apartment, I ordered him to strip in his living room. I did an inspection, still fully clothed. "Into the bedroom. *Now!*"

I removed my shoulder pack and took out leather cuffs, strapping them on his wrists, clipping them in front. I took off my shirt.

"*Down!*" I pushed him to his knees. His mouth was agape the whole time as I unzipped my pants. Not exactly enticing but still amusing. I slapped his face with my dick. He tried to put it in his mouth. For some reason I flashed on a nature documentary of a white shark with jaws open trying to grab a seal.

"*No!* Get up and go to your bed!"

Teasing an arrogant maybe corrupt congressman offered a certain satisfaction. I wondered if Anderson Cooper would want such details if I were interviewed.

I took out some silk rope from my bag, tied his hands to the headboard. I put on a blindfold. Then flipped him, face down, and slapped his butt.

"Stay still until I tell you otherwise. I need to get a special toy."

I went over to my bag and took out my gloves. I put the wood knot behind the headboard, then picked up his cell phone on the dresser and slipped the tiny device, almost like a tiny dried leaf, behind the silicone protective cover.

"*You moved!* You need to be obedient!"

"*Sorry sir!*"

One landline was on his desk. I inserted the device in the screw hole just like I was instructed. I removed and hid my gloves, slapped his ass and then used the paddle. I loved the constellation of red dwarfs. He'd remember this night. Why did some guys like this?

"Are you going to be a good boy? Have you learned your lesson?"

"*Yes sir!*"

I took out the dildo and slapped his butt. "More is coming, boy!"

"*Thank you, sir!*"

I oiled his crease, slipped in two fingers for a rough intro, put a rubber on the dildo and pushed it inside. His screams were epic. The evening was going rather well.

I flipped him back over, took off the blindfold, shoved inside him, pounding to a rhythm in my head, a drumbeat, hard and steady. When he came, I pulled out and exploded all over his face. He seemed in heaven. We went in and showered.

Moments afterward, his cell phone rang. He looked concerned seeing the name and wandered into the living room.

With just a towel over my shoulder I followed to listen and distract. It wasn't difficult. I slowly swayed my hips, kind of like hypnosis. His eyes moved back and forth as he sat on the sofa. He was talking about a dinner meeting tomorrow night at a Concord restaurant called DeAngelo's.

++++

"Good work," Agent Cortez said, sitting in Dirksen's den. "You really gave his butt a pounding." He guffawed like it was the most amusing thing he'd ever heard.

"Glad you're enjoying the entertainment." I felt my face flush. "Imagine what you missed by it being audio only." I knew he was just giving me a hard time but I didn't like being with the congressman. "Are you getting useful information?" I liked the money but I was fine with not seeing the man again unless something useful was coming out of it.

"Yes. We're grateful to you, Abel."

"Most friends call me Copperhead."

"Thank you. I'm honored. And you can call me *Ramon*. One Hispanic to another." He raised his coffee cup, I raised mine and we did a silent mutual toast.

"Was info from the dinner in Concord helpful?"

"We now have an identity for Mik. Actually short for Michail. He's an Americanized Ukrainian with ties to a Russian oligarch. We're doing a background search on him now and staking out his house. Fine work. I've also left two new pairs of shoes for you. Dirksen will explain. Now I need to go. Wilder wants to see you again." He stood and shook my hand. "Remember to be careful. As we get closer, they may sense a trap, get panicked and look for the leak."

We walked into the living room and I hugged goodbye to my own secret FBI agent.

"Copperhead, oh my brave Copperhead!" Dirksen's voice was playful. I liked that about him. Serious stuff but often jocular to lessen the tension.

I followed him into the kitchen. He made me a latte, just the way I liked it.

"You've been taking lessons from Walter."

He rolled his eyes. "No one bests my barista skills." He turned and pulled a canvas pouch from a cabinet. "First, another twenty-five hundred. In your investment account?"

"Pay Mama's rent forward if you can. Repay yourself for my salary, five hundred to Dr. Amos. Anything left over, yes, into the account." I sipped and sat on a stool at the counter. "Thank you."

He pointed to several boxes and clothes bags on the kitchen table. "Some additional appropriate attire I ordered from several stores. I gave them your measurements. Walter and I discussed the various styles and took advice from the young salesman. Since he was obviously gay, we assumed good taste. Nice stuff for school so you look special. Two casual jackets and another sports coat. I paid for them. Don't worry about it. Part of my expense and your role as my latest employee. Also I think Ramon mentioned shoes. They're FBI specials with secret spaces. One sleek Italian in style and the other kind of a hip tennis shoe."

He walked over to the bags, pulling out a small box. "No, I'm not asking you to marry me, although I do think you're adorable but you're barely younger than my son."

"I didn't know you had family."

"He's twenty-three and lives in LA. In the movie business. We can talk about him later." He opened the box. "Put this on."

He lifted out a ring. It was silver, pewter in tone, with inter-locking circles on each side. The background was pebbled. Very masculine. At the top was a modified Celtic cross with another raised circle at the center, and what appeared to be a green emer-ald-like stone. It was stunning.

"Give me your right hand." He slipped it on; perfect fit. "It's made to FBI specifications but my design. They implanted a GPS transmitter under the stone. That's the main reason for the size. Yes, it's an emerald, worth more than a week of nights with the billionaire, tips included, so treat it carefully."

He next handed me a small black plastic square with a cord attached. "Plug this into a regular outlet. When you get home at night stick your ring in here and it will recharge the GPS trans-mitter and unlock the secret compartment which I will explain. A charge is good for a week. This is important! Always make sure it's got full power."

"No problem. Can I make a call on it?"

With an eye-roll, he shook his head. "This next one is use-ful but in a very low-tech way. In case you need a weapon." He opened a shoe box and took out one sleek looking shoe with a raised heel. He turned the back side toward me. "Take off the ring and insert it backward into the right heel, about half an inch down." He indicated where.

"There's a hidden spot that you push in, triggered by the charge in the ring—here it is—and use the ring to hook the tiny clip extending from the edge of a knife. Pull it out." I took off the ring and handed it to him to show me. He turned it around and slipped the narrow side into the slit. "The knife is made of a special new material that combines the strength of steel and the moldability of plastic. Invisible to a metal detector." He pulled out the knife, showing it to me. "Smooth as a razor on one side, serrated on the other and can cut through metal."

He handed it to me. It had more heft than I expected. I lifted a hot pad lying on the counter and stabbed it. The knife sliced through with little effort. I reinserted it in the shoe and put the ring back on, twisting it around. I never wore jewelry, never could afford it. Now this stunning ring. "Thank you. I don't know what to say. Can I ask advice on what I should answer if someone wants to know how it got on my finger? Someone like my mother."

"One option is to say it's a cheapy you found on Amazon or on the sidewalk. Just don't let them look too closely. Or, how about something like this: A rich kid you became friends with at school who you helped in various ways, perhaps he had a crush on you, had to move back to Europe. He knew you admired the ring and gave it to you as a remembrance. Let's say his name was Edvard. That might work."

Not with Renoir but then he knew about my new line of work. Mama would be dubious. So I needed to work on it.

"Now let's practice again with the shoes and knife. You want to be able to access it with little effort should the need arise. Ramon tells me a second agent will soon begin working with you. The lessons will also train you on use of the knife."

Copperhead the knife fighter, like nineteenth century legend James Bowie. No, not my image.

"Remember your meeting with the Saudi princes this afternoon."

21.

Zachary

"How'd you get this?"

Zach was straddling Abel in bed, both naked, one hand holding their dicks, the other rubbing the side of Abel's chest. He had a serious bruise on his rib cage and winced when Zach touched it.

"I hurt myself at the gym," Abel reached up to pull Zach down.

It was the second time Zach'd seen a bruise. Two weeks ago it was on the back of his neck. He sometimes seemed a little stiff without explanation.

They kissed and rubbed each other. Zach flipped around and they sucked each other off. It was fabulous but something was wrong although not with the sex. Abel was hiding something. Zach knew he was working with two clients so his time with him seemed to diminish, but his ardor was always perfect.

Zach wanted to believe Abel was honest with him on everything. He had to be. He'd been with guys who were jerks, doing things behind his back. Abel was an escort and Zach accepted that. His boyfriend was also noble and generous, at least to his

150

observation the most selfless guy he'd ever met. Something wasn't right. Zach always tried to be upbeat, even cocky. But his insecurities were still there, if hidden most of the time.

Lying next to him he asked: "Please be truthful. Something's going on. The bruises aren't normal unless you're a WWE wrestler. You've been secretive on some phone calls." Zach rolled on his side and planted an elbow to prop up his head.

Abel swallowed and rolled to his side, the two facing each other.

"WWE is fake, but yes, these are real." Abel smiled before getting serious again. "I don't want to hide anything from you. I care for you very much." He bent over to kiss Zach's chest. Then he looked into the distance, thinking. "I'm involved in some things I can't talk about. They—" He paused, licking his lips and swiveled around sitting cross-legged on the bed. "They involve some work I'm doing with law enforcement."

"What?" Zach swung around and sat up facing him.

"I'm doing undercover work."

"You're not an escort but a cop?"

"No. I'm doing escort work for money. With three men. You know about two. The third isn't yet finalized but a decision soon. Please…you cannot say anything to anyone. I could get in serious trouble." He touched Zach's leg and looked into his eyes. "It might put me in danger."

"What're you doing?" Zach's heart was pounding. "I love you, Abel. I've been wanting to say that for a long time. Please be honest."

Abel touched a fist to his forehead, his mouth open as if awaiting instructions on revealing some secret. "I care about you deeply. But I cannot say more. Please trust me. At some point I'll tell you."

"And the bruises?"

"I'm taking training in various martial arts so I can protect myself and maybe take down the bad guys. The teacher is tough. I get slammed around a lot. I meet with a new instructor later this week."

Zach knew his mouth was agape trying to process this. He lifted his hands and Abel took them. "You're the sweetest man I've ever met. How did this happen? Can you at least tell me that?"

"A man under government surveillance approached Dirksen about my services. My role is to get inside this guy's operation. Lives could be at stake. I couldn't say no. In a weird way, it made me think there could be something positive about being a prostitute. Not just the money. I could do something to help society."

"Abel. Abel. My sweet, smart, fabulous boyfriend. Being an escort was a way to save your family and continue to pursue your dreams. But this...Now I'll be panicked whenever you're out."

Abel pulled him down on the bed and they held each other.

"Please be safe. Now that I've found you I don't want to lose you."

"I'll let you suck me next time," Abel whispered and licked Zach's nose.

Zach slapped his shoulder. "You let me blow you anytime so don't change the subject." He ran his fingers through the copper hair. "Deal."

22.

"Hold still! I'm trying to finish the sketch."

Renoir and I were in a small studio in the Art Department. It was payback time for his help. The room was overrun with paintings, clay torsos, bowls, flights of fancy sculptures and assorted art on tables. It smelled of paint and turpentine or some such solvent. He opened a window but it didn't do much so he turned on a fan. He was standing before a sketch pad on an easel, wearing a beret and drawing with an assortment of different colored pens and paint.

"Can't I stretch and take a pee? I've been posing for over an hour."

"No. You do not interrupt the creation of great art by taking a leak. Quit wiggling. Actually, lift up the dick of life. It's drooping."

"My arm's tired."

"Art often requires sacrifice."

I was having second thoughts on agreeing to let him paint me for his class final. He wanted to start early because, "great art is not created in a night." Or apparently a month. I was seated in a kind of throne, lots of gold leaf, faux carvings, red velvet seat and back, used in a recent Shakespeare production. One leg was over the arm. My business was center stage. I had some sort of toga-like cloth draped over my shoulder and part of one thigh. I was holding up a glass ball and staring at it as if I were a sorcerer. I felt silly.

"Remember, you said you'd obscure my face."

"I remember the request. I follow my muse."

"What does that mean? You're making me nervous."

Just then I heard two female voices giggling in the back of the room. I hadn't seen them come in since I was staring at the globe. They'd been quiet, at least quieter than the fan.

"What the fuck?" I flipped my leg over and pulled the toga over my lap. "I thought the door was locked!"

"Girls! You're interrupting art creation. This is a private staging. Please get what you need and leave."

They exited, carrying a canvas and laughing. They might have been watching for several minutes. I hoped they hadn't taken a photo for display on the Internet.

Renoir came up and slapped my knee. "Get your leg up." He rearranged the toga. "And put everything back into place."

"May I see the finished painting before you show it to your teacher and the class?"

"Please don't disturb me when I'm creating."

++++

Sam Black, an FBI karate instructor, met me at a private gym out in the Avenues, fortunately right next to a MUNI line. I had assumed Sam was going to be a guy. Samantha was her full name, but don't call her that. I'd thought Agent Cortez was rough in our round of self-defense and attack but she flipped me on my face in the first minute. She didn't hold back in punching my gut, my chest, literally kicking my butt. Embarrassingly, she was about five-foot-three and 110 pounds.

"If you sense something bad is going down, prepare yourself at the first sign of trouble. Take action, take it fast and make it brutal," she said. "Go for vulnerable points: eyes, throat, gut, testicles. Hit hard, there may be no second chances." She had me practice with a very lifelike dummy, gouging its eyes, hard elbow to the nose, kicking nuts and running like hell. "Get out of a bad situation. Don't wait around. You may have only incapacitated the enemy for a minute or two. Use that time wisely."

I punched the dummy. It barely moved.

"Don't be a pussy, Abel!"

"Really?"

She swung her leg and knocked me to the mat faster than I could blink.

"All right, now we'll practice with a plastic knife like the one in your shoe." She had one of her own and gave it to me, instructing how to hold it in my hand, stab, swing, punch. "Surprise is always best. Say you sense things are about to go down and you're sitting on a stool at a bar. Slowly lift up your leg and slip out the knife without drawing attention. Practice until it's second nature. Then hold it in secret to use when you need it. Knife fights are not desirable. They're chaotic. Stab and run. If the bad guy is truly evil, go for his throat or heart."

She was so casual about sticking a knife in someone's neck.

We agreed to meet twice a week. She gave me a book on strategy and methods and I limped home, changed clothes and headed to class.

Renoir was thumbing through the book when I got back. He held up a page on knife fighting. "Really? You do remind me a little of *Crocodile Dundee*. Or is it Steven Seagal? Are your tricks that difficult? I thought they sent you roses."

"Roommates are supposed to be supportive. I know you meant to say like Chris Evans as *Captain America*. Or Channing Tatum in *White House Down*."

"Maybe Tatum in *Magic Mike*."

I started to explain and then realized I could go to prison if I did. I was a secret agent. "As my fame spreads, I need to be able to protect myself from crazed fans."

"Like the two girls in the sketch room who saw your manhood. Remember, they were giggling."

23.

I dressed conservative as Dirksen requested, wearing a sports coat and jeans. I got to the Russian Hill house early in case he had any words of wisdom or warnings. I didn't want to be late.

Walter sat with me in the den and we talked about our school days as he set out bowls of dates and dried fruits, a crystal pitcher of filtered ice water. When the doorbell rang, he gave me a thumbs up and hustled to the front door.

I knew what the prince and his uncle looked like and a fair amount about their public lives and a lot more about their politics and the uncle's ruthlessness. Really interesting stuff for a poli-sci major. I still had no sense how Prince Ali would be in person, if we'd have chemistry.

The uncle came in first, Prince Abkar, dressed in a double-breasted gray suit with a colorful paisley tie. He had a neatly trimmed black beard with a touch of gray. Very dignified and self-important.

Then there was Prince Ali. He was about my height, walked with more of a dip and swagger than a regular step, bouncing to music in his head. His black hair was mostly covered in a red beret that said *Versace* in large gold letters. A handsome, clean shaven, sullen brown face, masculine, with a surly mouth, fitting the ultra-cool persona he was impersonating. Much of his face was partially hidden under a massive pair of black framed dark glasses. Even worse, he was wearing an electric T-shirt, another *Versace*— sky blue background, with a partially nude male Greek statue in gold on the chest with black and lime green and gold trim. Gaudy as only that company could do it and perfect for some people. Not this one. I wondered if there was a real person under all the fashion. He was clearly overdosed on style and unskilled at making it work. But muscular arms and narrow hips shone to perfection in very tight jeans. Oh no, white patent leather deck shoes. What to think?

I stood and turned to the men. Ali took off his glasses and his eyes seemed to widen, a smile captured his mouth. So much better. He walked over to me, his arms wide. "Abel you are here. Thank you."

His uncle cleared his throat just as Ali was about to hug me. He immediately stepped back, his eyes running up and down my body. "You are so handsome." His smile exposed large perfect white teeth and a brief glance at his pink tongue. One hurdle passed.

The uncle came up and Dirksen formally introduced us. He nodded to me as we shook hands, and I did the same. A nice firm shake. I worked at being butch. It was obvious the uncle was a little uncomfortable, a twitch in his lower lip gave him away. He turned to Ali and pointed to the hat. The young man took it off revealing black curly hair that fit his face. Nice.

We sat and Dirksen poured everyone ice water and a slice of lemon. He asked about the ranch and the older prince talked about raising Arabian thoroughbreds. Ali was next to me on the sofa, focused on his uncle while he pushed a foot against mine. At one point, he leaned over to me and whispered, "May we go somewhere and talk?"

"Dirksen, Prince Abkar, would it be acceptable if Prince Ali and I went up to your office and talked privately?"

"Yes," the older prince said, looking relieved. Maybe he didn't want to endure Ali and me talking about sex. Fine by me.

Upstairs we sat in opposing chairs by an antique walnut desk. I guess my facial expression was not what he'd hoped for.

"You disapprove of the way I am dressed, don't you?"

An unexpected opening statement. I could deal with it practicing some diplomacy. "Prince Ali, I'm interested in getting to know you as a man and how you dress is unimportant."

"I read the fashion magazines, ones like *Vogue*. This style is very popular." His tone suggested he was looking for acceptance. The rich prince was shy. He also had a touch of an English accent picked up, I presumed, from his time at Cambridge or just an affectation like the hat. No denying the accent was helpful, giving him an extra fifty points. "I want to please you." He looked up and smiled. "May I kiss you?"

"First, can you tell me why you immediately want to have sex with me? I'd like to know you better before we consider being intimate."

He frowned like I shouldn't or couldn't refuse him. "I've hired whores before and they just let me do what I want. Why are you different? I am paying more than I ever have."

That really pissed me off. I struggled to hold my voice level and not shout. "At this point you have not paid anything. I do get compensation for being with someone but it's a mutual thing. I will not do it with anyone I find uninteresting or who's rude. Think about what you said and whether it was insulting. I want to actually like the guy, someone who sees me and treats me as an equal. Know that I'm very selective." I kept my voice respectful and spoke slow. I waited. He looked surprised, struggling with a response for this kind of pushback from a rent-boy. I liked the idea of the big bucks but I was already busy enough and wouldn't be treated like property.

He stood up and pulled off his shirt, tossing it on the floor. He then undid his belt and pulled down his pants and underwear, raised his arms and asked: "Do you like me better like this?"

I started to laugh and covered my mouth.

"You...you think I'm unattractive, a joke?" He turned away from me, his arms crossing his chest, a loud exhale.

"Wait! No." I touched his thigh with an open palm, slowly running it up and down. "I smiled because of what you just did, showing me your remarkable physique. I just wasn't expecting it. And...I like what I see."

He turned back toward me and seemed relieved. "Thank you. I...I want you to like me. I think you are very sexy and watching you sing, your voice, the far-away look in your eyes, your passion, it pulled me to you. It was like I better understood my attraction to other young men. You reached me emotionally and well as physically. I feel better about who I am watching you sing. The idea of touching you, making love, connecting the physical with the emotional, it is something I never expected. I don't feel dirty or like a freak, someone disgusting, when I see you. I apologize for being rude. This is not my home country. You are right, we are equals." He moved closer. "You are welcome to touch me. I would like it if you did."

"Thank you for that." Such a beautiful declaration and unexpected. In that spirit, I reached over and lifted his balls, hanging nicely under a thick uncut dick. He started to stiffen. "Your body is very muscular. Do you play soccer?"

"Yes, I love it."

"Work out at a gym?"

"Yes. I have one attached to my bedroom suite in my home. A fine trainer."

I stroked him. He was clearly a hot man, better out of the gaudy clothes. I seemed a bit pale in comparison to his darker brown skin. I liked that. He was entitled and insecure at the same time. Also, a romantic. I'd read stories about what it was like to be gay in his country. I was tempted to be tempted. How could you not be? Hadn't I masturbated to this kind of gay fantasy, a beautiful man pulling down his pants, offering himself?

I stood, running my hands over his pectorals and abs. "Your body is beautiful," I whispered, leaning in, moving my lips across his. He groaned, putting a hand behind my neck and we kissed.

He was aggressive but so was I. He tasted exotic, my imagination suggested pomegranates. He wore musk, not unpleasant but a bit distracting. I moved my head and pushed my tongue into his ear.

He pulled back and removed the rest of his clothes. "Will you have sex with me?" He turned around—a fine round butt—facing me again, his dick hard.

Such a strange business to be in. It seemed off, me fully dressed in a sports coat and a naked prince in front of me wanting to get it on. I knew it would be rude to his uncle if we spent too much time here. Ali seemed frozen, waiting for me to respond. His ego would not accept rejection and, no question, I was turned on. If we dated, maybe I could urge some changes.

"The only way to get rid of a temptation is to yield to it." The quote seemed to find the perfect time to slip into my brain and out my mouth.

He grinned, his confidence back. "I remember that quote from school, popular with male students. Does that mean you will yield, that you want me?"

This man was more than most whores could hope to meet. I slipped off my jacket and opened the bottom buttons on my shirt, pulling it aside, showing my abs. I undid my belt and pants, slowly lowering them. He was staring, waiting for the show.

I pulled down my shorts. "Suck me off while you fist your dick." Not exactly romance but practical.

He dropped to his knees. "I had no idea it would be as amazing as the rest of you." He pulled back the foreskin and his mouth engulfed me. I thought about the busboy in Riyadh enjoying an extraordinarily fine suck from the prince until someone opened the closet door.

"You are magnificent," he said, catching a breath and taking me deep.

"Work your cock," I said, more of a demand; his hand started stoking in earnest.

I tried to time us together and it worked. He swallowed all of me, licking around as his hand worked out the last of his own load. He leaned back and seemed enraptured. I reached down, wiping off a patch of cum on his upper lip. I showed it and he took my hand and brought it to his mouth, sucking my finger.

"That was amazing. Will you see me again?"

"Is that what you want?"

"Yes. I don't get much chance to have a man in bed, taking time to explore bodies. I would like that with you."

"Go ahead, get dressed and let's talk some more. I enjoyed what we just did. You're a beautiful, desirable man." An odd way to say it but he seemed ecstatic.

He was grinning as he pulled his clothes on. When he picked up his gaudy T-shirt, I made a noise of disapproval.

"I wish I had something else to put on that you would like."

"Follow me." We went into one of Dirksen's spare bedrooms where he kept several outfits for his team. Ali was more muscular than I but still close to the same shirt size. A very nice difference. I went to a drawer with knit shirts and picked out a dark blue one, extra-large, holding it for review.

"You think I would look better in this? Something less flashy?"

"I do. I guess I'm conservative. You're beautiful with a magnificent body, also a romantic tongue. You don't need clothes that distract from who you are. Pick clothes that let your body and face speak for themselves. No beret, please. Your hair is perfect." A guy from Antioch was giving orders to a good looking, impossibly rich Saudi prince. Go figure.

He laughed, sounding joyous as he pulled the knit shirt over his head. A perfect stretched fit. I helped adjust the sleeves and turned him to a mirror. "Nice," I said.

"You can have my other shirt."

"How about a less flashy pair of shoes?" There were bins with different styles in various sizes. I found a stylish pair of dark casual shoes, size eleven. "Try these on."

He did so, exclaiming, "Perfect fit. You like these better. Of course you do." He set the old ones aside.

"I really like this look on you. Of course, you're also spectacular naked. Let's go back down."

He pulled me to him. "Thank you. Your reality matches my

dreams."

Oh my goodness.

The two men were in a lively political discussion when we entered the room. Both likely suspected we might have had sex but we weren't gone so long that it was obvious we did all that was possible.

Prince Abkar looked approvingly at Ali's change of wardrobe and put a hand on his shoulder. "I like you so much better like this. Perhaps this arrangement will work out if Ali and Mr. Torres are agreeable."

"Yes, Uncle. He is very special. Perfect in many ways. I would like it very much."

Dirksen watched me, his lips twisting to one side, clearly amused.

"I would like that too," I confirmed.

24.

"I need to do more detailed sketches," Renoir explained. "We can do it here in our room if I adjust the lighting. I'll just do one section at a time. Like your head or your hand holding the glass ball."

"Or my dick."

"Of course. Then I put them all together, make adjustments and use it as a template when I transfer it to a big canvas with oil. Life size will increase its impact."

"You agreed that my face will not be recognizable. Right?"

"Would I ever disappoint you?"

"That's not an answer." He was my friend. He was just playing with me. My phone pinged. Perfect. "I'm taking you to dinner tonight. Seven o'clock at Roland's Pizza in West Portal."

"Really?" Renoir replied. "Big spender with all that daddy cash."

"Don't smell like paint thinner. Take a shower. Use the lemon scented soap. Wash everywhere. Maybe some cologne but not too much. Dress nice."

++++

Roland's was a lively restaurant, all the wait staff sounding Italian even if they weren't. Great garlic bread. Spaghetti was good. Cheap wine. College student prices.

"We've a reservation. Torres."

She pointed to a back table where a young man stood and waved.

"How do you feel about Mormons?" I asked my roommate.

"Romney's not my type," he answered as we walked toward the table.

"Renoir, I'd like you to meet Alexander. Renoir is my art major, uber talented painter dorm mate. Alexander is Congressman Wilder's new intern. He's interested in art."

"Is that the politico you're fucking?" Renoir asked, looking all innocent.

They both snickered. If only they knew.

After dinner, we three returned to the dorm and I felt I'd done my job. Renoir exiled me to the hallway. "It's only fair, given what you did to that poor law student."

I settled into the lone chair outside, moving it close to the door, and finished an essay for English Lit on Walt Whitman and an astonishing poem written in 1855 as part of *Leaves of Grass*. "I Sing the Body Electric," used in the movie *Fame*. So gay positive.

The music from my room was inspirational, sometimes operatic. Renoir could sing.

++++

Another overnight with the Representative Wilder. Ramon asked me to push for it, actually to stop turning him down, so I could gather more intel. Wilder thought I had the hots for him and suggested I do it for nothing. "I've got bills to pay," I told him on the phone. "I am so worth it."

In the night, his phone dinged and he sat up in bed. I pretended to be asleep.

He was silent for a minute, just listening, then responded,

"The cash needs to pass through me and then to the dealer. That's the setup."

He listened again and I kept my eyes closed, pretending to breathe heavy.

"Don't threaten me. It's what we agreed." He hung up, scooted back under the covers and began to rub my thigh.

"Daddy, I'm horny."

Him calling twenty-year-old me Daddy seemed odd. I hoped Dirksen and Ramon understood the sacrifice I was making for my country.

25.

Zachary

The glamor of law school.

Zach doodled while the speaker droned on and on. He was a former U.S. Attorney General and never let us forget it. There were four hundred students in assigned seats in the theatre, all numbered, and all were full for this mandated course. Gilbert Behr walked onto the stage always a couple of minutes late, his lower lip pushed up along with his nose, showcasing a bulldog face, fat jowls and arrogance. He paced back and forth, never making eye contact. His topic was Constitutional Law and he had found ways, often blunt, sometimes imaginative, to violate the spirit and letter of the document when he was in office. He had been ruthless about hiding the truth, scorching his oath and silencing enemies of the President. At least that was Zach's view.

There had been a major fuss among students and faculty when Behr was appointed, apparently at a huge salary. The word was he would be expected to earn it and much more with his political contacts and beneficiaries of his actions, proving the school was open to all viewpoints, even destructive ones. He wore round wire glasses and had a stomach that overpowered his slacks. He always wore a baggy gray suit, white button-down shirt, long blue tie and tasseled maroon loafers. He was a bit duck footed in his walk, voice gravelly, like maybe he used to drink a lot, and it was often hard to hear him because he refused to use a mike and hacked a lot. Practically, it didn't really matter since the three teaching assistants did all the work, clarifying his comments so they better matched the law, and they graded the tests. The TA's said to follow their advice and ignore the guy. The three—two men and a woman—were talented. Grad students waiting to take the Bar Exam. Someday Zach might be doing the same thing.

Studying the law was often tedium, occasionally ridiculous and on rare moments riveting. Abel and Zach talked about their studies, how different they were yet how much they had in common. Abel was in poli-sci because he cared about politics. That was in large part about the law. The two had vigorous conversations about what was happening in government. For a singer he was one knowledgeable man.

The former U.S. AG continued to drone on while Zach focused more on his doodle, thinking he had talent, at least when sketching Abel. Naked, of course. He didn't have to exaggerate anything.

A guy next to him leaned over and whispered. "Very hot. A boyfriend?"

"He is and he is."

"Lucky you."

Zach would see him tonight. Abel was coming to his room. In some ways, Abel was part of his academic survival mechanism. Reading in law school was extensive, sometimes a hundred pages or more each night of legal jargon and precedents. But knowing he needed to finish before Abel arrived really improved his speed-reading and retention skills. Abel also worked with him on studying for tests. There were standard Q&As as study guides. Abel would ask the question and then see how well Zach answered. He insisted on doing it despite Zach's protests. Another reason to love the guy. Of course this was always after sex.

Abel was busy several nights a week, either with school or his side career. Zach often wondered who his lover was with. There seemed to be two regulars. At times he seemed upbeat when they got together, other times he seemed withdrawn, something heavy rummaging in his head. When Zach asked about it, he said it was nothing and changed the subject. He hoped at some point Abel would be more forthcoming since honesty and openness were critical in a relationship.

Abel's life was more glamorous than his because of his singing and his stunning looks. So many students wanted to sit in on his practice sessions with music tutors that they moved them into a larger performance room. Sort of like a Master Class. Abel said he was flattered but it could be distracting. Zach attended one after bugging him. There were at least fifty people in the audience. How could he concentrate? It was clear that his lover was held in great esteem by the school and a bit of awe from music students. He came across as humble and serious. Like he didn't realize his talent was so extraordinary. And it wasn't an act.

Zach's school life was boring in comparison. Yet one day, a few years from now, he'd be a trial lawyer, in the courtroom before a hushed jury and judge—riveted by his legal arguments—and they'd hear his fiery oratory about how this AG and his minions violated the law, sold out their country and how we needed to in-validate their criminal activity. He could dream. Abel's dream was arriving much faster. Kind of thrilling to be hitching a ride on his rocket ship, so to speak.

"Can I help you sir?" Zach said, all snooty, when Abel knocked on his apartment door.

"I believe you can, counselor." Abel pushed him back, closed the door, locked it and took hold of Zach's zipper, pulling it down.

"Your Honor! What are you doing?"

26.

Dirksen suggested we discuss any new findings in person at his place and, since he sent a car and offered dinner, I was excited. Plus he had more money for me.

Walter answered the door. "Ah, Master Abel." He displayed a slightly amused tightening of the lips that lasted for a half second before the butler face returned. He made me smile and I liked that feeling. "Mr. Horvath is on a call and may be awhile. Your usual?"

"You don't have to treat me special, Walter, I'm kinda on staff now."

"It is no problem, sir. You are special."

I went to the piano, feeling upbeat after Walter's comments, and opened a music book of Cole Porter. I thumbed through it and picked different songs at random, playing a few bars and finally singing the lyrics to "True Love".

"Beautiful," Walter said, setting down my latte. "Bing Crosby made it famous."

I had to think about who he was. Then I remembered Mama sang some of his songs at Christmas. You give to me and I give to you. Lovely lyrics. I found myself getting lost again, wondering if that's what I had with Bryan or might have with Zachary.

A few minutes later Agent Ramon arrived. He leaned on the piano and watched me, smiling as I worked through several pieces of Porter's work. When Dirksen stepped into the room I stopped playing and got up.

"What's the latest?" he asked as we settled onto the sofa and chairs.

I told them what I'd overheard and added: "Getting money in trade for military secrets—maybe he's a pass through for another purpose."

"Possibly. From what you said, someone in this chain is unhappy it goes through him," Ramon added.

"Ya know," Dirksen said, stroking his chin as he liked to do, "he's probably skimming and that's making someone unhappy."

"It's how he can afford me on a congressional salary," I offered.

"Afford us, you mean."

"This could be a new dimension. Maybe a more deadly one," Ramon said. "Like in the Iran-Contra scandal under Reagan, the U.S. secretly sold weapons to Iran to raise money and funded a rebel group in Nicaragua to destabilize a newly elected government." He leaned back on the sofa. "Even with the taps you put in, they're being cagey, talking in code. Nothing beats having someone in the room at meetings."

Dirksen nodded in agreement. "Cash from selling secrets could be funding something else. But what?" He looked at me and back to the agent. "This is getting dangerous for Abel. The more intel he provides, the more likely they'll figure him out. He's the only outsider there."

Ramon looked at me. "It's your call. You never asked for this."

"Actually, *he* asked for it by asking for *me*. He creeps me out. I'm trying to be creative in managing it, a professional. No kissing, for example."

"TMI but it must be working given the size of his tips. I have more money for you by the way. He contacted me earlier today about reserving more of your time, even making you exclusive. You were such a hit at the fundraiser that he wants to use you to up his status."

"An adoring boy on his arm who can sing." I grunted. "I'm only doing three men. *Only!*" I started to laugh then rubbed my face. "What's happening to me?" I inhaled, exhaled. "I actually like Chuck Markus. He's sweet in private. Ali is exotic and nice when you cut through the pretense. He also knows some English literature."

Dirksen smiled. "Our own male Dr. Ruth under the sheets. Markus's very rich. This is a business, at least theoretically."

Ramon shook his head. "Above all an undercover criminal investigation. Abel, what do you want to do?"

I was surprised when Walter spoke. "Abel is untrained for police work. You're putting him in danger. Please be cautious, sweet Copperhead."

I looked up at him and considered his breach of quiet service to express concern about me. Such a lovely man. "Thank you, Walter. Thank you more than you know." What should I do? My nervous energy popped me out of my chair and I stepped to the window. The church spires gave me a sense of calm and perspective before I turned around. I wanted to help my country. Could doing this also help my dad? "If I continue, is there any way it might help my father come home?"

Ramon looked thoughtful and perhaps a little pained. "As much as I'd like to say yes, I have no control over immigration. If you continue, do it because you think it's right and worth the risk."

I nodded, considering his words. Asking never hurts. "I'll take the risks. But no exclusive. I'll continue to see the loathsome congressman. I like Chuck, so if he wants to be with me, I'm good with it. The same with the prince." I sat down. "Also, I'm dating someone I really care about in the midst of my provocative new career."

"Zachary O'Brien?" Dirksen asked with Virgin Mary innocence.

"Absolutely. He's in law school, by the way."

"Nice. But don't wear yourself out with a non-paying customer."

"You're such a romantic. I do need an actual life. He's not a customer, he's my boyfriend."

His smile morphed into a bit of a good-natured chuckle. He liked me, was maybe even proud of me and enjoyed teasing like a favorite uncle. "The governor's office called to see if you were available to entertain at a small cocktail party she's giving in two weeks for her re-election campaign. You really caught her attention; she admires your talent and spunk. Unfortunately, she doesn't know about what you do or our rates. So, a freebie and, since it's a fundraiser, it may cost you if you are so inclined. Your call. Playing for free is more than enough."

"A freebie is fine because I admire her too. I'd like to make a contribution. A small down payment on her inspired support on immigration."

"Your dad would be proud of you. I know I am."

"Thank you, Dirksen."

27.

"Can we talk about something serious, Renoir?"

We'd both been quietly studying in our dorm room, him practicing French and me bonehead math. I felt a need to tell someone close to me about what was happening with my side job. Just enough without breaching my agreement on secrecy.

He set down his book and swung around in his chair, looking adorable as always. "What's up, Copperhead?"

"I want to tell you some of what I'm doing. Something that may be dangerous. I want someone not involved to know."

"Are you in trouble?" He scooted his chair to mine and took hold of my hands. "What?"

"My work with Dirksen Horvath isn't entirely about money. I mean it's money I need but there's more involved. I can only tell you a little of it because the FBI bound me to secrecy."

"The FBI? *Holy shit!*"

"For sure. One of the people I'm involved with is under investigation. I really shouldn't have just told you that and I can't say much more. I'm being paid to fuck, but I'm also in a position to overhear things, a kind of undercover agent. I've planted bugs as part of an FBI sting."

He stared at me, stone-faced. "Please say April Fool."

I just shook my head. "You can't say anything to anyone. I want to set up a check-in schedule with you if you're willing."

"What do you mean if I'm willing? I'd do anything for you. You're my best friend."

Only the broadest grin was possible with that kind of declaration. "I feel the same about you. It means a lot knowing you have my back. I'll give you a list of dates when I'm doing this stuff and times I should be back here. If I seem to be off schedule, try and reach me by phone or text. If you leave a message make it something unsuspicious like, *'Your mom called,'* something like that so I know you're just checking and I'll get back to you ASAP. I don't think anyone is hacking my calls. But I need to set up a safety line. Here's a list of names of key people you may want to contact if you don't hear from me. The FBI agent, Dirksen the pimp, Walter his butler if you can't reach Dirksen. And Zachary."

"Does he know?"

"Not everything. He knows something's up; I asked for patience. He knows it's a lot more than me working as a prostitute."

"You don't think he deserves to know everything?"

"Maybe after. He's generous enough overlooking my side career without me adding criminals and safety. Well, we're really just dating at this point. I...I told him I was working with police."

Renoir rolled his eyes. "This is serious, old man."

"There's more." I almost laughed thinking about the reality television vibe in my life. "Uhmmmm. This will sound...this will sound Cinderella but it's true. I've started seeing a Saudi prince in his early twenties."

Renoir's mouth dropped open again. *"Oh, my God!"*

"Stop it. His uncle brought him here for protection. Being gay there can cost you your head. His name is Ali, Prince Ali. The State Department is encouraging the relationship for reasons I can't tell you."

"Please tell me he looks like a camel and smells like a goat."

"More like Aladdin's better looking older brother with a body like Chris Evans in *Captain America*."

"Of course. I don't even know how to process this."

Ignoring his comment, unsure how to answer it, I opened my phone calendar. "Here, let me start filling out what I'm doing. And thanks."

He reached over and pulled me tight to his chest. "You're much too pretty to get hurt. Be careful."

++++

"So, where are we going?" I was in Chuck's small private jet, dressed in my tuxedo. He said it was a special secret. I leaned over from my seat and bussed him lightly on the lips.

"We can't do anything on the way down, not enough time and space is limited." He picked up a small control device and a screen dropped down in front, isolating us from the cabin and crew. A movie started to play.

The title flashed: *Pretty Woman*. I started laughing. "You're taking me to the opera in Los Angeles?"

"You mentioned you liked the movie and so do I. I assume a music major likes opera. You've been so nice to me, I wanted to do something entertaining and unexpected."

I slouched down in my seat and pulled down my zipper, inspired to be a bit nasty. "There is something we could do on the way down you might like." Was this an act only whores did or was it romantic? From his expression, it was certainly appreciated.

"I could offer similar service on the way back."

"Nice." He reached down to accept my offering. "I have *The Thing About Harry* on the way back."

28.

A black Mercedes sedan picked me up at school and drove me to Woodside, south of San Francisco.

We entered a forested area opening onto a vast well-manicured lawn. At the far end was an English Tudor mansion. Lots of intricate stonework, wooden cross beams, white stucco, a couple of turrets.

The driver stopped, stepped out and smartly opened my door, like you might see in a British movie. Standing outside the car, I glanced up and there was Ali, riding toward me on the biggest horse I'd ever seen, caramel colored, the long mane flopping, legs galloping high, the rider bigger than life, almost in slow motion. As they stopped next to me, the horse's shoulder matched mine. The prince was dressed in jeans, black riding boots and the knit shirt I gave him, his muscles stretching the sleeves. Another jack off fantasy.

"Welcome, handsome Abel."

"Thank you for the invitation."

He reached his hand down and nodded for me to get on the horse behind him.

"Ahmmm, I've never been on one."

"You'll love it." He extended his arm again. "Jump and I'll pull. Spread your legs as you leap."

"I can do that." He grabbed me and I did my best impression of Wild Bill Hickok mounting his stallion. I almost slipped off the horse's butt. Less than the elegant, butch image I was hoping to present. The animal moved but Ali held me.

"Wrap your arms around my waist."

He started off at a walk while I got used to it and the horse became accustomed to having me riding bareback on his hind quarters.

"Hold tight." Ali touched the horse's neck and we started to trot.

I pressed my head tight to his back and closed my eyes.

The horse started to run. I'd never been so petrified. I opened one eye. We slowed entering a wooded area. Then we stopped beside a pond. He swung a leg over the horse's head and dismounted before turning to me and offering his arms. I jumped down and was grateful to find the earth wasn't moving.

"Let's go for a swim," he said letting the horse's reins drop and opening a rustic storage shed. Filling a bowl with oats, he set it on the ground and used a hose to fill a trough.

"You need to get naked," he said, starting to strip.

I did, confident Oscar Wilde would approve.

Freshly trimmed grass ran up to the edge of the pond, cuttings suggesting it was done this morning. He dove in; I followed. It was surprisingly warm, my feet just touched bottom. He swam to me; we kissed.

"There is no one here to see us, Abel."

I splashed water in his face; we had a water fight followed by more kissing. He took my hand and we walked out through the soft mud. Behind the shed was an outdoor chase lounge. There was a backpack next to it along with towels. He tossed me one and we dried off, eyeing each other. He had carefully planned all this, right out of a romance novel. I couldn't believe he was paying me.

He dropped to his knees and took charge of my dick. I pulled him up and pushed him onto the lounge, rubbing and kissing like the world was about to end. I pulled on top and licked my way to his dick and engulfed it. The horseback ride, swimming in a pond had really turned me on. I grabbed his thighs and lifted them up, giving me an open view of his ass.

"Beautiful." I began licking and sucking. He groaned. I spit, inserting a finger. He shrieked; I laughed. "Like that, huh?"

"Don't stop, please!"

I edged him close, then eased off. Then again.

Two fingers. "I assume what I need's in the pack?"

"Yes."

I lifted it up, took out lube and a rubber. I squirted his ass and went to three fingers as I pulled open the prophylactic, securing it on my dick.

"Faster, inside me, please!"

"Patience, young prince." Wanting to be respectful and having no idea of his own experience, I followed my new post-Bryan technique, proper prep, in slow, rest, out a bit and in more. He ran his hands down my chest and I pushed his knees to his shoulders, grinning as I finished the forward lunge.

Watching him stroke himself, looking at the sheen on his chest, the perfect abs, hearing his groans were all inspirational and I began a rhythm, harder and faster.

"Oh yes!"

I bent over and shoved away his hand as he sounded near climax, pleased I was so flexible. He shot into my mouth and screamed. I kept sucking even as he tried to push me away from his tender dick. I grinned and picked up the pace, pulling out just before I erupted, scooted over him, coming on his face.

"*Yes!*" He shouted, opening his mouth, his tongue running over his lips, grabbing my cock and sucking me dry.

I moved beside him. We held each other and kissed softly.

"We can rinse off in the pond. I have lunch being prepared at the house. I had the grand piano tuned if you want to play and sing perhaps a different song than we just enjoyed."

"I look forward to all of it. Later if you have time, you could show me your bedroom."

"Can we talk about something?" He looked a bit sheepish.

"Of course." I lifted up on one elbow to look at him and he did the same.

"Thank you." He stared at my chest, not my face. This was something important. "In what we just did, you penetrated me. I enjoyed it and would like to do it again. Yet in my culture, that makes me less than a man. If you penetrate, some do not see you as homosexual. A gay is the one penetrated, a lower status. Islam is sometimes twisted by those in power or seeking more power, to damage or destroy their enemies. It is prudent not to be a target."

"I thought being gay was illegal in Saudi Arabia."

"It is. Yet it exists. Unless someone finds benefit in creating trouble, most don't care. At least that is my observation, certainly in non-public settings. Attitudes vary around the Arab world; views are not uniform." He looked up at me, his hand squeezing my bicep. "I know my uncle assumes I am the one fucking you. I do not expect it to come up, but I ask you play along if it does. Please lean into his assumption."

"Of course. Thank you for telling me. I don't want to cause you any problems. I value our relationship, our growing friendship. I respect you and know I've so much to learn. Most of America has accepted gays, either welcoming them as part of society or at least tolerating them. Some persecute homosexuality either for publicity or a need to have others they can mock and look down on. Our worlds have some things in common. The civil rights battle here largely embrace transgender issues. How are trans seen in your world?"

He smiled, rubbing the back of his hand against my jaw. "Not much visibility in my country but in Palestine or Lebanon. They are seen differently. Transgender women are often called *mokhannatheen* which means acting like a woman. Transgender men have a higher status because they are trying to be a man. A transwoman is going down the social scale. I don't agree with such views. I don't have the power to change them."

"Please tell me if ever I need to do something to protect your reputation. I know straddling two civilizations can't be easy."

He kissed my cheek.

He was a sweet man so far, a great client with the potential of becoming an intimate friend. A major movie studio set, porn themes, a handsome guy with an Olympic gymnast's body, lots of money and a warm personality. I could live with that.

29.

Trevor answered the door at the congressman's apartment. "Welcome, studman. Wilder's due back shortly. Come on in."

He was just as adorable as when I met him at dinner with Wilder and two other less captivating men involved in whatever was going down. He was about my height and muscular with black short-cropped hair. My type if I was looking.

He closed the door, shoved me against the wall and kissed me, pushing in his tongue when my mouth opened in surprise. I shoved him back.

"What are you doing? I don't know you like that. I'm with the congressman."

"No way you're dating him. How much?"

"You're being insulting to me and disrespectful to him!"

I started to walk away and he grabbed my arm. "I want you," he said. "I'm going to have you! *Plan on it!*"

I could feel the threat in his voice. Not a good man despite his looks. This could complicate my mission. "Wait in line," I snapped back, pulling away and moving to the living room, dropping into a chair so he couldn't sit next to me. I didn't want to make him mad but I was not going to be treated like that.

A moment later, the baby-faced man came out of the kitchen, the one I'd heard arguing with the congressman. He was holding a long-stemmed glass of red wine. He walked over to me, put out his hand: "Hi, I'm Clover. I about knocked you over the first time we met here."

I reached out to shake. "I remember." I thought I'd heard that he was going to lay low for a while.

He sat on the sofa across from me and put his wine on a small table. "So you didn't fall for Trevor's charm offensive just now?"

"I'm going to assume he mistook me for someone else and is feeling very guilty and a bit ashamed but has too much pride to apologize. Let's not embarrass him." I smiled, hoping an attempt at humor would help put a stop to what he'd tried. "Why are you guys here? I thought Danny and I had an engagement."

"Some business has come up. Want some wine?" His voice had a slight accent, one I couldn't duplicate with the FBI linguist.

"He's at that special age," Trevor said with a mocking grin. "Old enough to fuck but too young to drink. Being good-hearted men, we could make exceptions."

He hadn't seemed like this kind of ass at the restaurant. I reached over, picked up Clover's glass and sipped before setting it back. "I don't think anyone's checking IDs here. Nice wine." Boyish innocence and curiosity seemed like a good tactic. "Are you guys political consultants or something?"

"Or something." Clover offered his own boyish charm. "We're involved in a business transaction."

Trevor plopped down next to him, crossing his legs and continuing to stare.

"Oh, like real estate," I said. "I know he wants to buy a bigger place."

"Is that what you really think?" Clover asked.

"I have no idea what to think since nobody's told me what's happening. If I'm out of line to ask, please ignore me. Maybe we can talk about something less controversial, like the former not yet indicted President or your favorite ongoing war."

There was a knock at the door. Trevor answered and another man came in wearing a leather jacket and jeans. Maybe in his fifties, a lined, darkly tanned face and trimmed white goatee. He slipped off his coat and tossed it on a chair. Clover stood so I did too, not sure of the protocol. As the man rolled up the sleeves of his long sleeve khaki shirt, I saw a patch on his shoulder. It was green with what looked like crossed muskets and an eagle head. There were some letters, maybe a word or two from what I could see.

"Clover, good to see you," the man said shaking hands. His smile looked forced, a bit frozen.

"We're waiting for the congressman," Clover said. "He and Harold are meeting over the incident. Want some wine?"

"No. Cold beer."

"I'll get it," Trevor said, bouncing out of seat, appearing anxious to accommodate. So, maybe this guy was trouble.

"Who's this?" the man asked, looking at me, raising an eyebrow, his tone just shy of a snarl, laced with disgust.

"Abel Torres, this is Mark Wingman. Abel is dating Representative Wilder and *not* involved in what we're doing and is *not* in the loop. They were getting together this evening—for pay—when the issue emerged. Abel, Mark is part of our business group."

That was blunt, my rent boy status clarified, probably strategic. I offered my hand, wanting to appear friendly; he hesitated and then did the same. He didn't try and crush my palm but it was firm. "Nice to meet you, Mr. Wingman." He shook his head, lips curled like he just took a shot of cat urine and sat, dismissing me.

Trevor came back with two beers and a glass of red wine which he set in front of me. I just nodded with a whispered, "Thanks."

"We need to talk," Wingman snapped, his anger up front. "About next Friday. I don't have a lot of time." He turned and stared at me. The menace was obvious; he wanted me gone. Clover seemed flustered. I got the hint.

"Sorry. I really am scheduled to meet with the congressman but I can wait in the bedroom. Or just leave. What do you want me to do?" Play innocent whore, not secret undercover agent.

"How about if I take you to the bedroom and pull down your pants?" Trevor taunted.

"Leave him alone!" Clover sounded exasperated. He pointed a warning finger at the asshole then turned back to me. "Yeah, Abel, maybe waiting in the bedroom—*alone*—is a good idea."

"No problem," I said, picking up my wine and shoulder bag, exiting the room, grateful to escape the crossfire. Leaving the door slightly ajar, I listened:

"Is he Mexican?" Wingman spoke in a harsh whisper. Almost venomous.

"A mix," Clover answered, "let's move on, it's not important."

"Danny pays to fuck a damn half-breed?"

I heard more but the question made me feel faint. What kind of group was this?

Fearing I might get caught eavesdropping, I moved to a small desk and sat. There was mail and a yellow legal pad. Alert for any footsteps, hearing them arguing, I thumbed through the mail and found nothing of interest. I could see the outline of letters imprinted on the note pad. I ripped off the top page, held it to the light. Likely made by a pen pressing hard. Something was written, numbers and maybe an address. I folded it and slipped it into my vest pocket, ignoring the twitches in my back, my senses telling me I had just met a psychopath. Maybe Trevor was one, too. These were not good people.

I went back to the door and listened. Just murmuring. I moved to the king size bed, put my fancy glass on a side table, fluffed some pillows against the headboard, slipped off my shoes and sat, kicking out my legs. I scrolled through my phone to check the news, email and texts.

I'd started to nod off from boredom when I heard the congressman's voice. They were arguing.

"I will not!" Congressman Wilder's voice.

"I did *not* just hear that!" The tone ominous and threatening. The new guy with the beard. "Cross us at your peril, faggot!"

"Are you threatening me?"

"Enough!" Clover barked. "We know what we have to do.

Let's cool down and call it a night."

There were some strained goodnights. I slipped off my jeans and socks, took off my vest, unbuttoned my shirt while trying not to fall over in panic. The front door lock snapped shut and footsteps headed my way. I sat on the bed, opened my shirt further so my pectorals were prominent, and did my best to look excited to see him.

The door swung open and Danny Wilder entered—"Hello beautiful"—removing his shirt and standing there in all his white compression glory.

"Can you help me with this?" He turned around and this one looked like it was more girdle than T-shirt.

"Sure thing." I pulled it up with some difficulty over his shoulders. While he dropped it to the floor and took off his pants, I slipped off my shirt and leaned against the headboard, picking up my glass to take a sip then thought better of it and palmed my crotch instead.

He sat beside me, fully naked, stroked my chest and leaned down to suck a nipple. "Sorry I'm so late." He tried to kiss me and I brought my lips to his neck.

"You're going to pay for it. Get on your knees! *Now!*"

Thank goodness this wasn't an overnight.

++++

I texted Renoir that I was on my way home so he wouldn't be nervous. I called my personal FBI agent and told him what happened and about the paper. He said he was nearby and would meet me at the dorm. As my Lyft pulled up in front, Ramon Cortez stepped out of a car and waved me over.

I slipped inside his black SUV and told him everything I'd overheard, speaking into his cell phone to record it, giving descriptions of the men and the threat against the congressman. I gave him the yellow notepad paper and explained why I took it, also mentioning the patch on the man's shirt. "Does it mean anything?"

"Sounds like an insignia popular with one of the militia groups."

"Like National Guard?"

"No, one of the groups who believe the federal government is evil. You've heard of the Oklahoma City bombing?"

"Sure, in American history class."

"Some were also involved in the January 6th insurrection at the capital."

"That I do remember."

"The question is, what's this congressman's objective? Politically I wouldn't think he has anything in common."

"One more thing. While I was listening at the door, Wingman asked if I was Mexican. Clover said I was a mix and it wasn't important. Wingman disagreed calling me a...*a fucking half breed.*"

"That's a new element. It raises more questions. If this Wingman is a key player and a racist or white nationalist, what in hell is the congressman doing with him? At this point, be cautious and continue your role as plaything. Stay as docile as you can. Avoid Wingman if at all possible. Good work on the yellow notepad. I'll have the lab study it. Are you up for working with another sketch artist?"

"Of course. Maybe tomorrow." He agreed and I went up to my room.

Renoir met me at the door. "I saw you get into that man's car. Are you all right?"

"Yes. He's an FBI agent. I called him."

"Did anything bad happen?"

"I gathered some information. The case is getting more complicated. Nothing really bad. Not counting sex with the congressman, the worst thing was one of the bad guys shoved me against the wall and slipped his tongue into my mouth. I'm going to gargle."

"Aren't you a little late for that?"

30.

"Duck! Roll! Rise! Sprint!" Sam Brown yelled for the eighth time. "You need to get so used to fighting back it becomes second nature." She crossed her arms, fingers bouncing on her biceps. "Speed is critical in defense. See or even sense an attack coming, react, make it automatic. Practice over and over until it's instinctual."

I managed to avoid her next assault but then tripped and went face down on the mat.

"Not your finest performance," she said, scowling, helping me up.

Sam sounded frustrated and for good reason. I just wasn't anywhere near mastering her techniques. I was arguably better than making a fool of myself but my FBI fighter training did not a gold medal fighter make.

"I watch you walk and see a natural grace. I'm told your singing is powerful and deft. Your fighting ability is more like the elegance and voice of Elmer Fudd."

"Who's he?"

"Kids," she muttered. "Never mind."

I needed to release my frustration and did a back flip on the mat. It felt good, at least I could do something. A little showing off lifted my spirits.

"So you did tumbling in school?"

"High school gymnastics. I loved tumbling, flips, tucks, handstands, handsprings, pikes, all the floor action."

"Excellent. Gymnastics might be the world's most difficult sport but don't get cute, use it just to distract and get out of the way of a fist or knife. Not to get a ten from the judges." She gestured to the mats. "Show me."

I did a less than Olympic version of my floor routine, ending with a 360 backflip which included a full rotation, ending with me facing my original direction. I was breathless when I finished, my landing way off, a little shocked it worked. Our team had never won anything but we all had a good time. You practice so long and hard on these routines they get embedded in your DNA. I hadn't done this in months. No sprains, so that was almost as good as a win.

"That's impressive, Abel. Useful. Maybe we need some fight music to get you in the mood and it sticks in your head. Do some stretches and give me a minute at the sound booth."

She went into a small room with a glass window. I dropped my butt on the floor pushed out my legs and grabbed my toes. This I could do and it made me feel loose.

A heavy, pounding, thuggish beat started. Words incomprehensible. She spiked it to a deafening level.

"Ba! Ba! Death! Ba! Ba! Death!" That was what I sensed. It was way over modulated. Rap was not my sound and the mike was too close to the rapper's mouth. I could feel the spit. Yet the power was intoxicating. I tried to download it into my brain, through my body, my head nodding, shoulders twisting, feet tapping. My own fight song!

"All right, Abel." Sam said loudly over the din. "Use the music. What lyrics do you hear?"

"It sort of sounds like *Ba! Ba! Death!*"

"He's talking about a sex act, but if your definition works for you, great. Launch those words when you face a threat. Someone moves against you and the music hits, triggering your fists." She squatted down in a fighting stance, moving her hands, shifting weight from one leg to another. "Face me and charge as if your life depended on it!"

"Ba! Ba! Death!

I ran and dodged her foot, hitting the ground with a shoulder roll, faking her out, feeling the beat, bounding to my feet.

Ba! Ba! Death!

She twisted and came at me, swinging a fist.

Ba! Ba! Death!

I rolled back, swung a foot up that made her fall back, then continued the flip, onto my feet and ran. I screamed and threw my arms up as I cleared the mats. Of course I knew she went easy on me to give me confidence. I wasn't sure the screaming added to my ferocity.

Sam turned off the music. "Obviously that helped," she said with a pleased grin. "Music to fight and kill by. Music to instantly put you into high alert. Let's try this a few more times till you feel it through your muscles and mind. Snap it on in your head, like a light switch."

She wasn't so gentle the next time but after that I did improve. I lost myself—moving, jabbing, grabbing, rolling, kicking into any vulnerable area. As long as I faced an adversary who went easy on me, no problem. I'd practice in my room. Tossing Renoir might be entertaining.

"Next up, knife fighting. Let's get your signature blade, practice extracting it from your fancy new shoes, building speed, making sure any fingers you cut off don't belong to you and how to disable and kill if you have no choice." She walked across the room to the dummies and I followed, feeling like one.

31.

Zachary and I raced our bikes down the Great Highway early on a Sunday morning when traffic was minimal since there really wasn't much room for bicycles given the narrowness and the danger of drifting sand on the oceanside road. He'd rented the red wonders and planned the outing in Golden Gate Park. He had a picnic basket strapped behind his seat and a pack across his shoulder. I followed close behind.

He gestured for a right turn onto Lincoln Way and we pulled into a turnoff for a huge stone windmill.

"This is the Dutch Windmill. 1903. Seventy-five feet high. Isn't it wonderful? I love this place. You should see it in the spring when the tulips are in bloom."

We wandered around the site, took some selfies, then continued through the park, at one point stopping at the Bison Paddock. I'd never seen one live before. Magnificent animals.

Eventually he pulled to a stop by a large lawn edging a wooded area. No one was around. We put down a blanket and stretched out in the sun. He picked up his shoulder bag, took my hand and led me into the trees. A hundred feet in felt like we weren't in the city. He turned, took out two towels, laid them on the pine needle ground, turned and kissed me.

It seemed a little public but then again all I saw were trees. He pulled my shirt up and off. I did the same to him. Our hands explored each other. He really had a great physique.

"Yes, it's true I am more muscular and maybe a little better looking," he teased, "but I'm fine being seen with you." He laughed and I grabbed him. He may have bigger pectorals but I was stronger, or maybe just more strategic in my holds. I flipped him onto the towels and straddled him, holding his arms to his side. He really didn't put up much of a fight.

"So what are you going to do now, big boy? You have me all helpless and half naked in the woods. No one to rescue me."

I slipped further back, sitting on his thighs, and undid his belt, pants and zipper.

"Finally."

I moved to the side and pulled off the Bermudas. He wasn't wearing underpants.

"I thought they'd just get in the way."

I curled around and took him in my mouth. He was hard in ten seconds, one of his many great talents. He pawed at my back so I moved around so we were in a sixty-nine. He unhooked my belt. I lifted up and he pulled everything off, going to work on our mutual pleasure.

"I know you're not ready to fuck, but does that mean your butt is off limits?"

"Not at all."

"Roll onto your stomach."

I did and he straddled me, kneading my shoulders and working down to my lower back and my ass cheeks. He stretched out over my legs, kissing each side of my ass, separating them, working his tongue between them. I yelped when he reached ground zero. The sensation was electric, rippling through my body. Bryan and I had both liked this and Zach had serious talent.

He lifted up and put his dick horizontal to my ass and began rubbing, back and forth, a steady rhythm, kissing my neck.

He grabbed a bottle of lube by his pack and squirted some between my legs. He pressed his dick into the space, pushing my legs closed and pumped. He reached a hand under me and I lifted. He grabbed my cock with his lubed hand and stroked. Gay boys were so inventive.

I thought our screams might attract attention. But there was just the sound of wind in the trees and the chatter of a ground squirrel under a nearby bush studying the weird humans. Side by side, we held each other, smiling, feeling a bit naughty.

"Time for lunch," he announced and jumped to his feet.

"So romantic."

"When my stomach calls, I obey. Just like my dick."

32.

I was back at Dirksen's.

"A term you wouldn't use to describe the congressman is financial wizard," Ramon explained. "A Houdini of money he ain't."

"What's a Houdini?" I asked.

Walter answered. "A famous magician from long ago, an escape artist."

"He's pulling increasingly large sums from the trust his father left him and somehow that trust is made whole each month from a bank in London which just happens to have a large number of Russian and Ukrainian investors. He's also been observed dropping large amounts of money at casino card rooms."

"But that doesn't prove he's selling secrets, does it?" I didn't really like Danny but I was hoping he wasn't a traitor. Especially since he was a gay man and exposure of him would be seized on by the right wing as a reflection on all of us.

"The timing, our forensic auditors believe, suggests the money is in exchange for information on protected pieces of data, mostly troop and naval deployments, taking a cut to pay down his gambling debts and sending the rest to *God's Patriots*, the name of the group he's working with. Abel, you met their leader at his apartment, Mark Wingman. Your work with the sketch artist confirmed his identity. What you didn't see on the patch was the name of the group."

"Yes, the charming guy with the trimmed white goatee who hates Mexicans."

"That's him," the FBI agent confirmed.

"We've started feeding the congressman inaccurate data, working with a key staffer on the Armed Services Committee, hoping to see where it ends up." The agent shrugged. "At some point they may figure out it's bogus, so we need to make sure we've moved in before then."

++++

"Dirksen," I said after Ramon left, "I'd like to invite Chuck Markus to go with me to the Governor's fundraiser. I want him to donate to her campaign, although I don't quite know how to ask. I'll be donating the entertainment as you know. I don't want to charge him either. That would be tacky. Everything is not about money. Are you all right if I do it that way?"

Dirksen looked at me and smiled. "So cool the Governor admires you. Of course if you went home with Markus and did the gig, I suspect he'd gladly pay our fee and hers."

"Please, that's embarrassing. I want to help her re-election campaign, a thank you for her out front stand on immigration."

He nodded assent. "You're a good man, Abel. Enjoy the party."

++++

My favorite billionaire drove us to Sacramento in his sleek black two door coupe. He said it was a Maybach Exelero. Never heard of it but it was very luxurious and fast. I looked it up on my phone as we drove.

"Are you all right?" Chuck asked as I began to cough.

"Yeah. I'm doing good." I wondered if the car came with an

armed guard in the trunk.

"You mentioned this was a fundraiser," Chuck said, "How much do you want me to give?"

"You're my guest since I'm part of the program. But if you're so inclined, it's a hundred minimum and the max anyone can give to a statewide campaign is seventy-five hundred. I really admire her."

"You told me about your dad and her stand on immigration. It's cool you're supporting her."

The home was a classic old Victorian on a shady street in west Sacramento. We walked up to the table on the porch where a young woman, a bubble-haired brunette, likely just out of high school, asked my name. I handed her a hundred-dollar bill. I felt so cool, certainly my first time. "I'm the entertainment." She gave me a nametag and thanked me.

Chuck handed her a credit card. "Seventy-five hundred is fine and here's my business card for any information you need for your records. If you want more, text me with a form and I'll send it back." He had assumed his best CEO man-in-command voice.

She seemed flustered. "Oh, uhm, thank you very much Mr. Markus. Here's your name tag."

Chuck stuck it on his lapel and mine on me. I was feeling a bit ruffled, normally his MO. He put his hand behind my lower back and we entered the home. He was a man in charge, at least publicly.

The young woman at the table must have texted about the big donation. The campaign manager came up to us within minutes to thank Chuck. She was a slender Black woman, older with short hair and very sweet. We mingled with some of the hundred or so guests.

The governor came up and hugged me. "I'm so looking forward to hearing your beautiful voice again." I introduced her to Chuck. She thanked him for the donation. Money news got around fast. She winked at me, clearly acknowledging me for bringing him into the campaign.

The governor called me up to the piano, put two fingers to her lips and whistled. All conversation stopped. I loved this woman! My mouth was at full grin. After a sweet introduction on how we met, she said, "Abel comes from a musical family, his mother part African American, his father from Mexico. I asked him to honor us, honor them, with songs they enjoy."

It was easy to get overwhelmed by this kind of setting and the guests. I swallowed and assumed my stage voice. "I went to Catholic school as a boy and every Sunday to the African Methodist Episcopal Church known as AME. Talk about mixed messages and mixed styles of music. This is one of my mother's favorite singers and a song we didn't do in church." I began to play, Nat King Cole's love ballad, "Unforgettable." What you are, indeed. I nodded to the governor. She came up behind me, a hand light on my shoulder. When finished, enthusiastic applause and a few whistles, including her own.

"Last Sunday," I told the audience, "I was part of a Skype call between my exiled father in Mexico and my mother. They love each other so much. He sang to her, a classic Spanish ballad performed by a wide range of singers, including Andrea Bocelli, even Dean Martin. My version is different."

I began to play "Besame Mucho." Kiss me, kiss me much. So rich and velvety. I mixed Spanish and English. Kiss me, as if it were tonight. *Como si fuera ésta noche.* I remembered the tears in Mama's eyes. The last time they kissed through the immigration prison bars. Tears rolled down my cheeks as I sang. The audience was quiet when I finished, then erupted in applause. The governor said quietly behind me, "Beautiful, Abel, beautiful."

I wiped my eyes. Emotion should be in a performance but not delay it.

"In church as a boy," I said, "we sang many civil rights songs, the choir righteous, just like the governor. One of my favorites was by the late Sam Cooke, one of the great soul singers of all time."

I began, "Change is Gonna Come." There can be hope even in the darkest times. When you think you can't last any longer, something happens. Yes it will. My mind drifted as I sang, thinking of mother telling me about Bayard Rustin, one of the main organizers of the March on Washington that led to the passage of the Voting Rights Act of 1965. He was a gay man, she said, forced by prejudice in his own community to downplay an important part of who he was. Change was comin' but he died just as gay civil rights was beginning to move. Now many were trying to turn it back. Still, I needed to believe.

There was a tight circle of guests around me. And tears.

"Here's a song my mother picked for me for a grammar school talent show. Her life was not easy and the song spoke to her. It spoke to my father. It's both corny and wonderful, Don Quixote explaining his hopeless quest. I came in second in the contest, by the way, and we all agreed it was a perfect outcome. The winner sang 'Good Ship Lollipop' in appropriate Shirley Temple costume. She was wonderful." I raised my arm high and shouted: "Here's to Mama!"

I began "Impossible Dream" From *Man of La Mancha,* Don Quixote marching into hell for a heavenly cause. So powerful. I thought the governor would crack a rib when she hugged me afterward.

On the ride back, Chuck congratulated me. "You're an amazing talent," he said, squeezing my knee.

I thanked him for going with me and the generous donation.

He inquired, "Should I send money to Dirksen since you're spending time with me for this party?"

"What? No, absolutely not. You accompanied me to an event with the governor. I asked you. I thought you might like meeting her. Honestly, I'm thrilled by your generosity."

"What happens if I want to take you back to my penthouse, if you were agreeable? I would expect to pay. It's a business, although I like to think we have a friendship beyond what you do for Dirksen. You've really helped change my life by giving me confidence. I am grateful."

"I'd really enjoy going back with you."

33.

After a romantic seafood dinner, Zach and I walked slowly, hand-in-hand, lovers out for an evening stroll in the Castro, exploring the neighborhood of old Victorians and small shops, talking, whispering, sharing secrets, holding hands, giggling. It was a warm evening, lots of people on Castro but few on the side streets. We wandered onto 18th Street, past two restaurants and a bar, stopping when we started to kiss, leaning against a wall.

A pickup truck stopped beside us. Three men in ski masks jumped out from the back end of a small camper top.

"Fags!"

"Fucking Mexican!"

They slammed us against the wall.

"Fucking queers!"

I turned and jumped back just as a wooden baton struck the wall inches from my face. It took a moment to figure out what was happening. The guy pulled the weapon back to take another swing. Then the music hit, instinct, training, faster and faster.

"Ba! Ba! Death! BaBa Death…Death!"

I seized the man's arm and snapped my foot hard up into his

nuts. As he bent over, screaming, I grabbed him by his shirt and slammed his face into the brick wall with all my strength. The crunch was sickening. He dropped to the sidewalk, seemingly unconscious, his face awash in blood. The weapon rolled into the gutter.

"*Cocksucker!*" another man shrieked. I blocked his arm holding a piece of pipe and slammed my fist into his mouth. He tumbled backward, his head banging into the side of the pickup.

Zach was being held by his collar, a fist pounding into his gut, overpowered by the stronger man. He was landing a few blows himself but not enough to break away.

I bellowed and seized the man's hair, my music pounding in my ears, yanked his head back and slammed my fist into his larynx. The attacker grabbed his throat, choking, staggering, dropping to his knees.

The thug by the truck, ashen and wide-eyed as I ran to him, his lip red with blood, turned and grabbed the tailgate just as it started to move. He was not getting away.

"*Mike! Don't leave me!*" he screamed at the driver.

I wrapped my arms around his thigh and leaned back. He squealed as he lost his grip on the tailgate chains and dropped to the pavement face first, the pickup speeding away. As he attempted to push himself up, I stomped on his back and slammed his head repeatedly into the roadway with my foot until he didn't move. I gripped his hair and pulled back his head. His face was bloody, his lips badly split, exposing his teeth. He was unconscious. I let go and turned to my lover, my adrenalin pumping.

"*Ba! Ba! Death!*"

The attackers down, the threat momentarily gone, I ran to Zach. He was standing, leaning against the wall, holding his gut, gasping for air.

"*Are you hurt? God!* This is horrible! *Help! Police!*" I was screaming the words. We needed law enforcement.

"I'm okay." Zach wrapped his arms around me.

We caught our breath, holding each other. His nose was bleeding as well as his lower lip. "Thank you." Zach's voice was a whisper as he slopped his tongue across my neck. He was all right; no, he was perfect.

I lifted my shirt to soak up the blood on his face and shouted: *"Help! Police!"*

"Police!" a male voice nearby. Then there were more voices screaming.

I kissed Zach's cheek, the top of his head, his lips. "How could this happen? Here?"

The man who was holding his throat made a noise and started to rise. *"Fucking fags...!"*

I twisted around, landing my heel to the side of his head, holding nothing back. The attacker went limp.

"Bastard!" I returned to the embrace.

People started hollering, a crowd forming, phones aimed at us from all directions. I heard a whistle. Someone was on a phone a few feet away: "Police Department...I want to report a vicious attack underway... injuries..."

"Are you all right?" I heard it over and over as people rushed up to assist.

"Yeah! Thanks." I saw tears in Zach's eyes, not unlike my own. This could have ended so differently. Thank you, Sam Black, for the last months' worth of training and a rap singer who spit into his mike.

"You were amazing!" a young man yelled, running up to us. "I saw it. Got most of it on my phone. I'll give it to the cops. Fucking kick ass!" He turned and continued taking video of the chaotic scene.

"There's the truck!" someone screamed, pointing to a nearby cross-street, and a mob of enraged queers started chasing it. A beer bottle flew through the driver's window, hitting him on the side of his face. A dozen more bottles rained down on his window and roof. He banged into a parked car, backed up, and burned rubber, disappearing into the night, abandoning his fag hater buddies unconscious on the street.

Multiple sirens drew close from two directions. Three police cars worked through the large crowd and halted near us. People were running out of the bars. "Queer bashing!" someone shouted. More whistles. Red lights twirling.

Police nudged the crowd back as an ambulance pulled in close. Two EMTs jumped out and ran to us, focusing on the two of us before checking the attackers. A young female tech treated Zach's cuts. A male tech gave me a quick exam. Police were inspecting the thugs.

"*Holy fuck!*" a twenty-something Black police officer said, walking up to us. "Nice to see some justice for creeps like these. Someone knows how to fight. Can I shake your hand before I get official and you tell me what happened? I want to remain impartial here." His grin was so welcome.

"I'd be honored. By the way, the driver's name is Mike."

He turned to the crowd. "If you witnessed what happened, please come here and give me your names."

Another cop, Hispanic, squatting over one of the still unconscious men, holding a wallet, shouted: "He's from East Bay. Teens out for some thrills. Well, they found 'em."

When the medics finished, the crowd applauded as we walked to a police cruiser, my arm around Zach. I waved, "We're all right. Thank you! Thank you so much."

Cell phones were everywhere, recording some excitement for Facebook. A tall bearded man, in red sequined dress and impossibly tall shoes, moved close and did a selfie.

"We're all just glad you survived. You're kick ass!"

"Thank you for being here for us, for the community." My brain was on automatic at this point.

We slipped inside the car, holding each other. The crowd, still growing, parted as we passed through, whistling and applauding.

"We're proud of you, man!" an Asian man hollered into the still open window, whistling.

"Thanks for doing us proud!" a young dyke with rainbow hair yelled as she pumped a fist skyward.

We waved at everyone, appreciating the support, feeling a little better about what happened. Across all the barriers that divided society, the Q community seemed like family, a weird, diverse mashing of people you didn't know but who understood how they were different and stuck together. Most of them, anyway. Sadly, not all the time, I thought, remembering the congressman.

We were at the police headquarters for two hours. I called Renoir and Dirksen to let them know. Mama screamed in horror when I told her. "I'm fine, please don't cry. These things just happen." But they don't, not really. Politicians elsewhere proclaimed a sense of entitlement for hatred, thinking it helped their election, their personal benefit more important than someone's life. Sick. Some churches were infected as well, God taking a back seat to politics and hate or maybe hijacked by it.

The Black cop, Sergeant Kearns, showed us the video which caught most of what happened. The guy seemed to be taping the streetscape when the attack started. "Mighty impressive, Mr. Torres. Most of the police and staff watched it. Seeing the bad guys lose—well, most of our work is much less satisfying than you might guess. The media's here, talking to them's up to you. Two attackers are conscious, all of them concussed. You were not gentle. Nice to see. They'll recover and be prosecuted. We have a lead on the truck and the Contra Costa Sheriff dispatched a unit to talk to the parents. That should be quite a conversation. Yes, his name is Mike. Looking at some street cameras, these punks were tailing you, thinking you'd be easy targets. We haven't seen an attack like this in the Castro in about a year and then it was skinheads. These were clean-cut white suburban teens. Haters exist even in a place like the Bay Area. What makes them come out of their caves?"

Eventually, after we signed our statements, Sergeant Kearns said: "You're free to go. We'll be in contact for the pre-trial work. A deputy police chief gave a statement to the media. They know what happened and what you did. They've seen one video and were given copies. There's a podium and microphones in place. If you need a ride, a dozen officers would be happy to take you home."

"Thank you, sergeant," I responded. "I think we'll be fine."

A young woman walked over to us. "This is Sally McIntyre," Kearns said, "our Public Information Officer. She'll exit first, announce you're coming out and ask that they treat you with respect given the hell you've been through tonight."

"Good luck to you both." Sergeant Kearns offered his hand. The Hispanic officer, Corporal Hernandez, gave us each a hug as other police and staff, standing behind desks and coming out of offices, applauded while we waved and walked out into the hallway. At least a score of reporters, some with TV cameras, started shouting questions.

Renoir and Dirksen were waiting and jumped up when we emerged, running to us. The reporters still were shouting. "Hold on, first things first!" I said holding up a hand. Zach joined the four-way hug and quick conversation.

"I've got a car and driver downstairs," Dirksen said, "You should rest and be in a quiet place. I'm so sorry. You were magnificent, Abel. Oh, and your favorite congressman called, worried about you and pleased you didn't mention Zach was your boyfriend."

"But he is!" I kissed Zach on the cheek. A photographer snapped a photo.

"A technicality. We want to keep our customers happy." Dirksen laughed, rubbed my hair and patted my cheek then did the same with Zach. "My boys! Did they give you some pills for your nerves?"

"Yes," Zach answered. "Thank you."

After we finished answering the reporters' questions, Dirksen took us to Zach's apartment and then Renoir back to the dorm.

It hit when we were finally alone. I started to shake. "You could have died," I said, snot rolling with the tears, both of us embracing and dropping to our knees. I felt helpless and folded down until my head touched the floor. I couldn't stop crying.

Zach wrapped his arms around me. "Thank God you're okay. You saved me! Saved us!" He kissed the back of my neck. "Abel, I love you."

++++

Various versions of the attack were posted and went viral. Someone had used the original witness attack video, images from a street camera which captured the whole episode from a distance, added audio and video from the press conference. It was mesmerizing if you forgot about being a participant. I trembled when I saw it, still not believing it was me. Zach refused to watch. Our names were included, since we were adults, in the print stories and some postings both of us identified as college students. I was also ID'd as an up-and-coming singer. One post showed me singing at the fundraiser and then the attack and press conference. It was unsettling being the victim of a random attack and what might have happened.

Hundreds of comments. Some praised me, one woman labeled me the aggressor for being so brutal.

"Why do people have to be so violent? Why can't they settle their differences peacefully?" she posted.

A guy responded: "Get real! Because they were attacked and wanted to stay alive! One guy had an iron pipe to smash their heads." Other comments on her post were less charitable.

Bryan sent me a text,

Bryan: Thank God you survived. This was horrible.

You are such a special man. I still love you.

I wasn't sure quite how I felt about this, the first message I'd had since he broke us up.

Friends of Zach's called and texted to show support. Some attached segments from local newscasts, several web news channels and even one national newscast, the pitch being the victims beat the crap out of the thugs. Actually, not quite the words they used.

When I turned the lock at my dorm room the next day, Renoir ran up and pulled me into a python embrace, still teary. "I was so worried." He leaned back, looking at my face. "Your eyes are puffy. Not your best look."

"Thanks. I'm better now. Except for the rib you just cracked. Hopefully all cried out." I looked at the room. There were bouquets all across our desks and on the floor.

"The huge one is from Dirksen. He actually called and came

by this morning to make sure I was doing all right, not hyperventilating like when I talked to him at the police station. So sweet of him. I like the guy. You got flowers from your personal congressman and Senator Wiseling. The fancy arrangement of those stunning blue delphiniums is from Chuck and Reggie Markus. Whoever they are—clients, I assume. But you don't do brothers, do you? Or father-son?"

"Keep going."

"Some of our fellow students brought them too, maybe classmates or even strangers wanting to show support. Everyone on campus seems to know and that I'm your fabulous roommate. When I came back from lunch and a class, there were flowers at the door, like a memorial. Some had notes, thank-yous for being a stand-up queer and role model. I lost it, Abel, and cried for an hour. It just really hit me; kind of a delayed reaction, how bad it could've been for you both."

I put my arm around him; we just stood there before he pulled back and seemed once more to be his regular self. "Also, two amazingly handsome men brought flowers too. I suspect by their looks and the sophisticated way they talked, that they may be FOD, Friends of Dirksen. If they do freebies, I'm available."

34.

The congressman greeted me at his door with a fuck me now look and lunged to kiss me. I grabbed him around the chest and blew into his ear. He laughed and pulled me inside.

This was an after dinner, three-hours only affair; I had classes and he had a hearing in the morning. He dropped to his knees and opened my pants, clearly not interested in foreplay, which was good. He growled as he pulled out my cock. I tossed my jacket on the sofa and pulled off my shirt. He liked to play with my chest. I liked giving him distractions from my lips. I imagined myself as part of an *avant garde* improv group. My assignment was to get the man asleep ASAP so I could go home.

After a few minutes: *"Enough! Stand up and strip!"*

He did so, looking like it was his birthday; the cake coming his way.

I spanked him in the bedroom, always an audience pleaser, and was less than easy when I pushed inside him. He screamed. When I asked if it was too much, he responded, as expected, *"No! No! Keep going!"*

As we lay next to each other on his bed, I decided to get pushy.

"Who were all these weird guys at the restaurant and here in your apartment when I came to see you last week? That one guy with the white goatee was really rude, almost threatening. But I was here for you."

"Yeah. He's kind of a jerk. He heads a pressure group that hates government. I'm trying to find a way to pull them into the system, not just angry outsiders."

"That's really cool," I said, knowing it was bullshit. "If anyone has the skills to make America great again, it's you."

He raised his eyebrow, likely not happy with my choice of words. "Thanks."

When he put his head down on the pillow, I decided to try a little more. "But you're so nice and they're nothing like you. I asked if they were political consultants and they just laughed and sent me into your bedroom." I kissed his cheek. "Not that this is a bad place to be."

He lifted up onto his elbow and I did the same, face to face. "You're one beautiful young man, Abel. I'm pleased we're going to that political event next month. Lots of queer voters and you seem to have your own growing constituency because of what you did to those gay bashers and your fabulous voice."

"And you," I said, placing my hand on his chest.

He smiled, almost shy. "Thank you."

"All right. We both have early morning appointments. I have something special I want to leave you with that will make you think of me almost constantly while we're apart." I rolled over him and stood, walking to my shoulder bag. "Stand up, hands at your sides."

He did as I asked.

"Remember when I measured your dick last time?"

"Yes, sir. It was very erotic."

"Good. For me too. I want to keep things sexy between us because you're such a hot man and deserve it." I took a small box from my bag, opened it, and held up what I hoped he would find exciting, given his BDSM proclivities. Agent Ramon wanted me to stay close so this might be a useful technique.

"This is a silicone cock cage, a beautiful male chastity device made of medical grade polycarbonate material. Very echo friendly." I moved it around, showing what it looked like all together and then I took it apart, ready to install. "I want to know you're thinking of me; and no one but me can have you. No masturbating in the shower. It's all for me."

I sat on the edge of the bed and pulled him facing me. I held out the ring, ready to start. "This wraps about the back of your nuts and over your cock." I slipped it into place, picked up some lube and rubbed it over his dick before I pushed it inside a clear tube. A nice fit. "This is important for your initial comfort in getting used to it. I like the fact it's clear so it lets me see all of your special place. Then I use this lock to hold it in place." A nice loud click for the metal lock. "There's a slit for pissing, but you can't get a hard on. I have the only key." I moved it around to make sure no skin or hair got into it.

"My God! That's amazing. I've seen them advertised but I never thought I'd wear one."

"You never had me in your life before."

Standing and wrapping one hand around the trussed package, the other on his shoulder, using my command voice, I said: "You'll wear this, understood?"

"Yes sir! Thank you, sir."

Turning it one way, then another, examining my handiwork, I said, "So very sexy."

Grabbing my phone, I stood. "A photo seems appropriate to show just how sizzling you look."

He stood there, offering no objections, perhaps dazed. He seemed lost in his head, perhaps thinking about wearing it to work, sitting next to other congressmen in a committee hearing, constantly turned on.

"It's a large and fits so, so…astonishing." I'd had to get the smallest size. I showed him a closeup.

"I like it."

The improv segment was over.

++++

Sleep was not my friend. Just too much happening in my life. Being strong and sassy was my MO, but really just a front. Insecurity was always just behind the showman. Performing on stage was a release, pouring my emotions into the music, a secret whore celebrating being alive. Was hate rising and I'd just never noticed until it hit me? Being too distracted from your surroundings can be dangerous.

Three a.m. Renoir was snoring. Good for him.

I sat up and hugged my knees, thinking about what was going on. The attack. Zach could have been killed. Or both of us.

Fucking for money. Fucking for money and the FBI. Slapping around a congressman, for God's sake, and spying on him. What kind of nasty was he up to? Screwing a Saudi prince. What was I doing? Would I get killed? I was being fetishized as a kind of sexual he-man when I felt more like a regular guy who likes sex. I read that sexual projection was not uncommon for people watching a performer on stage and some of my reviewers spent more time commenting on my body and looks, the way I moved, than my voice. All part of a package and I needed to accept it. My singing voice—the career I wanted—was part of what made me get the big bucks for my side career as a prostitute. That and my dick, if I listened to Dirksen, what certain rich men wanted once I stopped singing. The life of a college freshman.

All my classes, a full-time load. Bonehead math was so deflating but at least no mention about the evils of masturbation. All the great opportunities to sing and improve my art. The department chair a big fan. The expectations on me were crushing. Play the mature lead in a major musical when I'm still a kid to many people. I looked younger than my age. Good for some things, less for others.

What would Mama think if she found out what I was really doing? Did she suspect? Had we been able to cover the source of her rent money? I couldn't handle it if she thought less of me or was ashamed. Or my dad, struggling just to survive after being kicked out of the only country he ever knew. What would he think? I had no idea. Yeah, I did. He'd be appalled; they both would.

Zachary. For the first time, I was dating someone I connected with beyond the bed. It was so different from high school. Bryan and I were just horny teenagers willing and anxious to try anything. Yet my heart hurt when he left for Chicago. It felt like my world had ended. Now, a new lover. I smothered a laugh. Zach and I were horny young men too—me just a few months past being a teenager—with major libidos. But there was more there, such potential for depth of affection, sass, compatible careers and histories that had much in common. What if I went exclusively into music instead of politics? How would that work?

There had to be a limit on the time Zachary would tolerate me fucking other men for money. It had to be bothering him. It would me if our lives were reversed. Sure, he'd done survival sex but that was in the past. This was now; he'd been so understanding. Even saying he admired my family loyalty. Did I deserve a man like this? Could I end up hurting him?

College should be enjoyable, stimulating, a space to grow up.

I jumped when the alarm went off at six a.m. and fell back asleep.

Renoir dropped a cold wet towel over my face.

Time to re-attach my nothing-bothers-me, confident-swagger-mask.

Where did I keep it?

35.

Smith's Landing was in what the Chamber of Commerce called "historic Antioch," on the water, overlooking a boat harbor with a view of the southern Sacramento Delta. Not a place we visited often. For our family pocketbooks a bit expensive, but very popular.

"Technically," I explained to Zach as we came in the front door, "this's an expansive inland river delta and estuary at the western edge of the Central Valley where the Sacramento and San Joaquin rivers come together."

"My, aren't we formal."

"Smartass. I grew up nearby, I can be an expert." I pointed out the window. "That's officially the San Joaquin River past the harbor. Beyond that is Kimball Island, a cool place to hike." I pointed to the left. "Over thataway, is the Dow Wetlands Preserve, farming land and marsh areas loaded with migrating birds."

I spotted Mama at a table overlooking it all. I'd intended to walk up all casual and cool but found myself fast stepping to her with my arms wide.

"Mama!"

She waved, stood with open arms and moved around the table, flashing a major grin. She enveloped me, kissing my cheek a half dozen times.

We pulled back and looked at each other as if it had been months, not just a week since I'd last seen her. Being attacked by crazy homophobes can change your perspective. She wet her thumb and wiped lipstick off my face. "You're so beautiful, Mama. New hat?"

She swatted me. After wiping her eyes, she whispered, "Yes, after all that gaybashing news and getting a chance to meet this handsome man beside you, I decided I needed a new hat."

"Mama, this is my boyfriend, Zachary O'Brien. I think I told you he's a freshman in law school."

She took his hand, then pulled him into a hug. "You were hurt."

"Yes, ma'am. Some. But thanks to your son, I'm alive. He saved my life."

She smiled, pride in her eyes, and pinched his cheek. "You didn't tell me he was *this* handsome."

"Lovely to meet you, Mrs. Torres. He didn't tell me you were a model."

"Please, call me Raven."

"Isn't that a cool name?" Grinning to hide my nervousness about what she might bring up, we sat when she did.

"How's Renoir?" she asked. "He is such a sweet guy."

"Doing good," I responded. "Painting, getting good grades."

"Give him my love."

"For sure." She was dressed for church and that pleased me. She liked having a reason to dress up; today it was to make a good impression on my boyfriend. She wore a warm caramel-colored jacket, a darker skirt, and a large dark brown scarf with caramel stars draped around her neck. Her hair was pulled tight into a bun and topped with a woven black hat and caramel ribbon.

"I'm so happy my boy's found someone special. He's told me so much about you. It's wonderful you both have an interest in the law. Compatible careers are important in a relationship. Now, what're your intentions?"

Zach's eyes widened.

She crossed her arms, tilted her head and stared.

I just watched him, curious about his answer. "Yes," I prompted. "What are your intentions toward me?"

Leaning forward on his elbows, facing Mama, very serious as if suddenly having to give his closing argument to the jury, his every word was slow and dramatic: "Raven, I intend to take very good care of this son of yours and be the best boyfriend possible. I'm crazy about him."

I laughed in appreciation of his skill. "Good answer." Good boyfriend.

She patted his arm. I could tell she already liked him.

"Now, what's the big news, Mama?"

"The Buckhorn Casino hired me as a full time, permanent entertainer. No more second shift restaurant work at the truck stop." Her grin took up her whole face, eyes glistening.

"*Oh, Mama, that's wonderful!*" We clasped hands. "You're so talented."

"I start next Saturday. I'm so thrilled about that entertainment company you work for that's booking you for small gigs. I'm proud of you. Your father is too." She sat up straight when she said that, her eyes misting.

"Abel is a very talented singer," Zach said. "I love listening to him practice. I'm not saying that just because he's my boyfriend."

"What's the news on the auditions at school?"

"I've been prepping every day with the two coaches I told you about. I'm going to give it my best."

"You'll knock 'em over with that voice."

Zach told her, "Abel said I could watch but I have to hide in the back of the auditorium so I don't make him nervous."

"I talked to your father this morning and he also has news. He's just been hired by an American owned construction outfit in Mexico City. He finally found an employer that let him show what he could do. He starts in two weeks. So this is a twofer day."

"That's so good to hear."

She looked at Zach as she spoke, giving some background.

"He's been having a tough time in Mexico City. He knows the language but still speaks like a Gringo, he says. He told me some charity has been sending him money, several thousand dollars so far. It let him get a little apartment by himself and not sleep with a dozen strange men in a single room in a dangerous neighborhood."

"Yeah," I said easily. "Dad was telling me about it. So generous of someone."

"An admirer of my singing, apparently a regular at the restaurant, has been paying my rent. Also a stunning show of generosity. Also anonymous."

"Also amazing."

"I like your clothes, Abel. A nicer look for you."

"Uhmm. My boss gives me an allowance for clothes so I'm presentable when I do my sets at various events. This is one outfit."

She just watched me for a minute. The waiter came, thank goodness.

"I'll have panko prawns," I said. Mama nodded. "Make it two."

"Oooh, the crab tower looks dramatic," Zach said. "I'll try it."

Giving our orders was a respite but I could tell with the way she was watching me, she was not done with the money topic.

"Yes, such a coincidence that a secret fan pays my rent anonymously, saving me from eviction and, at the same time, your dad gets money to stabilize his life from a charity nobody ever heard of. Now you're dressed nice and working in music. Anything you want to tell me?"

I just looked at her, then down at my plate, not sure what to answer, stunned that I hadn't hidden it better.

"Raven, I think this family was in line for good luck," Zach said. "You've raised a remarkable son. He's told me about you and your husband. It was time for fate to get it together for you three."

He was perfect.

"Fate. Uh-huh."

She let it go with an amiable shrug and we talked about school, her new job, dad's job, mean-spirited politics, and we enjoyed our meal. In a trip to the restroom, I gave the waiter my credit card so it could be handled discreetly. Until I became a prostitute and secret agent, I never had one. This one was co-signed by Dirksen so I could qualify.

As we finished lunch, she looked at her watch. "We need to go."

We walked to a separate room in the restaurant, behind the bar. Sadie Watkins from choir was at the door.

I took her hands. "Sadie! What a surprise! Sadie is the super-star at my church. Sadie, this is Zachary, my boyfriend."

"I've heard all about you, young man. You better be good to this special friend of mine." She gave him a squint eye and then laughed.

"Oh, no problem."

I heard applause. Behind her were all my private voice coaches and school music teachers in the East Bay, *The Posse*. Sometimes several of them would listen as I practiced, huddle and then offer suggestions. It was helpful in improving breath control for the long drawn out segments and ya-yaing I loved. After being accepted to the university, I'd called each of them and sent notes of appreciation. I saw a few when I visited home. Now they were all here after my misadventure. It was nonstop introductions and small talk for the next hour. Zach seemed to enjoy it or was a decent actor as lawyers sometimes had to be.

"Thanks, Mama,." I told her and kissed her goodbye

++++

When the congressman was asleep, I slipped out of bed, watching to make sure he remained in that blessed state, the way I liked him best. When I'd earlier suggested I was open to an overnight, he seemed almost giggly.

I slipped on my rubber gloves and imagined myself a top MI6 sleuth protecting the Queen. He'd hidden his desk key brilliantly behind a Lincoln head bookend. Sitting in his chair, I unlocked the file drawer. It squeaked; I froze. He snored; I continued. Using my cell phone light, I flipped through the titles of a dozen files.

Donor list.

Bills pending.

Important Birthdays.

Passwords.

Special Project.

Amazing. He had a written list of his various passwords and kept it in an easy to break in place. I took a photo.

Special Projects sounded tantalizing. It listed various names, some looking to be eastern European or maybe Russian, and contact information. Even more enticing were pages with columns of three-letter codes, a number next to each and a date. Some codes were repeated. The numbers were often different, perhaps an amount of money for some special account. Not sure. Let some FBI expert take a look. Photographing each page was easy. As I put everything back, his snort startled me, one of those ready to spit up phlegm wonders. He had sleep apnea so there was a chance it could wake him. Closing the door and locking it, I moved into the bathroom and flushed the toilet, walking back to the bed, my phone and gloves held out of his sightline.

"Get back in bed, Daddy. I want you to fuck me."

I sat on the edge, slipping my phone and gloves onto the rug and using my foot to push them under the bed. "Sorry if I woke you, sweetheart, but nature calls." I picked up a rubber and lube and lifted the covers. "Roll on your stomach, baby." Flooding my brain with images of Zachary was now SOP and reassuring myself that I was fucking for my country.

When he was again asleep, I got up, took my phone back to the bathroom and forwarded the photos before erasing them. I quietly put on my clothes, stuffing the gloves in a pocket and leaving the chastity cage on his end table. He had orders to always put it back on. I left him a note about an early class, how much I enjoyed our time together and went home. Enough heroics for one night.

36.

"Abel, I've an unusual one for you," Dirksen told me on my cellphone.

"Dirksen, I think each one has been unusual. And it's six-thirty in the morning. Why so early?"

"An opportunity just came up. It could make money but also give you a different kind of musical exposure. An important connection. I tried calling last night but you were out."

I sat up in bed. "I was out? Really. Where do you think I was? Did you hear any of the tapes from my time with your favorite representative?"

"Sorry, no. So your excuse for not returning my call is accepted. Are you sufficiently awake to learn about this new prize?"

"Is the prize better than the congressman's butt?"

"I really have no experience with that or a fair way to compare but listen to this. A rich Brit is in town preparing for a fundraiser for various environmental and wildlife preservation groups. He's scouting locations and visiting friends. He was knighted last year. Sir Frederick Toland. About forty-five-years-old but looks a lot younger. Senator Wiseling, one of the co-chairs, shared that video of you playing at Equality America. Yes, he's gay. He called me and I shared some of your other tapes. He wants to meet you and have you play live for him at his hotel. If he thinks you're as good in person as on the tapes, he may slot you in as part of the program."

"But he also wants to fuck, right?"

"I'm not sure who would top. He didn't express anything one way or another. He thought you were charming, talented and, yes, sexy. The senator did indicate that you were a few bucks shy of a twenty and that I represented you."

"What kind of statement is that?"

"I was trying to be funny."

"Please don't, particularly before sunrise."

"The sun has been up for a half hour."

"Not in my room." I rubbed fingers at the corner of my eyes to remove the dream dust. "When?"

"Could you do it around seven?"

"Tonight?"

"I'll text you the address and tell him you'll be there. Also the compensation stats. If you don't feel motivated for the sex, no problem. A sports coat, open shirt and jeans are fine. He'll still compensate you for your time and the short notice."

"Can I sing stuff I've already been doing?"

"No problem. Enjoy yourself."

I hit the shower. Renoir was still snoring when I left and went to the cafeteria for yogurt and wheat toast.

Modern Political Theory was a little tough to take at nine a.m. but I managed to pay attention. I wondered if what I was doing might make a good case study someday. Afterward, I practiced a half dozen pieces at the Music Department, some old, some new. The afternoon was light so I took a nap.

++++

Sir Frederick Toland was staying at the Four Seasons Hotel near mid-Market. At nearly nine hundred a night it was not one I frequented. I was struggling to understand my situation. Sex was an extra three thousand on top of fifteen hundred for just playing and singing. Surreal was the logical word to describe how a poor kid like me could draw such lavish interest from important people. Ridiculous was an even better term. My dick was remarkable according to some, and I liked it, but this guy wouldn't know that until my pants came off. He saw some videos of me singing, gets a call from the senator, and suddenly I get big bucks for sex. Plus, if I spent the night, I could experience what this kind of hotel might be like should I ever get rich and want to come back.

The front desk man called up to the room and I was admitted. When the door to a suite opened, I was surprised. He did look familiar and was boyish for his age. Then there was the British accent; those European sounds were always sexy and added points to most any guy.

"Welcome, Abel, thanks for coming on such short notice."

"No problem, Sir Toland."

"Please call me Frederick. May I take your coat and satchel? Can I get you anything to drink?"

"Yes, thank you. Cranberry juice is great if you have it."

He took my jacket and shoulder bag. "Please have a seat."

The suite was in tasteful pale colors, several bouquets of flowers amid antique furniture mixed with the new. I sat carefully on the sofa trying to look upper crust, not an almost teenager of the night. The grand piano was just across from me. He returned quickly with my juice in a Steuben cut glass tumbler, just like I'd seen at Dirksen's. He held a tiny cordial, an after-dinner drink.

He asked about my life, school, music, how I met the senator and Dirksen. I was honest since he already knew about my side gig. We talked about favorite musicians, movies, and why he was so involved in the environmental movement. I expressed admiration and then asked something I immediately regretted even as I was saying it: "So how did you get so rich?"

He smiled indulgently. "The old fashioned way, I was born rich. Inherited wealth is the best way to go."

"I suspect that's true even in America. I was born poor; my family ripped apart by a white supremacist government. But my parents love me and that makes me happy." I shrugged.

"I envy you that."

He watched me and I him for an extended period. Finally, he pointed to the piano. "Would you like to play?"

Seated at the keyboard, I looked at several playbooks. "Anything in particular?"

"No, things you've done before, maybe for class. What you did at the gay fundraiser. Your choice. I'll just sit and enjoy hearing and watching."

Also evaluating my talent. So far he'd not put the moves on me and was very polite, almost formal, very PBS. His eyes seemed to be always on me but I was used to attention.

"This is from one of my favorite old-time movies. I played "As Time Goes By" from *Casablanca*.

He just sat and watched, saying nothing, just nodding, taking a sip of his drink now and again. So I went on. "Governor Bowfield asked me to sing this one at a party given by Senator Wiseling. It's not one I usually do but I'd worked on it with my mother and so I gave it my best. A Johnny Cash classic." Did it sound like I was name dropping?

I sang "Ring of Fire," my heart pounding as I finished. It was such a high to sing and think of the great Johnny all dressed in black. Still no reaction, just another nod. This was disappointing, entertainers thrive on getting reaction. If the audience doesn't respond, how do you judge your own performance. "More?"

"Do you have one that was a particular challenge? You handled these very well and heartfelt. Yet I would like to experience your range."

"This is one I started working on last week. I don't have percussion or a chorus but this Brit tune is certainly at the higher end of the register for a male singer." I thought of Bryan driving away the morning after our last time together, convinced he was all I'd ever need, as

I sang Sam Smith's haunting and sad "Stay With Me."

Frederick walked over to the piano and clapped, saying something sexy in Italian before switching to English. Clearly he was showing off his linguistic skills. His elocution added yet another layer of seduction. "You have a remarkable voice. Hearing you in person makes me realize the videos don't do justice to your talent and, maybe just as important, your presence. You have star quality. That's rare." He gestured to the sofa.

We sat next to each other, an arm's length apart. "I enjoy promoting up and coming talent when I can and, if you're interested, I'd be willing to slot you into the program. The Secretary General of the UN will officially host. We've not finalized a venue. A crowd of about a thousand will be there, possibly many times that if we go big. A gaggle of Hollywood types will attend and it will be taped and edited for later showing on PBS. Ten thousand dollars a seat to start and I expect to turn many away. I'll underwrite your fee as directed by Mr. Horvath."

"Ten thousand dollars to attend?" I shook my head, feeling a little under-funded. I thought movie tickets were expensive.

"The full entertainment bill is yet to be finalized. It's about six months out. There might be a major headliner, a performer who won an Academy Award has expressed interest. I cannot, unfortunately, reveal her name or the group at this time. I think your style of music would be well received. Important for you is there will be Hollywood types, including music agents."

The man oozed sincerity and he'd made no moves on me. I was feeling a little frisky and decided to play this a little different than he might expect.

"So is this a casting couch recital? Dirksen said you wanted to fuck. Is going to bed with you part of this deal, part of your research for talent?" I tilted my head and smiled, raising my eyebrows, hoping the contrast between face and words might draw a reaction.

He looked surprised. "My goodness. You are to the point. I did tell him I thought you were beautiful and someone I would love to experience sexually. But the two are not mixed. Each is independent. I'm interested in your participation in the program and there would be some set of songs, maybe three, not yet determined, you would perform. Having sex with you is separate. As

I understand the issue, it's financial. For me, it would have to be something you're interested in. I'm likely old from your vantage point. You should feel no pressure. I think you're a talented performer with a bright future if you can make the right connections."

"You're saying connecting with my penis is not part of the singing proposition?" Zachary had said he accepted this line of work, encouraged me to have fun, and if I did it with Sir Toland, a knight of the realm, it was not an act of love or passion, but a coupling for renumeration. Business with long term potential, an investment in my future. I'd never been to bed with a man this old, perhaps around my dad's age, which was unsettling, but he was attractive and fit. Yet, mitigating even further, aside from the money, was his ability to talk Italian in my ear. Best not over-analyze if I was going to be a successful businessman, as Dirksen might advise.

His smile was broad and showed good teeth. "You are delightful. Mr. Horvath said you had personality."

"Ah, more flattery." He moved with a certain grace, not like most middle-aged men. So maybe he was younger than dad. His voice was perfect dick candy. He wore a knit shirt that showed nice arms. "Show me your teeth."

"What?"

"It's a thing with me. I like nice teeth and a clean mouth if I'm going to kiss."

He laughed and leaned toward me, taking two fingers at each side of his mouth and spreading wide. He stuck out his tongue. *"Ahhhhh!"*

I began to giggle. Then he did too. I reached toward him and put a hand on his shoulder. As I returned to normal: "I top."

"No problem."

Who knew my freshman year in college would be so interesting?

37.

Stories and photos on the attack had run in both college newspapers, and even two weeks later I got stopped or pointed at on my way to classes. Zach said the same with him at law school. Lambda Legal, the national queer law group, called and wanted to schedule me into a future fundraiser. "Bring the congressman if you want. Or the hot guy you were with." I agreed to perform and did not commit on who might join me.

Zach and I needed to escape so I did some Yelp research. It needed to be local. I emailed him my best suggestion and included a link to get him appropriately excited.

We bicycled into Golden Gate Park—a new favorite place given the good time we had on our first visit—to a spot I hoped was as enchanting as the reviews, a site to cuddle and continue testing if we were meant to be a couple. Stow Lake was man-made in 1893, I'd read, with its own island and a Chinese pavilion. Lots of trees, mature vegetation and flowers, at least in the photos. As we pedaled up the hill early on a Tuesday morning, it came into view.

"Wow!" we cooed together.

"Look at the ducks! There must be a dozen. Hey, a swan."

Zach sounded upbeat. "This is amazing in the middle of the city."

"There's a black bird with red stripes. Never saw one before." We locked our bikes in a rack and then meandered down a dirt path.

"Check out the heron over on the island," Zach said, grinning. "This place is cool. And nobody with cell phones pointing at us."

We went to the boat rental and the old man seemed thrilled to have some business. "Really slow day," he said. "You're my first customers."

We got a paddle boat for two, white with a green keel, made of fiberglass, with a short divider between the paddlers' seats. But still easy to hold hands. We stepped into it from the dock, it rocked a bit, and the agent gave us a push. We put our feet to the pedals, sort of like riding a bike, and we began to move.

"There's a turtle," Zach said, like a kid at his first park visit. We moved the boat toward the rocks to get a photo. The turtle slipped into the water, not interested in Facebook glory, so we moved back to the center of the channel.

"Look," I said.

"What?"

"At those beautiful lips."

He turned and blushed. We kissed lightly at first then it got heavy. "This may not be the best place," he said, pulling back. "Later. I can't believe I'm the one saying that."

No one else seemed around, except a couple of joggers, which made it even more special. The ducks were friendly, coming right up to us, quacking for treats. A stone bridge loomed ahead, Roman in design according to the brochure we got at the dock. We turned the boat around and did a selfie. We continued as I read the map.

"We should find the Chinese Pavilion around the bend. It says you can pull up on the sand and walk around. There's a waterfall. That might be fun."

We stopped at the sandy edge, got out and tied the boat. The Pavilion was right by us. Perfect for more photos and a long make out session. We held hands walking up a path toward the sound of falling water.

"If there's no one here in the woods," Zach said, "we could…"

"Sounds good to me."

We could hear the waterfall and, as we passed a stand of trees, there it was: a lush green hill with water cascading over rocks and dropping into a small pool before meandering through a stone causeway and into the lake. More selfies.

"I don't really see anyplace I want to pull my pants down," I said. "Let's head out, finish the paddle boat ride and get an early lunch maybe at the DeYoung Museum."

We skipped back toward the boat, two young men singing and having fun. "Follow the yellow brick road…"

Two figures stepped in front of us from behind some trees, fifteen feet out. They were wearing black ski masks; one had a rifle over his shoulder, the other held a pistol aimed at us.

I felt a sting on the back of my neck and swiveled around. A man was behind us with a weird pistol. I pulled a dart from next to my spine. I stood motionless for a moment, examining it, trying to figure it out, then I felt faint and grabbed Zach.

"What the fuck?" he said as we began buckling at our knees.

Holding a tree didn't help. My strength was draining and I slumped to the ground.

Zach ran at the man who shot the darts, grabbing him by the arm, swinging his leg. *"Son-of-a-bitch!"*

I heard a muffled gunshot; Zach screamed and collapsed.

The three came up to us. I tried to kick one and got the tip of a boot into my back. I yelled, *"Zach!"*

There was laughing. Then nothing.

++++

I heard multiple voices; men arguing. My head was pounding like a major hangover, my brain working at half power. It was warm; no it was hot and I could feel and hear air whistling. I tried opening my eyes but they were sticky. I was face down on a blanket that reeked of horse shit, arms above my head. I pulled a hand to wipe my face. My wrists were tied with a leather strap and attached to some kind of rusty metal ring in a rough wooden wall. Like you might see in an abandoned shack. Instinct told me to remain still.

Gradually I started to remember. We were attacked. There was a shot. Zach! Someone drugged us and kicked me. I was picked up and carried, someone laughing. Now here I was. What about Zach?

"Well look who's awake." Trevor, the cute asshole working with the congressman. He stooped down and rolled me on my back. "Hi beautiful. I said I was going to have you."

He took out a switchblade and clicked it open in front of my face. I watched, trying to suppress the shaking in my knees and teeth.

He reached down and pulled up the bottom of my knit shirt and started slicing all the way to the collar. Then he opened up one sleeve, starting to hum some tune, then the other sleeve. He yanked the shirt off. "Nice," he said, running his hand over my chest.

I was desperate not to pee my pants.

"Get him up!" someone demanded. "We aren't interested in fag fucking. We got important work to do. I want him standing for interrogation." It was the voice of the guy with the goatee, Mark Wingman.

Trevor stepped back and Wingman unhooked my wrists from the ring and they both lifted me to my feet, pushed me against a wall and tied my hands overhead. The man was in a sweat soaked wife beater. He had a tattoo on his right arm, a clenched fist in a black field. My horrible day just got worse. I'd seen the image in a story about the rise of white nationalism. This was a symbol. There was a ding on Wingman's cell phone. "Fuck," he said, perhaps eloquence for him, and walked off. I forced myself to focus on my situation and if or how I might survive.

It looked like I was in a large barn, sun shining between the wood slats, a building clearly in need of major repair. The main doors were open and I could see open land, like a ranch. The wind was strong, raising dust outside the doors and whistling through the wooden walls. I counted maybe fifty men and a handful of women. From those I could see, they all wore holsters; many had rifles that looked like AR15s over their shoulders. Clover was there, talking to someone. Most were old and angry looking. But there was laughter, some seemed excited, even giddy, ready for an adventure in a theme park. I noticed a handful younger than me.

"Please," I said. "Where's Zachary? What happened to him?"

Trevor poked me in the stomach. I tightened my gut in time and it didn't hurt. "Your hot little boyfriend was left behind on the island. I shot him in the leg and punched him a few times just for fun, to see him bleed a little. We had no use for him. Anyway, you'll never see him again."

He came up close to my face. "I will have you, just like I promised, Copperboy, once they're done with you. I know the congressman is finished having you." His lips curved up; his eyes malicious. He reached down and squeezed my crotch through my pants. "It won't be long."

Sweat dripped from my forehead into my eyes.

He picked up a copy of the *San Francisco Chronicle*, holding it toward me. The headline said, *Gay Hero Kidnapped; Boyfriend Shot!* "It seems tourists found your boyfriend just how I left him. They figure it's connected to that fag bashing in the Castro. That means no leads and no posse coming to rescue the beautiful Copperhead. Oh, and your precious Zachary said he was your boyfriend. The congressman is pissed. Just to make you feel better, your real boyfriend will recover. But you won't."

Clover watched from nearby, playing with his phone. Trevor got a call on his cell and disappeared into the barn. Another guard, maybe early sixties, stepped up and sat on a wooden barrel, a semi-automatic rifle on his lap.

An hour went by, maybe two. Hard to tell. My bladder was ready to explode. "Excuse me sir. Sir!"

The tall man, dressed in camouflage, looked up at me. "What?"

"Please, could I go to the bathroom? Please, sir?" I tried to make my face look as desperate as my voice. I did have to go but I also hoped it would let me see more of what was happening.

"Sure," he said. "Mike, come over!"

Another man—no, younger—maybe a boy about fifteen, maybe thirteen, came over, dressed in a school T-shirt that read *Go Titans!* He had a shaved head and a pistol in a military holster. "What ya need?"

"The privy. Let's walk him there. Maybe let him eat."

"Can I punch him if he gives us any trouble?"

"No problem."

The boy held a cocked pistol to my head and his friend undid my hands, turned me around and tied my wrists together. Mike held his weapon on me as we walked through the barn. The older man had his rifle on a sling pointed at me. The barn was old, leaning a bit, some of the siding missing. I'd been held in what looked like part of an old horse stall. There were stacks of boxes on pallets and a small forklift moving them around as men with clipboards shouted orders to teams of workers.

We stepped outside, the sky near sunset but still bright enough to blind me. There were three wooden outhouses. The teenager opened the door to the one on the right. "Don't take long."

"Uhhh. Could I please have my hands undone. It's kind of hard...."

I was turned around, the kid holding the pistol to my head while my hands were untied and then I was pushed into the outhouse. The smell was about what I expected and, given that it was in the sun, the heat oppressive, and these were clearly not Honey Bucket rentals with a regular cleaning service.

Afterward I slowly opened the door and both were waiting for me, the kid holding his pistol. They marched me to a nearby portable sink and I washed my hands and face.

"Face me, fag," the kid said. He again tied my hands in front. Next to us was a rustic open cooking station with a few tables. Some men and women were sitting down eating, others preparing meals.

I was taken to a wooden picnic table, like you might see in a park, and told to sit. The tall one walked over to the cooking area and returned with a metal plate full of some kind of stew, a glass of water and a fork.

"Thank you, sir."

"*Eat,*" the teenager said, sitting across from me, resting the pistol on his forearm, the barrel pointed at my chest.

It actually tasted good, all things considered, and I cleaned the plate.

"May I ask where we are?"

"You can ask," the kid said. He sniggered, clearly enjoying his power position. "I guess it won't hurt. Central Valley. South of Yosemite."

"Thank you. May I ask what's happening? I have no idea what is going on or why I'm a prisoner."

"Like I believe that. We're gonna make America free." He laughed, his blue eyes staring into mine, challenging me to disagree.

"Back to the stall," the tall man ordered.

There was a sense of excitement around the barn, people moving with purpose, many with smiles on their faces. All armed.

"You need to lay down. Sleep if you can."

I didn't argue with the tall one.

They took me back to the stalls, ordering me to sit on some hay across from where I was before. Two blankets were there. I opened one out and pulled the other over me. The kid brought a rusty metal collar and attached it to my neck with a lock. A short chain hooked it and me to the wall. I had maybe three feet of leeway.

"Sleep tight," the kid said with a giggle. They both left.

Some bright lights were turned on. The terrorists—a name that seemed appropriate—worked for hours doing God knows what, sometimes arguing, I even heard a fist fight which was over fast. Eventually I drifted to sleep.

I awoke when a bucket of water splashed over me. I jumped up and almost choked when the chain stopped me and the metal collar bit. A young woman stood over me, looking satisfied.

"Wake up, traitor." She was maybe twelve, dressed in jeans and a western style purple shirt. Two gunmen were nearby, chuckling at her bravado. I was unhooked from the wall, the metal collar still locked around my neck, taken to the outhouse, allowed to wash up, then breakfast. Undercooked bacon and eggs but the potatoes were good. I ate it all, not sure if I would have this chance again.

I tried to start a conversation with her but a man behind me barked, *"No talking."*

Back at the stall, my arms were attached to the wall over my head. They didn't hook the collar chain to the wall which was a relief. Take your blessings where you can.

Thank God Zach was alive.

If I died here, which now seemed plausible, was it worth it? My goal had been to help my parents. Short term, they'd benefited. If they knew what happened, what I did, Mama would likely have preferred sleeping in the church basement or a tent. Dad would rather clean sewers than have this result. I did what I thought was necessary. Saving my family, my goal, was more important than being squeamish about the means. We could all dream of *The Trio.*

They'd never know. I'd simply disappear, a lost boy. Maybe Dirksen would continue to help them. Yeah, I think he would. Or will.

38.

Zachary

There were voices somewhere in the distance.

Zach's eyes began to open and memory of the attack hit him—Abel collapsing from the dart, three thugs in masks, slipping into darkness, taking a swing and kicking at one of them. A pistol shot. Pain. Zach screaming as he went down. Laugher. A boot kicking his arm as he reached for a man's leg. Another slamming into his gut. Fists pounding his face. Zach starting to wretch. Then nothing.

"Abel?" He sat up, yelling his lover's name. He was alone, in a bed. A door open into a hallway. There was a man standing next to him gently touching his cheek.

"Zachary...Zach. You're safe, you're safe."

He turned towards the voice. It was Walter, his eyes all scrunched up. He enveloped him in a hug and he took it, soaking in the good vibes. "Where?"

"San Francisco General Hospital." He pulled back, smiling in that special way of his. Zach knew Abel loved the man and he understood. "You've been shot and drugged."

"How long?"

"About eighteen hours. The boat manager and some tourists heard the shot and called police."

He started to get up and Walter stopped him. "Please rest until the doctor comes."

Zach touched his own face. His lip and cheek were swollen like a prize fighter who'd lost. "My leg!" He pulled back the blanket and touched his calf. It was wrapped in a bandage so big and tight he could barely move his leg. Strangely, it didn't hurt as much as it should have. He must be on pain medication. "Where's Abel??"

Walter texted something before looking back at him, picking up the blanket and pulling it around him like a father might. "Dirksen's on his way. He's just down in the cafeteria having his hundredth cup of coffee. An FBI agent and policeman need to talk to you."

"Where's Abel?" he demanded.

"They got him. A huge manhunt is underway. Try and stay calm. Please."

"Who's they?" Zach's voice was a squeak. His arms trembled as he tried to sit up. Walter leaned over and held him, pushing Zach back into the pillows as if trying to absorb his fear.

"The press thinks it's friends of those thugs you thrashed in the Castro. Police haven't offered any alternative scenario. Because of the gay bashing attack on you and Abel, it's a major story here and in the national papers." He kissed the top of Zach's head and leaned back, keeping one hand on his shoulder, another on his forearm.

Dirksen came running into the room, out of breath. "Thank God you're awake. Are you in pain?" He reached for Zach's other hand. It was reassuring but overwhelming. "The lawmen are right behind me. You were a brave man, taking on three armed men." He leaned over, put a hand around Zach's neck and kissed his forehead. "I'm proud of you."

In walked Sergeant Kearns, one of the police officers who came to the Castro after the attack. He was in uniform, his black face in a wide smile. "Hello, Zach." He reached out to shake his hand. Zach grinned back.

"Hey, Sergeant Kearns, take a number."

Dirksen let go and Zach shook the sergeant's hand. It was a firm shake which was good, they weren't treating him like some delicate flower.

"How do you feel?"

"A little groggy and overwhelmed and panicked. Where's Abel?"

No one answered as another man in a suit and tie walked into the room and stood at the foot of the bed. He was a no-nonsense kind of guy, obvious from his stiff demeanor and stoic face. He was in his thirties, brown skin, black hair, clean shaven. This had to be FBI.

"Hello Zachary. You're looking good considering what happened in the park. You took quite a beating."

"And you are?" Zach's jaw felt stiff as he talked.

The man came around the side of the bed, standing next to Walter, offering his hand which Zach took. "I'm FBI agent Ramon Cortez. I head the team that's been working with Abel."

"Please tell me Abel is safe."

"How much do you already know?"

"Not much. I could tell something was happening, really bugging him. Plus all the bruises on his body. I confronted him about not being totally honest with me. He said he was doing undercover work with the FBI and getting fight training. He said that was all he could say. I had to keep it secret or it might put him in danger."

"That's appropriate on his part. We assumed you'd suspect and want to know. You deserved at least a partial answer. He couldn't tell you everything because we swore him to secrecy and he wanted to protect you. He's one hell of a brave young man."

An older man in a white medical coat came in and Walter and Sergeant Kearns moved aside. He pushed back the blanket on Zach's leg and lifted it up, bending it at the knee.

Pain shot through Zach. "That really hurts."

"You can move it. That's good. The bullet came in just below the knee, missing the tibia by a fraction of an inch. It could have been much worse. You're on light medication to ease pain. It will take two weeks, likely longer, till you can walk unaided. You should make a full recovery." He put the blanket back and came up beside him. He lifted some kind of gun-like device to Zach's ear. "Your temperature is normal." He ran fingers lightly over his face. "It'll take a week or two for the swelling to go down. Longer for the discoloration. Same with the lip." He nodded and left the room.

"Nice bedside manner," Walter commented acidly.

Certainly efficient and maybe he needed to be that way in this emergency hospital. The four men regrouped around Zach.

"All right," he said. "Lay it on me. Please."

Cortez explained what Abel was doing with the congressman and the white power group he was infiltrating through his sexual relationship. The more intel he provided, the higher the danger. "He really opened up the case," the agent said, "and wanted to take it on since many lives could be a risk. Your boyfriend's a real deal hero. It had to be that group that took him and shot you. We have a few leads—some from his great undercover work. Tell me what you saw in the park? Can you describe the attackers, anything about accents? It's important. Even a small detail could be helpful."

Zach described what happened. But it had all been over so fast he felt useless because there wasn't much to say. Then he had to ask what was really burning him. "My mixed race, brown skinned, sweet natured boyfriend is the prisoner of white nationalists. How could you put him into this kind of danger?" He dropped his head back on the pillow, a pained gasp punching up. He might never see him again.

The agent patted his shoulder. "Because we didn't know. He's the one who figured out who and what they were. Knowing that, he wanted to continue. He knew the danger. Walter tried to give him an out. He didn't want one. He is a patriot in every sense of the word."

"We'll leave you now," Sergeant Kearns said. "To look for him."

"We'll tell you as soon as we know anything," Agent Cortez promised.

Now it was just Walter and Dirksen. He felt totally deflated and helpless.

"What do I look like?"

Walter dug through a duffle bag and lifted out a small mirror. Always prepared.

Zach's right cheek was swollen and a dreadful black and purple. His lower lip was sticking out, split in the middle with dried blood. He handed back the mirror, raising his eyebrows and tightening his lips. "Oh, well. Not really important. What's important is finding Abel. Alive."

39.

I wondered if police would ever find my body. Not if I was buried out here, wherever I was in the Central Valley. California's breadbasket to the nation was a massive area, bigger than many states. It looked desolate, a stand of trees in one direction, a house in the distance and then just open land. Not any crops I could see. After they were done with me—after Trevor was done with me—this was where I'd be left. I always tried to be an optimist but this time it was all but impossible. I'd die here so I needed to make what time I had left count. Rolling through my head was a prayer answered: Zach could live his life. Mama and my dad would be fine. I was happy for that note of grace.

Would I be brave when a pistol was raised to my temple? Did it matter? Yeah. It did. I'd not give them the satisfaction of seeing me break down. I had to fight back even if my only option was to stand tall waiting for the bullet. Who knew what I'd actually do when the time arrived? Who knew just how you'd react if facing death?

On my feet for what seemed like hours, listening but not seeing all the movement around the barn, I sometimes nodded off, only to find myself falling, my arms painful. I heard a group of men approach.

Wingman walked into my stall, stopping inches from my face, hands on his hips. *"Mexican half breed,"* he said. He spat in my face. I turned my head. Not much I could do about it. "You think you're so clever, little faggot whore."

He slammed a fist into my gut. I didn't see it coming and it hurt. Then a second fist. I started to retch. Clover held a bucket in front of my face, smirking, like he knew it was coming. When I'd finished, he took it away and wiped my face with a towel. The other men just watched, smiling, enjoying the show.

"Who put you up to it, boy?"

I started to talk and couldn't, my mouth still coated with vomit. I spat off to the side.

"Here," Clover said, holding a bottle of water to my lips.

I rinsed my mouth and drank until he said: *"Enough."*

"I don't know what you're asking."

He slapped my face so hard I had ringing in my ears. I tasted blood in my mouth.

"Don't fuck with me, boy! Don't fuck with these fine patriots. I know you're a whore and you were so clever in planting a listening device at the congressman's condo. He dropped a phone and a transmitter popped out. How did it get there, boy? *Who gave it to you? Local cops? Feds? Blackmail? Talk!"*

My head was reeling, my mind flashing scenarios of my death. I tried to focus. What should I say? If I was truthful, would it put Dirksen in danger? Did it matter if they knew it was the FBI? If I told them, would they have all they wanted and turn me over to the mercy of Trevor? I was not inclined to be helpful and recalled some of my favorite television crime dramas.

"Go ahead and kill me. I don't know what you're talking about. *Yes,* the congressman paid me for sex. I need the money. My family is poor. You're going to murder me anyway, no matter what I say."

"Please, Abel, tell what you know," Clover said, stepping closer. "It'll go easier if you do."

"Are you the good cop? I thought you were a nice guy, trying to protect me from Trevor. I don't know what you're asking. Please believe me." I hoped my face looked as pained and innocent as I was trying to make it.

Trevor walked up and sucker punched me in the nuts. I screamed and tried to lift my legs, wanting to drop to the ground in a ball.

"Oh, God!"

"That's helpful," Wingman said. He turned and slugged Trevor in the mouth, knocking him to the ground.

"You heard him! He disrespected me!" Trevor held his jaw in shock.

Wingman: "Maybe the kid doesn't know anything. But we gotta kill him anyway. No loss."

They talked among themselves. I took the pain, non-stop, roiling through me. I couldn't think but I had to. Eventually, blessedly, they left me alone. Turning a certain way, I could see the double barn doors open. A truck rolled by every so often, time was a little hard to judge. I started to nod off.

++++

A slap on the side of my head.

"Wake up, you self-righteous, deceiving asshole! Were you planning on blackmailing me?"

A bucket of water was thrown in my face. Someone grabbed my hair and shook my head.

It took a moment to reach full consciousness and recognize the congressman. "Hello, Danny." My throat was the Sahara. "Could…could I have some water?"

He looked around and brought a metal cup to my mouth. I drank deeply before he pulled it away.

"I really don't know what you're asking. I'm a broke college kid needing money and got picked up by a talent agent. We met. I thought it was special what we had going. I always looked forward to it. Blackmail? I don't understand." I worked hard to show tears.

He moved tight to my face and spoke in a harsh whisper. "Do you know I set off an alarm going though security at the federal building? I had to drop my pants so two guards could inspect your little toy. I've never been so humiliated."

I struggled to keep a straight face about what I'd attached to him. How lovely. Some good news at last. I still had a sense of humor.

"I thought it was sexy. You said so too. I'm sorry that happened." I wish I could have seen it. Maybe it was on surveillance video and on the Internet. "I really have no idea what's going on. Can't we go back to your place and have fun?"

He ran a hand over my chest, looking at me, a glint in his eye. His dick was interested.

I heard the sound of trucks, several of them, coming to a noisy stop just outside the barn door. A dust cloud blew through the barn and I caught a glimpse of men gathering around what I guessed was an eighteen-wheeler. Also two SUVs. The congressman turned away from me and walked across the barn to join in the inspection.

Pulling at my binding, I tried to work myself free. It was impossible, the rope was stretched too tight over my wrists.

++++

I was left alone for hours, impossible to judge how much time. The old man came back, took me to the outhouse and to the table for some food. Then back to my stall, reattached to the wall at a ground level, I tried to sleep.

The sun was rising the next morning when the Nazi kid came back and the outhouse and food routine continued. Neither of us were in a mood to talk. He and another man attached me to the wall again, arms up. Time was hard to measure beyond the most basic night and day terms.

My head snapped back. There was an argument. Nasty. Between Danny and Wingman by their voices. I heard the pounding of fists.

"Hit him good!" somebody yelled.

There were laughs.

I heard Danny shriek. *"Don't! Please! I did my part!"*

More arguing. Another scream.

The group parted and the congressman was half walked, half carried back to my wall. His face was bloody, his head lolling, his hands apparently tied behind his back.

Wilder had his men drop him next to me and tie him to the space where I was before. He was on his knees, facing out, hands to the wall.

"Let's go, check the equipment." The order was given by an old man in camouflage with a rifle over his shoulder. The group walked away, all except Clover.

He squatted down, looking at Congressman Wilder. "Sorry it's ending this way, Danny. I like you. But you got greedy. Wingman's not a man to cross. Taking five percent is one thing. We expected that and it's reasonable. Just expenses. Trying for forty crossed the line."

"You had nothing without me!"

"We needed cash to buy the equipment. Now we have it. We don't need you anymore."

He rose and strolled out of the barn.

Danny muttered, "They're going to kill us both, Copperhead. You know that don't you?"

"Look at all the blood on me. I kind of got the message. They wanted me to confess but I don't know to what. The ever-charming Trevor will be the one to kill me, probably fucking me to death."

I kept my voice steady. "If we're both going to die, I'd like to know why. I'm a college kid in need of money. Now I'm endangering some plot. What's going on? Please." I looked down at the back of his head.

Danny turned his face to me, as much as he could. A look of total defeat. "I'm not proud of anything I did. It all started because I'm a gambling addict. A lobbyist for western agriculture approached me about meeting someone. Wingman. He bailed me out financially. Another lobbyist introduced me to an eastern European."

"A friend of Putin, I'll bet."

"Probably." A defeated laugh. "He was generous. But started asking questions about American military strategies for Eastern Europe and the Middle East. Offered more money, a lot of it, if I'd be a financial conduit to Wingman. I could take a cut, big dollars. The info I gave him provided the funding for the patriots. They were working together."

"So you committed treason?" I struggled to hold my voice steady. With a word like treason, soft had more punch. Better than screaming, *"You, a Democrat and a gay man, gave aid and comfort and support to white supremacists and enemies of our country and our LGBT community?"*

"I didn't see it that way. At least not at first. It seemed to me that most of what I passed on was wasn't all that critical to our national security. When that changed, there was no way out."

"Why would a stranger, likely tied to some Russian oligarch, care about some crazy American militia group?"

"Russian meddling jacked up to the next level. They want to really mess up our politics. Beyond doing it online, fucking with elections. They want something dramatic to make Americans think our way of life is finished. Create dissent, fear, distract people from real issues. Panic is key."

I thought: *And knowing all that, you were willing to put your own self-interest above country and community?* I was almost afraid to ask the next logical question. "Danny, what are they planning to do?"

He coughed and took a breath. His voice wavered. "I only just found out. They...they have rockets and dirty bombs, high explosive military grade rockets with a load of low-grade radiation. Getting those rockets were what took so long. Not easy to get your hands on."

I looked at him in horror. Danny spat and shook his head, blood oozing from his lip. "They want radioactive waste over a wide area, mass hysteria. They've got three rockets. That's when I realized. One's for Sacramento because it's the state capital, another for Los Angeles. The third's supposed to go back to DC and go off at some spot, probably the Capitol buildings. Iconic structures collapsing, panic over radiation."

I gasped for breath, my emotions breaking through ahead of common sense. "My God." My voice was a whisper. "How could you be part of this?" How was this possible? When he didn't respond I continued, "But then again, I'm only a whore." I was beyond pissed. Could I have done more? I couldn't comprehend this kind of depravity.

"No, Copperhead. You're nothing like me."

"These are white nationalists of the worst kind. How *could* you, a gay man, work with such people? And...and killing a congressman would create a huge issue, bring in the FBI—"

"Shut up, fags!" Wilder swaggered over. He spat on the congressman. He seemed to like doing that. Maybe he thought it was the source of his secret power.

How could Americans hurt their own country? I stared at Wilder. How did this man become like this?

"You got a question, boy?" Wilder slapped my face and spat on my chest. My face had to be badly bruised, not that it mattered. He was gloating with his power over us.

"Yes, sir, I have a question." I kept my voice submissive and struggled not to scream at him. I wanted answers and knew he wanted to talk; to brag. "If you're patriots, why help Russians, why kill people? I...I can't comprehend it."

"Of course an establishment big city college boy, a liberal, a half breed, a fucking queer wouldn't understand. You've all been brainwashed. The federal government violates the Constitution with everything it does. California government is illegal. This state, all western states, need to be separate, their own country."

He was spitting as he talked, his head high, like he wasn't really speaking to me but to persuade some huge unseen audience.

"We're sick to death of Mexicans and Middle Easterners, coloreds of all kinds taking over our America. This nation was founded by Christian white men and women. We need to create enough chaos that true patriots see their opportunity for freedom. And act. God is with us. It makes good sense. We've been planning this for decades, building our nation of true believers. This is the launch of our revolution. A white revolution. All videotaped live for the Internet."

He stopped, catching his breath, and looked at me, daring me to say something. So I did.

"Why not just use elections? The nation's a fractured mess and the right wing's stronger than ever. Why kill people when you can win elections?"

He looked at me, anger visibly building. I closed my eyes when I saw his hand heading to my face.

Damn it hurt.

"Boy, understand your history. My uncle was part of the Sagebrush Rebellion in the seventies, those ranchers back then demanding massive federal land holdings be turned over to states and private enterprise. Never happened. Decades later, same deal and real Americans are angry about the coloreds getting preferential treatment. Now guns are easy to get, mostly legal, and it's time for it to stop. There are millions of us, more pissed off every day. We just need a spark. I'll provide it."

I just gaped at the man. He thought this would launch a war? What was happening to America? Here I was, a brown faced immigrant's kid, worrying about helping the country that kicked out my dad. Because it was *my* country, my mom's country and my dad's. These were criminals emboldened by all the crazy bullshit on the Internet, all the crazy talk radio jocks. Not to mention politicians that should know better.

"Take 'em outside. There's a gully a hundred yards east. Bury 'em there."

"Wait!" Trevor shouted. "You promised I could fuck Abel before you killed him!"

"You're disgusting. Okay. When we're at the gully, do your thing. Give the men a show. Then we'll end 'em. That work for you?"

"Yeah. That's perfect." Trevor walked up to me and lifted my chin to face him. "I told you." His smile was beatific.

There was shouting by the big truck; some kind of argument.

"Fuck!" Wingman said and swaggered to the doors.

We were left alone for the next hour. Three men I didn't know stood guard. One grandfatherly looking man in his sixties, gray hair, cut short, looked at me.

"Do you have grandkids, sir?" I wanted to make a connection.

"Yeah. Two boys, one girl."

"How old?"

"Fifteen, eighteen and ten."

"Wow. Your oldest is about my age. Please, sir. Could you let me put down my arms? I've been tied up like this like for hours. It's really painful. Kind of like my last request before execution. You all have guns."

"I don't see why not. But if you try anything, we'll end you right here. Understood?"

"On my word, sir, I won't do anything."

With one man pointing a pistol at me, Grandpa undid my hands and let my arms drop.

I bent over. "Oh my God, my arms have no feeling. Thank you, sir."

He untied my hands, gave me two minutes to rub my limbs.

"That's enough. Turn around and put your arms behind you." He re-tied my wrists but not as painful as before or maybe I was just numb.

I knelt, rested my butt on the back of my shoes. It took a few minutes of moving my arms and hands as much as I could for feeling to fully return. He got distracted by his phone. Two men wandered off, including Grandpa. Another guy, maybe thirty, very pale with buzzed blond hair, grabbed a stool and sat, holding his rifle in his lap. He did something to the weapon; I heard a click.

"I just put a bullet in the chamber. This does thirty rounds a minute. Don't mess with me. Either of you." He leaned back, shifted in his chair with the barrel now pointed directly at us.

I rubbed my hands, checking to see if the ring was still on my finger. It was. I slowly pulled it off, looking straight ahead. If I dropped it, this option was gone. Slowly I turned it around, the backside forward and tried to find the magic slit in the heel of my special shoes. My heels were tight to my hands in this position. I rubbed it up and down the right shoe. Then I felt the slot retract and pushed the back of the ring inside. Slowly, with a silent prayer, I pulled out the end of the knife. I put the ring back on, not sure why, but I wanted it on when I died. Maybe someday that's all someone would find left of me and wonder how it got there. I extracted the rest of the knife and held it in one hand.

Now what to do?

I pulled up the end of my jeans on the right leg, thinking I could put it by my ankle, the end embedded in my shoe, the jeans covering it. It sliced into my shoe and cut my heel. Damn. A bad idea, anyway. How would I get to it with my hands tied? I'd have to hold it in one hand when they marched us to the gully.

I pulled and twisted on the leather straps around my wrists. I examined Danny's backside and saw how the knot was tied, three strands, a Boy Scout classic square knot. Maybe mine was similar. I thought of how I could cut with the knife in such close quarters. I sliced partway through one strand and stopped. I needed to finish at the right time or maybe I could just try and rip it off. I moved the knife to my lower hand so it was better hidden and held it tight to my wrist.

I was going to be murdered but maybe I could take out one of them. Two would be even better. Not much justice but you do what you can for your country, and this was for my family too, and Zachary.

What was he doing right this minute? He must be panicked. Police had no idea where I was. Would Renoir or Dirksen contact him? I hoped so. Did I love Zach? Yes. I never told him. My mind drifted remembering good times; my hand kept a death grip on the knife.

++++

"Are you scared?" the congressman asked, face still to the floor.

What a stupid question, I thought, and answered, "How could I not be?"

The armpits of his shirt were drenched. He was trembling. "I'll try and think about the hot sex we had as we face the firing squad." He gave an ironic laugh. "About as close to heaven as I'll ever get."

"Don't they know there'll be a huge manhunt for a missing congressman?"

"There's no way anyone knows I'm here. I'll go missing but police won't know where to look."

"Wow. You may be the lucky one, Danny, and just take a bullet. I'm getting fucked by slime-ball Trevor before they do whatever they have planned."

I noticed the guard was distracted by a group of men walking by.

"Danny." He looked up. "Remember the words of the American Revolution's greatest naval hero."

"What?" His teeth pinched his lower lip, unsure of my meaning.

"John Paul Jones."

After a moment he nodded understanding.

Locked in a desperate battle with a British frigate off the coast of England, the enemy captain called on him to surrender. Jones shouted—*"I have not yet begun to fight."* And he won. Our situation might be hopeless but we'd never meekly go to our deaths. It was useless bravado but Wingman had to be stopped.

40.

The grandpa guard took a bottle of water and opened it, offering it to each of us in turn, held to our lips. "You guys must be thirsty." We each drank as much as he allowed. It was warm but welcome.

"Thank you, sir," I said. It would give me energy.

A short time later, Wingman returned, his strut ridiculous. Trevor, Clover and two middle aged men were behind him. "Let's finish this." He reached behind Danny and undid the loop to the wall tie, yanked him forward to his knees then prodded him to stand.

He reached for me and stopped. "You're not tied to the wall." He pulled a pistol and aimed it at my head. "Stand up."

I did, falling back to the wall. "Please let me get blood into my legs." I pressed against the wall, lifting one leg up and down, then the other, trying to restore feeling and keep them from looking at my hands.

Trevor grabbed me by my metal collar and I stumbled out, almost falling, doing my best to keep my back to the wall and away from my kidnappers and ignore the pain. I held the knife in my left hand holding it behind my right forearm, hoping it was hidden. He pulled me out and turned me toward the door. The congressman moved right behind me and stayed close. Maybe he saw the knife and was trying to help. We walked and shuffled in single file. It was at least ninety degrees outside as we exited the barn. By the sun, maybe early afternoon. There were dozens of men doing various tasks. Several turned and smiled.

"I'm going to have such a good time with you," Trevor threatened, his voice joyful.

"Kill the faggots!" somebody yelled.

"Maybe not the cute one!" a woman hollered and there was laughter.

We were marched down a dusty dirt road, past some old growth eucalyptus, dozens forming a glen. Almost funny that my blood would feed an invasive species of tree. I saw the gulley just ahead as the road turned. Lots of weeds and rocks. We stopped at the edge. The drop down the hill was maybe twenty feet before it returned up the other side. I noticed a lizard scamper past. My future neighbor.

"I want to fuck him in front of the congressman," Trevor said.

I look the lead by turning my back away from the group to face him. He didn't notice.

"It'll drive him crazy seeing me screw his whore."

The man was joyous in his depravity. Was he always like this or had I just misread him?

"All right. Do what you want but make it fast. Fag sex isn't my thing."

"Maybe you'll learn something." Trevor put his hand on my shoulder. "Down on your knees pretty boy."

I slowly dropped down. Since no one was behind me, I swung my knife around in a now or never dash to cut the leather strap.

"Please be gentle," I whined, hoping it would compel him to show off and give me time.

I felt the end of the knife nick my wrist. If I winced, I hoped they just thought it was a reaction to his dick. He pulled his pants and shorts down, lifting out his package. My muscles tensed, my breaths deep, getting ready as he stroked his cock to get hard.

The leather strap broke. I pulled my hands free, rubbing them, trying to remain stationary, careful of the knife, moving it into my right hand, turning it with infinite care. No guns were pointed at us as they waited for the show, knowing we were helpless. They seemed uninterested, maybe repelled, and looked away. Homophobia finally being useful. They were all armed except Trevor. He moved his dick to my face. I was more disgusted than scared and it triggered the music and full adrenaline download. This was the time.

Ba! Ba! Death!

"Ya know what venomous snake bites the most people?" I growled, just so he could hear, looking up at him, getting ready for justice.

"What the fuck did you just say?"

"Copperhead!"

I whipped my hand around and severed his cock before he or anyone else knew what was happening. I shoved him down the hill. Springing to my feet, I lunged to Wingman just three feet away. Before he could realize what just happened, I drove my knife into his chest, the blade cutting deep, snapping bone as I twisted it and pulled down. He stared at me, mouth agape, no sound, frozen in place, a confused look, blood spurting out all over me, his life and hate finished.

The man beside us pulled his rifle up just as I used the embedded knife to twist the dying Wingman toward him and the terrorist fired. The bullet lodged into Wingman's back. I shoved him aside, pulling my knife free and used it to slice into the man's gut as I slipped and fell.

Danny charged the other man. The traitor fired and Danny took a hit, collapsing onto his back, screaming. This was the end.

A series of rifle shots from behind us.

Clover stood frozen, his mouth open, red spurting from his temple, and fell sideways. Both gunmen took it in the head. I was face down in the dirt and spider-crawled, pulling the congressman back to the edge of the gully. I undid his shirt and encountered his male corset concealing the wound. Something told me I needed to get to his actual flesh to stop the bleeding. I cut him free, keeping my head low, hearing bullets close overhead, not sure what else to do, not certain what was happening but focusing on the task at hand. My hands were shaking. With the girdle off, I bunched up his shirt and pushed it against the wound.

"It's your shoulder. We need to keep up the pressure." But what did I know? It sounded like what someone would say on a Netflix show. It looked dreadful but I wanted to be positive. My hands were covered in blood.

"Thanks, Abel."

There was a major firefight by the barn. I heard what I assumed were mortar shells and the buzz of what I guessed might be a drone overhead, a big one, firing into the not real patriots. A huge flash; it sounded like the barn collapsed. A deluge of shots from the wooded area all around behind us.

"Who's shooting?" Wilder groaned, cringing at the noise and pain.

"The cavalry," I replied.

41.

We both stayed low, not wanting to be a target, and surrounded by the dead—except for Trevor screaming in the gulley. There was the roar of engines converging on the barn at high speed from all directions. An armored personnel carrier stopped beside us, raising dust. Two medics jumped out and ran to us.

A woman stooped down with her medical bag. "Where're you hit?"

I sat up, seeing my chest red with the blood of three men and lots of dirt.

"I'm okay. Help the congressman." Wilder was quiet, staring up, blood soaking his shirt.

Trevor was still screaming.

"There's a guy in the gully missing a dick. Please don't help him find it." I watched her work, cleaning the wound and adding a compression bandage.

"If you think this is going to get you out of rehearsal for your *Les Miz* audition, you're sadly mistaken," said a voice from behind me.

It was Dirksen J. Horvath, dressed in Army camouflage and

holding a long crazy-looking rifle and scope. Next to him was Walter, dressed the same and with a near identical rifle. They both had sergeant stripes on their sleeves and helmets. Dirksen was a buck sergeant, Walter a sergeant major.

"*What the fuck?*" I staggered up.

"Watch the language," Walter admonished.

A Jeep stopped behind the carrier, kicking up more dust. I stared and then laughed with comprehension.

"*Governor?*"

"If you think I'd miss this fight in my state you're sadly mistaken, young man." She was standing up on her seat, a little like Patton, in Army fatigues, also wearing a helmet with two stars on front and on her collar. Her handsome young driver, very serious and seeming to enjoy my reaction, looked straight ahead, working to suppress a grin. She jumped down and started to hug me and thought better of it, her nose wrinkling. "Maybe I can hug congratulations later, after you get cleaned up. You do fine work, Copperhead, I saw it all through my binoculars. We had to wait until the Sheriff's unit was in place. The damn FBI insisted. I sweated bullets when I watched you moving that knife. But we had to wait, all these traitors with weapons, knowing they were about to kill you. Mighty fine for a college crooner. You're a hero. You're my hero."

I couldn't talk, just held my arms open and stared, frozen, trying to make sense of the craziest day of my life. They were all grinning like they'd had three strike balls in a row. I don't know why that came into my head.

She stood in front of me, a hand on each of my shoulders, apparently the only bloodless part of my front. "You know I spent thirty years in the Army and Army reserves before I got into politics," she said. "My time overlapped with two of the best snipers in the Army."

"So you called out the National Guard?"

"For sure, to back up the FBI team and the local sheriff. This was my fight. I deputized these two characters to help. Sure glad I did."

"You're needed by the barn, General," someone hollered from down the road.

"Gotta go. We'll talk later, sweetie."

++++

Congressman Wilder stood, his shirt off and shoulder covered in a bloody bandage. His eyes were glassy, his thoughts far away. Two MPs walked up and led him away. The medics were helping an almost delirious Trevor from the gully, his pants off, a bloody bandage around his crotch. "We gave him a morphine shot," the medic said. It was unclear if his cock had been reattached. Or even found. Maybe the lizard got it. I liked the image.

Dirksen put his hand on the back of my neck and checked on the metal collar. "Does it hurt?"

"Hell yeah!"

He pulled out a handkerchief and wrapped it around my neck to give some protection.

"Thanks, Dirksen."

"We'll get it off as soon as we can. For now, we need to clean you up." He was grinning and it gave me strength. "Ramon gave us a basic rundown from info the FBI got from the taps you left in Wilder's room. We knew it was a dirty bomb and one single word—'rocket'—on one call is why half an army's here. That yellow notepaper you took gave us the name of this ranch but no precise location. With the help of drones, we picked up the limited range on your ring."

I looked at it, twisting it around.

"Thanks Dirksen. I seem to be saying that a lot." My hands were covered in red and, looking down, so was my bare chest. It made me nauseous, this mess from people I stabbed.

"We saw the knife when you turned around," Walter said. "We knew you were going to try something. We made sure to have your back."

"You shot Clover and the two others?"

"Yeah," he said. "Me and Dirksen. We divided the targets.

Wanted to take 'em out as soon as you reached the gully but the Sheriff's unit hadn't confirmed they were in place. It was chew your nails crazy. Finally the governor said...actually I shouldn't repeat her more colorful words... *'Take 'em out!'* "

"Would you have fired without the order?"

"Absolutely. She knew it. We figured she'd ignore orders to wait. She's rather fond of you, ya know."

42.

We walked toward the wreckage of the barn, much of it still burning, past scores of bodies and as many prisoners in handcuffs. One
man had open eyes staring at nothing and nothing below his ribs.
The reality was too frightening to witness. Twitching began in my
knees then up my back. I saw the governor working with a group
of soldiers around the trucks with the dirty bombs. It looked like
some kind of military lab truck was pulling in. A few civilians
were in hazmat suits.

"*Copperhead!*"

I looked around.

"*Here!*" Agent Ramon was running toward me. He wrapped
his arms around me and stepped back, probably from the smell of
me. "Were you hit?"

"No, just beat up," I said, wincing.

"Sorry about grabbing you. Man, I was so worried. Your inside work made this possible. The nation owes you much." He
took out a camera and I tried to smile but my face ached; I knew
it was swollen.

"Maybe not a great time for a photo. Hey…you're covered in

blood," I said, pointing at him. "My blood or blood on my body."

"Wearing it with pride. Photos will help you remember this day and what you looked like. It's important for the case file. The white cloth under your metal collar is showing blood."

Not surprising. "Uh, my face is bloody too, isn't it?"

"Black, blue, red and hot cocoa. Don't worry, you're still handsome. More or less." I heard joy in Walter's voice.

"I don't think there'll be a problem remembering. I don't want to see my face."

Ramon took several photos.

The shaking intensified; my knees buckled. Both Dirksen and Walter caught me.

"Medic!" all three hollered. They helped me to the shade of a tree.

"Your adrenalin's running down," Dirksen said. "You're likely in shock."

A different medic stooped beside me, stethoscope in hand. Within minutes I had a needle in my arm attached to a bag of something and was riding a gurney being pushed to a military ambulance. I felt sleepy. Ramon took more photos of me. After some discussion with the governor, Dirksen and Walter rode with me to a nearby field. The three of us got into an Army medical helicopter. My first time in a helicopter and I was strapped down and couldn't appreciate it, staring up at the ceiling, feeling hot and woozy.

Dirksen was working his phone. "Sending a group text to your mom, Renoir and Zachary."

The chopper lifted off, holding steady for a moment and then lowered the cockpit, tail up, headed somewhere at a high rate of speed.

My favorite pimp's phone rang. "Yes, hold on just a minute. He's a little groggy."

He showed me the name on his phone and held it to my ear. "Hi beautiful," I croaked.

Dirksen moved it away a few inches because my boyfriend was screaming and crying. I loved it. Music to live by.

Music to survive.

43.

The Governor and the FBI, featuring Agent Ramon Cortez, held a joint press conference the next morning. There were maps and multiple photos of the militia camp. Other photos included Walter and Dirksen and those of me, bruised, swollen and covered in blood. My battle face was contrasted with my regular photo. There were photos of me on a stretcher and in the helicopter. I watched it live on CNN from my hospital bed. A major national story. Hordes of reporters and cameras.

Zach, Walter, Dr. Amos, Dirksen, Renoir and Mama were with me. So was Dean Schultz, a lovely surprise. She was one of my biggest boosters.

Agent Ramon explained how I'd gone undercover at the request of the FBI to infiltrate the congressman's circle of criminal connections. "It was his work, his bravery, putting his life on the line, exposing key details of their plans, brutally beaten, almost killed, personally taking out the lead terrorist, that brought this network down. He likely saved tens of thousands of lives. Maybe even American democracy. I can't say enough about what this remarkable young man did for his country. He just turned twenty years old. Think about that and what it promises for the future of America in the hands of our children."

I almost lost it, burning under the national exposure, hearing that kind of praise and remembering the gore, the feel of a knife slicing into a man's chest. My peanut gallery all clapped and whistled.

An hour later everyone left except Mama. Zach excused himself, saying, "I'll be in the hall."

Mama and I sat quietly. She wrapped her fingers in mine and watched my face. She put a hand on my cheek, tears in her eyes. "I was so frightened. That nice FBI man, Ramon, called and said they had a lead but couldn't give details. That gave me hope." We had been through so much together. "Your father and I talked several times. He was panicked. You know how much he loves you. He's supposed to call again soon, in just a few minutes. He wants to talk to you."

"I'd love that."

We sat for a time, recalling memories of good times. Eventually, she said, "You were in the middle of all this and you found time and a way to help me and your father. *My boy!*"

"I love you both so much."

Her cell rang. "Yes, he's right here." She handed me her phone.

"Hi Dad!" We talked only for a short time because he had to go to work. He just wanted to hear my voice. "I'm all right, really. Just a little bruised." He said he was proud and told all his friends about me who saw stories in local papers and in the news. It was so amazing to hear his voice again. A day ago, I thought I never would.

I spent the night under observation. The next morning I felt mobile and asked if I could leave. The doctor brought me three bottles of pills and explained their purpose. After we did the paperwork, I was pushed in a wheelchair to the front door of SF General, Zach at my side. I'd finally convinced Mama to go home.

When we went to my dorm, a camera crew and reporter were interviewing Renoir just outside the door. He was clearly at his theatrical and artistic best, talking all about our friendship. I didn't want to take away from his moment, so we turned back before they noticed us and headed to Dirksen's.

Chuck Markus was there along with his brother Reggie. Prince Ali arrived a few minutes later. We all had a good cry.

In the next days, as I tried to regain my life, people stopped me on campus wanting selfies. My phone rang so often I turned it off. How did my number get so widely known?

I focused on my rehearsals and classes, but it wasn't easy. I was late to Poli Sci 101, a huge class in an amphitheater. I entered and the room went silent before erupting in applause and cheers, everyone standing. What do you do? I kept repeating, "Thank you," doing the Queen Elizabeth wave and nodding until I found a seat. Then the teacher said, "You're a credit to the school, Abel, and to America, proof of what one brave man can accomplish. Thank you." I nodded, wiped a tear, put my head down and opened the book, anxious for the lecture to begin.

I kept wondering if the fact that I was a whore would come out. Reporters were looking for new angles. Would it make a difference? Did I want to continue doing it? The money was nice. Zach and I needed to talk.

After considerable cajoling, I agreed to do a joint interview with the governor. I was still wrapped up in my head over what happened and hoped I wouldn't come across as a fool. Details were vague but I knew it was CBS and a major production. Her office set it up.

She wore her buckskin jacket. I donned my favorite blue sport coat and tie, very conservative and Middle America. My face remained a mix of purple, green and other horrible colors but the swelling had come down. The shirt hurt my neck because of the bruising and cuts from the metal collar. When it was cut off at the hospital I'd almost cried. The makeup artist and director decided much of my face should be left as is, not covered up. My first time on television and it was *60 Minutes*.

Reginald Broker, an out gay man and contributing reporter, did the interview. I wanted to be honest and direct yet my nerves didn't cooperate—I gripped my seat, clasped my hands tight and my voice was not always steady. The governor placed her hand on my forearm to provide calm support. I answered directly, it was so painful, and Broker kept coming back to explanations of exactly what happened at each point, how I felt, how I controlled my fear while infiltrating the operation through the congressman, when it was that I realized it was a white nationalist group and me the son of a Mexican immigrant. Sometimes I was on the verge of losing it, it was all still so real.

"It's all right, Copperhead. Take your time. You can do this," the governor said.

"You killed the ringleader of the terrorists and wounded two others," Broker said, waiting for me to speak.

"It was now or never. I had no idea the FBI and military were there. I believed I was the only one with a chance to derail this thing if I could kill him. I had only the one chance. How did it feel, is that your question? I felt like I was doing something I had to do for my country. Now I have nightmares over what I did."

I knew I looked dreadful with all the bruises on my face. He asked about that as well, the beatings, the attempted rape, stabbing three men, killing one. How it felt to learn that a gay United States congressman had betrayed his oath to his country. I choked up twice, pulled myself back together and continued. I didn't mention the whore issue.

"Where did you get that knife?"

"The FBI told me not to reveal that secret."

"This young man is one of the bravest people I know," the governor said.

Towards the end of the interview, he asked the question. "I was told by a source that you pretended to be a prostitute after you got the congressman's attention performing at a swank cocktail reception. True?"

I wanted to be truthful, up to a point. This was easier to answer than killing a man. "Yes. When the FBI and associates found out he was sexually interested in me, I posed as a prostitute with the help of a friend to get inside the operation and plant listening devices. I was also able to sit in on various meetings since I was, as the congressman stated, *'Just a whore.'* I wasn't seen as a threat and played dumb. They ignored me as if I were invisible, until I wasn't."

"I assume you had to meet the congressman's sexual expectations for this to succeed."

This guy was not going to make it easy. "Well, I'm a few months past being a teenager, after all." I smiled, raising my eyebrows. He laughed.

"Any personal discomfort was nothing given what was at stake. I'm the son of a Mexican immigrant father and mixed race mother. We're poor but proud. I wanted to be the son they raised me to be. We all must do what we can for our country."

"Abel, you're receiving lots of kudos for what you did. If you could think of one thing that would being you the greatest joy, what would that be?"

"To have my father allowed back to America, as an American citizen, to be with Mama and me." I couldn't help it. Tears ran down my face.

The governor leaned forward and kissed my cheek.

That concluded the taping. It would be the entire program.

The segment ran on Sunday. The interview followed a report showing photos and videos, including a long shot of me stabbing Mark Wingman in the chest. My jaw dropped, my heartbeat jabbing my rib cage; I lifted from my seat and settled back down. Who'd filmed this? I pressed my fingers over my eyes and took deep breaths. They showed a clip of me playing and singing at the LGBTQ political fundraiser and the congressman kissing my cheek.

As the segment ended, the camera had zoomed in on my face, using a freeze frame to capture a single tear on an eyelash.

Zachary wrapped me in his arms, pulling me onto his lap, kissing my forehead, running his fingers through my hair. Seeing it all again, watching me nearly fall apart telling the story, made me feel naked to the world, embarrassed and stressed.

"I'm so proud of you," Zach said kissing my nose and smiling. With him, Mama and my posse, I was hopeful I would get through this and put it behind me. Especially the nightmares. I lifted my head and our lips touched. Some distraction would be useful. He ran his palm over my crotch anticipating how he could help.

44.

My friends insisted I meet with a psychiatrist to handle my depression over killing someone and all the other traumas. Sometimes I just shut down, curled on my bed, not wanting to talk. My mind took me on walks through the bodies. The blood. The smell. Maybe a soldier was prepared for this carnage. I wasn't.

I went to a psychiatrist, a man, who offered a few tips on how I could change focus when the horrors started, but mostly talked about himself. Plus, he was big on pills that left me rummy. I stopped taking the drugs and got a therapist instead, an older woman, very empathetic and friendly. She helped calm the evil spirits.

Time even better spent was talking with Dirksen and Walter. Once when I went over, the governor was there, helping them prepare *enchiladas suizas*, guacamole and margaritas. I had to drink Diet Coke again and we all thought it was funny. She was more like a salty grandma than the top elected official in California. She was real, telling endless ribald stories about Army life and tales of what Walter and Dirksen did on some of their missions. After an evening of margaritas, it was good she had a driver to take her back to Sacramento.

Publicity continued and I was approached by dozens of publications, television programs and blogs about telling some aspect of my story. I declined because there was only so much I could say and I was just repeating the same things. I was surprised seeing myself on the cover of *Time Magazine* and *The Atlantic*, part of larger stories about home-grown terrorists and home-grown heroes, the reporters often calling me an icon for everyday citizens stepping up even in dangerous times to protect their country. I also had become a cause celebre around the disgraceful immigration standards of the country, given the reprehensible example of my deported father. Two book publishing agents approached me—one by knocking on my dorm door, the other in the library. They both said they could find an author to write it for me. So, how would it be my book? I referred them to Walter. Flattering as it was, it was also a distraction from the rest of my life. I had to hold my ego in check. I knew too many arrogant jerks and didn't want to become one.

Mama collected everything that mentioned my name, sharing it all with friends. In Mexico, my father was thrilled when he came across stories about me. I was pleased to be offering a little joy in his life. My East Bay singing posse sent texts and snail mail letters saying they were proud of me. I called each of them back, all of them important in my life.

Zach was my anchor, often by my side and in my bed or his.

Prince Ali sent flowers and many texts expressing his concern. I invited him to dinner and introduced him to Zachary. I wanted him to know I had a lover but I would still enjoy being with him. But I did feel guilt, considering that the State Department was pushing me. I had some money saved but no other income. Was I being greedy or strategic, knowing things could go to hell again any time? I thought it was important for Zach to meet him. He knew this was another underground effort and said he accepted it. Awkward, just like him meeting Chuck. At dinner, Ali was a charming gentleman and never did or said anything to suggest we had been intimate. We hugged and did a chaste kiss before his security detail drove him back to Woodside.

All this rolled through my head as we jogged back to Zach's apartment after a grueling workout at his university gym. My body had been desperate for exercise, too much time spent talking with friends, therapists, law enforcement, reporters, students wanting to connect, being held on death row by a bunch of white nationalists. There was also vanity. I expected a certain look in the mirror, now that Dr. Amos had transformed my appearance, and I wanted to be at my best for Zach. I did mostly free-weights, he did machines, and we ran until our workout clothes were dripping sweat. We were playing games as we finished the last half mile, slapping each other's arms and butts. Without discussing plans in the locker room, we pulled on our jackets, grabbed our shoulder-bags and ran to his place a few blocks away.

I slipped off my shirt, shorts and jock, turning toward the shower. He was right there. "You're all sweaty," he said, pushing me back until my butt reached the counter. He was also naked and pressed tight to me.

"Let's shower," I suggested.

He turned and had the water on in seconds. "It's cold so we have a minute. Can I—?

"You're impossible," I told him, pulling him close. He began running his tongue over my chest and lower until he dropped to his knees. The room was filled with steam when I pulled back. "Shower now!"

"So bossy."

Somehow we rinsed, soaped up and rinsed again, with minimal touching, stepping onto the floor mat and toweling off. We were watching each other, randy-eyed, and held hands walking into the bedroom. He shoved the comforter back and pulled me onto the bed. We kissed and wrestled, still playful, and he rolled on top of me, slowly rubbing our dicks.

"I love you," he whispered in my ear, his tongue sliding inside.

"Without you," I told him for the first time, "I don't think I could have gotten through this." I kissed the end of his nose. "When I was expecting to be shot, I kept thinking of you, happy you were alive and could have a life without me."

"And now we can have a life together." He bit the end of my nose. "I really do love you."

"Strange way to show it, attacking my nose." I felt relaxed, safe and with someone I loved. I needed to say it. This must be real, given my emotional and physical attachment to this man.

"I love you, Zachary O'Brien."

We both had said the three words and meant them. Bryan and I had whispered them many times, pressing our lips together, believing this was forever, what we had was genuine, but in the end those words meant nothing. He'd moved away and found someone else within weeks. Holding Zachary in my arms felt different, was different.

"Does this mean we can fuck now?" he asked.

45.

Zachary

"Aren't you Copperhead's boyfriend?"

Zachary looked up from his phone while leaning against the wall waiting for the cafeteria to open. The man was serious looking, early twenties, blue knit shirt over a tight frame, African American, smiling like a lawyer trying to butter up the jury.

"You mean Abel Torres?"

"Sorry. Yes, Mr. Torres." He looked apologetic and decidedly earnest.

"Yes, I know him." Why not brag about it? Who else could say that he dated *the* Abel Torres? "And, yes, his boyfriend."

He held out his hand. "My name's Darryl Tanner. I'm second year law. I've seen you around. I was at the Q fundraiser he sang at with the congressman. I thought his singing was breathtaking. Then the gay bashing and what he did with the white supremacists. I'm in awe."

"Me too." Zach gave him a hurry up look. The gate just opened for lunch.

"I've an idea to honor him and maybe help his career."

"Okay." Always willing to listen to people offer useful suggestions while they crush on him.

They grabbed trays, went through the line and Zach decided not to object when he asked if he could buy lunch.

"What if we used social media to set up a seemingly spontaneous Abel Torres appreciation hour?" His words were tumbling out, and he seemed not to pause for a breath. "Create a national happening, a single hour in a future single day, every radio station, music channel, social media channel, all play his music, clips of him talking and the voices and faces of millions of admirers. All America talking about Copperhead." Another quick gasp of breath to get it out. "He wouldn't officially be involved, no role in setting it up, but his fans would. The thousands and I expect millions who know his story and think he's the real deal, platforms to play his music on a specific date and time." He paused to take in more air and maintained his infectious grin. "We'd need the okay of his management team, of course, if he has one, to grant legal release of his music. I don't think he's made any records, just recordings in public settings."

His eyes were wide, expectant. He did a fast series of mini-nods, also endearing, waiting for Zach's reaction. A good litigator. Grandmas on juries would love him.

It seemed crazy but it was just weird enough that it might work. Abel would be appalled and would never agree to it. In advance. If it was seen as his own promotion, then tacky.

"Give me your card or at least your number and name again. Let me talk with his manager." This might go viral. It might help lessen his depression. Of course he really didn't have a manager. Well, maybe Dirksen, but he managed Abel's body, not his music.

"Can we talk more after you talk with him?" The grin was still at full blast. "I can always buy lunch or dinner."

Always words of magic.

++++

Zach called Dirksen and Walter to get their take. They liked the idea and Dirksen said he'd find a lawyer to handle any legal issues. They agreed not to tell Abel until it started to come together which at this point still seemed sketchy.

The campus radio station was the tip of the PR spear, as Darryl explained, and it was immediately on board. It offered to hold a "Copperhead, Our Hero" hour in a month's time. It would ask every student to post the notice and help it go viral. Also to start pestering every station in town, every talk show host, and the *San Francisco Chronicle* and other newspapers. Guaranteed to become a city wide phenom.

Abel was adorable the first time a reporter, a television reporter, asked him about the movement.

"What?" he asked.

The reporter explained.

"Really?"

His expression of genuine confusion, then embarrassment—he actually blushed—was priceless. A volunteer turned it into a GIF. No way his sincerity, or preciousness, could be faked.

One call from Dirksen and the governor was primed, stating her full-throated endorsement as part of her weekly press conference. The Legislature passed a resolution making the designated date Abel Torres Day and supporting special programs about the dangers of white supremacy, domestic terrorists and the need for heroes.

Several talk jocks with national audiences, always hungry for something new, started talking about it, pledging to take part. CBS Network Radio announced a special program at that hour. Then other networks.

Darryl was right in the middle of it all, working with a small army of his friends and contacts in civil rights groups. Renoir too. LGBTQ groups were immediately involved. Abel's "Somewhere Over the Rainbow" rendition, so slow and emotional, was used as a hook to get everyone's attention because it was breathtaking even if wildly different from the original.

Dirksen contacted a big public interest PR firm in the city

to organize non-profit outreach to get resolutions of support, contacting newspapers to editorialize, and do some targeted advertising. The agency had many civil rights groups as clients and networking was easy. Dirksen pledged big money. Zach called the exiled Prince and Abel's own billionaire. They signed on, clearly thrilled. The agency hired Daryl as a PR spokesman to lessen the call volume to Abel who was uncomfortable in his blushing bride role and to distance Zach's boyfriend from the event creation.

A special website was created and volunteers recruited to man a phone bank for answering questions about the effort, about his life. Volunteers also edited interviews he'd done and repackaged them for stations and sites to use since there was no way Abel could do hundreds of interviews on the big day. Nor did he want to.

Senator Wiseling introduced a resolution in Congress setting aside the day for Abel. It passed within a week by an overwhelming voice vote. Even the racists in Congress voted for it so they couldn't be pointed out for what they actually were. Plus, voting for Abel's day was easier than actually doing something about racism. The president issued a surprisingly upbeat statement when he signed.

There seemed to be a small army of GIFs and memes showing up online. Some Zach's group helped launch, but most just appeared from fans. A few were sexual, some downright dirty, and Zach saved them even though he officially expressed his disgust. Abel looked horrified and worried his mom might see them. Zach suspected Raven would see them as would his posse. But she would pretend otherwise knowing it might embarrass her son. When Zach was thinking about calling her, she called him.

"I know you've got to be involved," was her opening line.

46.

The never-ending hour honoring me was a real mix. I was humbled, horrified and almost afraid to be seen on campus. I met Darryl a couple of weeks before it all came down. Sweet man, we clicked on various topics and became instant friends. He had a sticker on his shirt that said "Copperhead Day." He offered me one and I declined. Graciously, I hoped.

The day of the event, I never left my dorm room, telling instructors I needed to hide. I only had three scheduled classes that day and two of the three were understanding. The one that didn't was Math. Not a bad ratio for college professors.

Slowly the craziness ebbed.

It took a couple of weeks, but I was grateful to finally get back to class without creating a sensation. Rep. Danny Wilder was in custody, no bail, his life ruined, repudiated by his constituents, his country and his community. I decided it was best we not talk, despite his numerous calls through his attorney, since I'd lied to him on so many levels. What he did disgusted me. His trial would just rehash the treason of a gay man, granting salacious tidbits for clerics and politicians who lived for hate. The FBI said I shouldn't anyway, or it'd create a problem at trial. On some level, I felt sorry for him, a weak man, a traitor who got double-crossed by his terrorist bedfellows and they'd been ready to dispose of him, detritus in their grand revolution. I'd have to face him in the courtroom and that was soon enough. I wondered, as he sat in jail, if he wished he'd died in the Central Valley.

The audition was six weeks to the day after the firefight and stabbing. Forty-two days since I murdered someone.

I felt melancholy, rethinking what happened, the scene in a constant loop in my head. They deserved what they got but I felt a splinter of understanding of what it was like for them, big dreams, even if evil, crushed by the military and yet a few would live on with the pain, likely in prison. I thought of my own dreams almost cut short by their planned revolution. *Les Miz* was a perfect foil for my emotions, soldiers killing the revolutionaries, crushing their hopes, almost crushing mine. But it was the soulfulness of one song that spoke to me. I had no love for those killed at that remote ranch, but I understood the pathos, felt it.

I pushed away the images of carnage when I was summoned from the green room. I walked out onto the stage at the Orpheum Theater near Civic Center. There were only a handful of people in the vast empty space, all in the first row, a table in front with paperwork. I suspected at least one other person was out of sight in the balcony. There was a professional-looking television camera in the aisle along with an operator, set up if the director wanted to review the singers.

"Focus on the camera," said a man I could scarcely see. "Pretend it's the audience. Ignore us."

I was the twelfth and final person, all of us anonymous. We were not allowed to hear our competition or know their names. We were asked to perform a song from the show and I chose one that seemed appropriate although not sung by Jean Valjean. Directors may have their own idea about how a song should sound for a particular character, so I thought it might be prudent to perform one done by another character that would give a sense of my talent. Or not.

My name was announced by a woman, a stranger to me. "State your selection for the director, why you chose it and nod to the pianist when ready."

Dr. Benjamin Moss was there along with two others from the Music Department, the director, three I didn't know. I nodded in respect but said nothing in greeting. No need to play the piano this time. It seemed strange, like I was naked. What would I do with my hands? I picked up the microphone so I could move it as I moved.

"I'm auditioning for the part of Jean Valjean. Despite all the remarkable songs he performs, I decided on one for another character which, at this moment in my life, resonates with my own feelings." I nodded to the man behind the keyboard. After his intro, I began "Empty Chairs at Empty Tables."

As I sang, emotions of loss and death rolled through me, into my voice, rising higher, deeper than what I had rehearsed, tearing through me. I was out of control, all the faces of the dead taking me out of this reality into another, their voices channeled into mine. This was a catharsis. I felt like my soul was bare, vulnerable, embedded in this tale of loss and yearning. The music ended and it took a moment to come back to where I was.

"Thank you," I said, putting the mic back on the stand, clapping to thank the pianist, otherwise avoiding all eye contact, and walked off stage, through the dressing area, making a pit stop to wash my face, do the regular, and regain my sense of normalcy. Taking dramatic liberty with a famous song could be a major mistake. Leaving in silence after a performance was a discombobulating feeling. I saw the exit sign ahead.

When I came out the stage door, Zachary, Mama, Renoir and Alexander, his new Mormon boyfriend, Dirksen, Walter, my favorite billionaire, Chuck Markus and my number one Saudi prince were there, applauding and screaming as I walked up a half dozen steps. Then they were on me. Whether I got the part or not, this made it worth the effort. It also helped lift the gloom. The song felt like a rite of purification.

All of them seemed emotional. My mother hugged me. "Oh,

my God, Abel. I've never heard it sung with such passion and range."

"Mama, did you just swear?"

Later that afternoon, Dr. Moss called to tell me I got the part.

47.

Zachary

They were in the living room, lounging on the sofa, having coffee, just in undershorts, Zach's favorite way to look at Abel except when he was naked. Abel reached over and picked up Zach's left leg, pulling it toward him, running his hand over the scar where his lover took a bullet during his kidnapping.

"I feel so terrible about this," Abel said. "I never thought you'd be at risk. I saw what you did—trying to protect me" He bent down and kissed his calf. "You're my hero."

He couldn't say this too many times. "Thank you, Abel." Zach was so in love. "And you're mine."

There was no question in his mind that Abel was going to be a major musical celebrity in a short period of time. His talent was thrilling. So many opportunities were opening up that he would be a wealthy man. They'd talked about Zach's discomfort about him continuing in the escort business. He had no reason to do it anymore given all the money he'd saved. Not to mention that he was now far too famous. Zach accepted the one-off meeting with the big Brit impresario and possibly playing a major international event. He found it amusing. Of his regular clients, one was in prison. Another had found a boyfriend. The third, well, that would be only once in a while to help the State Department. Zach just wished the Arab prince were a little less spectacular.

Zach felt in a strange place. His boyfriend would become a star, a talent someday burning brighter than a supernova. Would he lose interest in a man trying to make it as a young lawyer, maybe just a law clerk? Did other couples have this kind of angst? Careers out of sync? Zach guessed his expression said it all.

Abel just looked at him. "We talked about this. Trust me. We'll be together forever."

He wanted to believe him. His eyes said it was true. Zach thought about Abel's mom and dad. Even with the father in exile, what they had was real love, two people so perfect for each other, the forever kind.

That night they went to dinner with his mother, just the three of them. As they walked into the Greek restaurant, people pointed. Really pointed at Abel, the handsome star. Zach waved too when they held up their entwined hands. It made him feel special.

When Abel went to the restroom, Raven turned to him. "He's so in love with you. You know that, right? That makes me happy for you both."

"Thank you for saying that. I do love him." He felt his heart thump.

"You're a perfect couple, Zach. You complete each other and I'm thrilled for him. Thrilled for you. You're part of our family now. My husband and I've talked about it. He agrees and really hopes to meet you some day."

She kissed his cheek.

Zach smiled, just shy of tears. "Having a family again means everything." It hit him, the power of her words and his grin became ridiculous. "Should I change my last name to Torres?"

She laughed just as Abel returned to his seat.

"You want to change your name to Torres?"

"Maybe."

48.

Walter called and said I needed to be ready for a ride on Thursday and I must wear a sports coat and tie. Zachary should come too, dressed the same.

"Anything else you want to add, like...say...where, why and what?"

"We'll swing by at nine a.m." He disconnected.

We were standing on the street waiting when they pulled up in Walter's old dark green Bentley. I waved at the Highway Patrol officer observing from across the street, one of several silent watchmen still seeking to protect me from crazies. Police and the governor took the threats seriously. He smiled, started his cruiser and followed us as we pulled onto Interstate 80.

"So, what's up guys?" I asked Dirksen.

"I've booked you a jailhouse conjugal visit with your favorite congressman," he offered deadpan. "Said he misses you so I agreed."

Everyone laughed. Except me.

I got a text from Renoir.

Renoir: Good luck on whatever this new adventure is about.

Your painting is finished.

Zach looked over and read the message. "What painting?"

"He used me as a model for his final project in one of his classes. An oil painting. Life size. I've been posing for him."

"It's nude, isn't it?"

"Ah, it is. But he promised to obscure my face."

"From the paintings I've seen, his style is detailed realism." He shook his head and pointed at my nose. "How could he possibly distort this beautiful face?"

I snapped my head up and bit his finger. We laughed, looked at each other and I pulled him tight and put my lips on his to shut him up. It got intense.

"Guys! Guys!" Dirksen said. "Can you do that later? I don't want Abel's lips all red and puffy."

Kissing being outlawed, we rode in silence, admiring the traffic jams. Ninety minutes later we pulled into downtown Sacramento and headed to the Capitol building. In the parking lot, a police officer stopped us. Dirksen gave his name and we were waved through to a private stall. Inside, I saw a sign for the Governor's Office ahead but we stopped halfway down the hallway and entered another room.

A young woman stood up from her desk as we entered, welcomed us, shook my hand, and opened a side door. Television cameras and lights were set up in a studio. Four seats were in front as technicians did sound tests. There was a single chair in front facing the others, and maybe twenty seats behind the cameras, all part of the set.

We were offered sodas or coffee and the hostess gestured to a group of seats to the side. Reginald Broker, star of *60 Minutes,* walked into the room. He stepped over and welcomed us and I made introductions. "We're taping a coda for the interview and story we did before with you and the governor and we want you all present, not just me reading a rundown of what's happened since you foiled the terrorists," Broker explained. "It's going to be different from what we usually do as a follow up because our initial story has drawn massive public interest. This is not live and we'll edit a shorter piece for the actual program."

"Wow," I said, feeling my throat constrict. Zach put his arm around my shoulders and stuck his tongue in my ear, a surefire way to get me to change focus.

Broker touched my shoulder and smiled. "So, just relax and be natural, at least as calm as you can in this kind of setting. Go with the flow."

A makeup man walked up and pulled him over to the empty chair, adjusting his mike and makeup. He shrugged. "Got to get beautiful."

Zachary and I looked at each other. "I have no idea," I said, touching his thigh.

"I love you." Zach said. "I know you'll make me proud with whatever this is."

"Don't be too sure. You know I get emotional."

The same makeup man came up to me and work on my face. "We decided to make you mostly natural," he said. "The bruising is largely gone. Don't worry, you'll be very handsome." He added some makeup and winked as he attached a mike.

One camera crew with a shoulder mount was taping the goings on as well as at least two studio cameras. I assumed all this would be edited into something coherent.

The governor walked in waving at us, blowing a kiss as she took a chair up front. The door opened again and Senator Amanda Wiseling entered, smiling at us, waving, and taking a seat by the governor. A technician came over to me and said, "This way, sir, take the third seat."

I tried not to look at the cameras and did as directed, looking out at an audience that was filling up the back but I couldn't see because of the lighting and equipment. I smiled at the governor and we touched hands. It was reassuring. The senator winked and I got up and we hugged.

"I'm so proud of you, Abel," she said.

"Thank you, ma'am."

I returned to my seat just as another aide led Mama into the room.

"What?" I went to her and we embraced. "What is this?"

"I don't know."

"You're beautiful," I told her.

She slapped my shoulder and grinned.

The aide pointed to the last empty seat and she took it. I could see she had already been in makeup and a microphone was attached to the lapel of her blue high collared jacket. She looked spectacular, her hair pulled back, a subtle touch of rainbow color over her eyes—I knew she did it just for me—and someone had given her a corsage.

"Thirty seconds," someone said. "Quiet on the set."

A red light on a camera behind us turned on. I was jumpy in my chair, nervous, maybe a little afraid of whatever was about to go down on a national television news program with my mother.

"This is Reginald Broker. When we last met American hero Abel Torres—son of an undocumented Mexican immigrant father and a mixed-race mother—we witnessed what he did to thwart a terrorist attack." Broker paused, a pensive expression. "Here's a brief replay."

On the screen was part of the original video, me with my hands tied behind my back, shirtless and bruised, being marched to the edge of a gully and forced to my knees. Other scenes followed, including me covered in blood, standing with Governor Bowfield. It ended with a clip of my singing and playing the piano, with hope in my heart, "You'll Never Walk Alone."

Broker returned to the screen. "Imagine having the calm and determination if you were twenty-years-old and in such a situation." He shook his head and continued: "I asked him what would mean most to him as a thank you from a grateful nation." A clip played on a nearby monitor.

"I...I would like to see my father allowed back to America, as a U.S. citizen, to be with Mama and me."

There was the freeze frame, the governor kissing my cheek and the tear dangling from my eyelash.

Broker continued: "Two of the women before me, dedicated

elected officials on a mission, went into overdrive to see what they could do. California's senior U.S. Senator Amanda Wiseling, and California Governor Lucinda Bowfield." They both nodded to the camera with broad political smiles.

"To Abel's left is his mother, Raven Torres." She looked surprised for a half second before her lounge singer façade returned. She also reached for my hand.

Then I stopped breathing as a side door opened and my father stepped towards us.

"*Dad!*" I screamed and jumped up, arms outstretched, tripping over a cable into his arms. "*Dad!*"

"*Abel!*"

My mother was two steps behind. The three of us jumped up and down. We held each other, faces red, tears unchecked, embracing so hard it hurt. But it could never really hurt hugging your dad and mom. My parents were now locked in an impassioned kiss. So beautiful.

I noticed the senator and governor were grinning, clapping, moving closer. The small audience was on its feet. My rooting crew was shouting my name, as if in a chant. The governor handed me a tissue.

The cameras moved around capturing us from all angles. Reginald Baker joined the governor and senator behind us. I noticed my poli-sci advisor, Dr. Amos and Dean Schultz in the audience at the back as a camera moved. Next to her was the Music Department Chair, Dr. Moss. They were tearful and clapping like maniacs. Soon they joined in the chant, "*Abel, Abel, Abel!*"

My mom and dad were together and I had the most amazing adopted family.

Broker waved his arm. "Zachary O'Brien, Abel's boyfriend and partner in life: *Come on up!*"

Zach sprinted to us and we embraced, kissed, and the world was good. I saw Prince Ali in the back, staying off camera. He was clapping and smiling, dressed all conservative in a sport coat and tie. Next to him was Chuck Markus, my favorite billionaire, dressed in an open shirt and jacket. He pointed at me with an impossibly wide grin. I pointed back.

How was all this possible? Who could have imagined the cascade of crazy events that changed everything? A boy who understood poverty, experienced homelessness, who felt wronged by his country when it took away his dad, grows up to become a whore to save his parents, makes important contacts for his music, is recruited by the FBI, goes undercover, kills a man and is declared a national hero. The father returns, a family reunited. A teenager, burned in romance, afraid of losing his heart again, finds love. The current is with me for sure. Shrimp Boy wins. I rested my forehead against Zach's cheek. "I love you."

"I top tonight," he whispered in my ear, all guttural. We both laughed.

My parents gripped my arms, looking at each other then back at me, eyes gleaming, tears of joy. I watched the senator wipe her cheek, smearing her mascara, heard the governor blow her nose and shout my name, her fists pumping the air, and listened to the applause, Zachary's cheers, my mother's lipstick likely all over my face, the joy, laughter all around me.

The music of family; the melody of love.

-0-

Acknowledgements

Special thanks to my longtime editor and friend, always an inspiration, Katherine V. Forrest, author of the acclaimed Kate Delafield mystery series. Appreciation to David Nathanson, always smart, funny and wise, for his advice on two important characters: Dirksen J. Horvath and Renoir. And to my husband Greg, always offering an honest view and encouragement. Writers need that. I am grateful to you all.

I can be reached through my web site:

www.StevenACoulter.com

About the Author

Steven A. Coulter writes speculative fiction. He explores issues of consequence embedded in fast paced adventure, exotic settings, nasty bad guys, reluctant heroes, and the audacity of love. His work is enriched by his varied careers—soldier, teacher, journalist, state legislator, corporate executive and library commissioner. He has a BA and MA in Journalism and was a Lambda Literary Fellow in 2008 and 2013, later spending two years on the Board. He lives in San Francisco with his husband, Greg. They favor bittersweet chocolate.

Other Books by Steven A. Coulter

COPPERHEAD *(Book 2)* (coming soon)
LGBTQ Fiction/New Adult

Abel Torres is now one of the most famous young men in America, a national hero, a sophomore in college with a musical career beginning to launch. As he prepares for the opening of *Les Miz*, a stranger threatens to make public his life as a prostitute with multiple clients, not just the congressman, which could crash his career and humiliate his family. Who betrayed him? Who can he trust? The white supremacist underground, enraged that a mixed-race gay man thwarted their revolution, has him in their crosshairs. And, as always, his voice soars.

THE PASSAGEWAY (Coming soon)
Science Fiction/Fantasy/LGBTQ Fiction

Darwin McQuaid runs into an urban forest as he flees thugs from his high school. They're gaining when a young stranger steps behind him and confronts them. Within seconds they flee in terror.

Darwin discovers that his champion is of indigenous heritage, his own age and with a mental and physical prowess far beyond his own.

The teenager, called Daruk, greets Darwin by name and claims he was sent by a family friend, Uncle His, an old man who lives in a nearby cabin. They are members of the Ohlone tribe but often vague on specifics

Daruk offers to train Darwin in his brand of fighting which includes mind stimulation to enhance skills and mental capacity. Skeptical but trusting Uncle His, Darwin allows it and is surprised he is faster and doing better in school. As their friendship deepens, Daruk offers to take him to his village.

Daruk and Uncle His are Guardians of The Passageway, warriors who protect the crossroads of three parallel universes, three

Earths, each five hundred years apart that touch together deep underground in San Francisco. The two are from the distant past and selected by leaders in the future who discovered the link and began an audacious experiment to preserve one Earth from the environmental and political catastrophes destroying the other two. In Daruk's world, America will never exist because Columbus was forced back and Cortez captured by the Aztecs. The New World was left for the natives. It is a complex, often fractious world. Eleven Guardians keep the peace. They want a twelfth.

Daruk takes Darwin to the Ohlone village where he was born five hundred years in the past and invites him to become a Guardian. The teenager is overwhelmed. Even if he gained the skills, Darwin has family and friends who could never know. Daruk's earth is a paradise but not everyone wants peace.

RISING SON—CHRONICLES OF SPARTAK *(Book 1)*
Speculative Fiction/LGBTQ Fiction

Weaves sci-fi, fantasy, and a hunky hero in a future eerily extrapolated from today's political reality.

The ruling elite see Spartak as a trophy; the people see him as their best hope. By the year 2115, twelve families control all wealth in America, the middle class is myth, democracy a con game and the Supreme Court has just legalized a new entertainment option for the bored elite. Spartak Jones is kidnapped and forced to become the first legal slave since the civil war, a souvenir birthday present for the eldest son of the richest family. Handsome, seductive and athletic, he is not shy about using his talents to survive and protect those he loves.

When a war erupts within the ruling class, he proves to be a lethal warrior, fearless, resourceful and photogenic. His swashbuckling exploits awaken a long dormant liberal underground hungry to restore democracy. In a world both familiar and horribly twisted, Spartak becomes a symbol of hope, a flesh and blood icon for an America that used to be and might be again, if he can survive. A riveting tale with a powerful political undercurrent.

REVIEWS

"Brilliantly written...creating superheroes of substance!" **Grady Harp**, Amazon, Top 100 Reviewer

"If you love The Hunger Games, and you want a bit more of a gritty and adult feel, you may love Rising Son." **Queer SciFi.com**

"A multitalented, bisexual, teenage slave becomes a symbol of freedom in this debut sci-fi saga... with energetic action scenes and sharply drawn characters, and the result is a vigorous tale." **Kirkus Reviews**

"Straight up Ayn Rand stuff...Holy Shit!...So shockingly different from the literary icon for searching youth...Holden Caulfield of Catcher in the Rye." **Jack Saunders**, author of *Baseball Comes Out: A Revolutionary Novel*

"Highly imaginative and creative, action packed, with a fascinating young protagonist who combines the physical and moral attributes of both Spiderman and Superman in his remarkable body and psyche." **Katherine V. Forrest**, author of the Kate Delafield mystery series

"The treacherous world of 22nd century San Francisco as imagined by Steve Coulter would be a challenge to anyone but to 16-year-old Spartak Jones it becomes the stone on which he hones his athletic skills and his bravery. Coulter's writing can make us feel both at home and uneasy at the same time as he skillfully reveals a future we must fight against at all costs." **Jewelle Gomez**, author of *The Gilda Stories*

"Totally absorbing. I stopped everything else and read the book to completion in one setting." **Amos Lassen**, blogger

FREEDOM'S HOPE—CHRONICLES OF SPARTAK *(Book 2)*
Speculative Fiction/LGBTQ Fiction

Fighting to restore the America of legend, Spartak Jones becomes one. By 2116, the war between the ruling elites is now full frontal and the seventeen-year-old has become its celebrity warrior and icon for an America that used to be.

Is he a pawn or hero? How much evil is acceptable if you believe your cause is just? Love may be his greatest weapon.

From the Space Elevator, 22,000 miles above the earth, Spartak and Zinc McClain launch an audacious scheme to thwart a religious war and a military coup.

Fast-paced, disturbing, heretical, uplifting, and ultimately romantic, the novel weaves science fiction, fantasy, politics and a strapping hero telling his own story.

REVIEWS

Great speculative fiction. I could not put this one down once I started. Swashbuckling adventure in a dystopian 22nd century America. This is not really science fiction as much as speculative fiction, reminding me of Margaret Atwood (Handmaid's Tale) or George Orwell. This is only the second book by this author so I am excited and look forward to see how he grows... There is a serious political underpinning with action, romance and great characters. And it makes you think--the author talks about the future we are shaping by our actions today. In this era of political division, fake news, social inequality, concentrating wealth and other horrors, this may be the world of our grandchildren. **Stargazer,** *Amazon reviewer*

Wow. This is a glorious love story. Spartak and Zinc are the perfect match for one another; they bring out the best in one another, their love giving them strength to face impossible odds. But it is so much more than a love story - it is set in the future, yet the message about freedom and justice and equality reflects what our world needs today. It is emotional and thought provoking. I can't wait for the next book. **Lisa Marie Davis**, Amazon reviewer

The protagonist is a young and renowned athlete in a society that tolerates him for its entertainment. The writing is literate, direct, and a pleasure to read. There is a fascinating plot point—the return of slavery to the United States of America. **Dennis Myers,** Reno News & Review

CPSIA information can be obtained
at www.ICGtesting.com
Printed in the USA
BVHW061538120522
636888BV00005B/73